TO KILL A DRAGON

MATT BANNISTER WESTERN 12

Paperback Edition

KEN PRATT

Published in the United States by Wolfpack Publishing, Las Vegas

CKN Christian Publishing
An Imprint of Wolfpack Publishing
5130 S. Fort Apache Road 215-380
Las Vegas, NV 89148

christiankindlenews.com

Paperback ISBN: 978-1-63977-213-1
eBook ISBN: 978-1-63977-212-4
LCCN 2021922374

TO KILL A DRAGON

I want to dedicate this book to the people who have faithfully been following the Matt Bannister Series. I want to thank you for the reviews, emails, private messages, and the friendships I have made. Countless are the times when my spirits were low and an encouraging message from you wonderful folks not only made me smile but encouraged my spirit. I am very thankful for you all. This one is for you!

Author's note

To my new friend, Lanee – Thank You for your help. I appreciate you very much.
I want to thank my son, Keith for always taking an interest and assisting where he could with this book. I appreciate his insight and help a great deal. I also want to thank CKN Christian Publishing for all the work they do behind the scenes to make this book possible.

*"We do not make requests of you
because we are righteous,
but because of your great mercy."*

Daniel 9:18

It was Monday morning and Lucille Barton had not felt so excited about anything since leaving her in-law's home a year before. She had hated living with her husband's family, and their leaving Utah to create a homestead of their own in Oregon was exciting. It was frustrating to learn they misjudged the cost and hardships of the journey and found themselves stranded in Branson. The Lord provided a job and a home for them and their two small boys at the Slater Silver mine. Lawrence was caught under a rock and lost his lower leg in the mine when two Chinese brothers angry at the world, sabotaged the mine with explosives. Their life at Slater's Mile was tough, but it had become home, as they adapted to living there. However, Lawrence was now unemployable and they lost their income and home. They had reached their lowest point of their lives, but the Lord Jesus was faithful through his people in the community and provided a home and a future for the Barton family. The people in the community were strangers to them but not to Jesus; those fine people reached into their pocketbooks and provided in a miraculous way to help them.

The grand opening of the Barton's Pottery Shop was one week away, and Lucille was excited to open her shop to the public. She had been working long hours since the brick woodburning kiln had been made, but it was overwhelming to try to fill the shelves with merchandise. Lawrence helped, but he was limited in his skills and knowledge. He was recovering from having his lower right leg amputated, which was still painful at times. Lawrence spent more time inside the house playing with the boys and teaching Michael the alphabet and elementary arithmetic. He helped her mostly by keeping the boys busy and cooking the meals while she worked in the shop. It was a humbling experience for Lawrence to change roles with his wife, but he had come to terms with his limitations, and was thankful for the gift of their home and business. They were blessed and they knew it.

To form a lump of clay into a sellable product desired by others was a laborious skill set with a soft touch and an artistic eye. Lucille wished she had a complete inventory to spend more time on each piece, but for now, making a variety of pottery of various glazes and designs was about all she had time to do. She hoped the people of Branson liked her work enough to be able to support her family. It was scary to start a new business and not know if it would succeed or not. It was even more frightening to depend on a pottery business in a community where most folks were just practical enough with their money to get by. Unlike some people who had money to invest without much risk, their business was the lifeline of their survival. She worked knowing it was so. Like any business, though, the product had to be attractive and affordable to catch someone's attention.

A knock on her shop's door startled her. She looked towards the door and there were four Chinese men standing outside peeking through the windows. She had drapes to cover the bay windows, but they needed to be open to allow the sunlight inside. She kept the door locked to keep any curious people from interrupting her work, but one Chinese man persisted to knock, with a wide grin on his round, friendly face.

"We're not open yet," she said loud enough for him to hear. She was sitting at her spinning wheel, forming a vase. "Come back next Monday. That is our grand opening."

The Chinese man knocked again.

She wiped her wet hands on a reddish-stained apron around her waist before walking across the shop to the door. She repeated in a friendly manner, "I'm sorry, we're not opened yet. Come back next Monday for our opening, please."

"Hello," the Chinese man said in well spoken English. "My name is Wu-Pen Tseng. This man is my friend, Jinhai Zhang. You may call him Jin. May we have a moment of your time, please? I believe we could help you."

Lucille had never spoken to a Chinese man before, but in her heart, a thin line of resentment hovered in her chest. The two Chinese brothers that caused her husband to lose his leg had soured her view of the Chinese people. "How can I help you?" she asked through the door with a touch of resentment coming through her voice.

Wu-Pen offered a friendly chuckle. "No, we came to help you. Let me show you." He motioned for Jinhai to turn around and Wu-Pen reached into a wicker basket that the man wore on his back. He pulled out a small tea pot with the most exquisite artwork on its side. It was a nature scene with twirling small vines and blue flowers encircling a shallow stream flowing around rocks under a stunning arched footbridge. It was a stunning work of art glazed on the tea pot. Wu-Pen held it out for her to see. "Please, take a look at the workmanship."

Lucille was impressed and opened the door to get a closer look. She held the tea pot and appreciated the artistic beauty which surpassed her talents. The design was unique and had a decorative hook for the lid to anchor to so it could be lifted, but not fall off. "It's wonderful," she said as she handed it back to Wu-Pen. "Did you want to sell it?"

Wu-Pen shook his head. "Please, may we come inside and talk business?"

She was hesitant. "Business?"

"Let me explain. I represent the Chinese Benevolence Society. My friend, Marshal Matt Bannister, has told me all that has occurred to your family, and yet, he did not ask me if we would be willing to help such a wonderful family. I would like to help. Jinhai is an artist of such skill that he created this tea pot and is giving it to you to keep or sell. I am here to make an offer to you and your family. Jinhai is old and needs easier work than we can give him. He can work for you and create magnificent pieces of art and teach you to make unique and beautiful things."

Lucille smiled hesitantly. "I'm sorry, but I can't afford any help right now."

"Of course not. You need not pay Jinhai until you can. Say a month or two and then you can pay him what he is worth. In truth, he needs to stay busy more than paid. He loves the art and is unmatchable in his skills. He will increase your business and has a lifetime of knowledge to share with you."

"I don't know. I'd have to ask my husband and..."

"Please," Wu-Pen said, "I understand your reluctance. You have four Chinese men standing at your door offering our most gifted artist for nearly free. I'm sorry, what is your name?"

"Lucille."

"Lucille, may I will be honest? I know your husband lost his leg in the mine disaster that two of our countrymen caused. We are very ashamed. We are good people despite those men. I feel an obligation to help the families that suffered because of our countrymen. You owe us nothing, but we owe you and your wonderful family. Please, accept Jinhai as an employee to help make your business a success. He is reliable, quiet, and works with great care. He can use your equipment, supplies and work long hours. If you let Jinhai do what he wants, he will make lots of money for you. I promise."

"Does he speak English?"

Wu-Pen crinkled his nose. "No. But I can translate any work you want done or questions he may have. May he come inside and look around? Maybe you could give him one hour to paint a picture on a bowl? If you like it, you can keep him. If you do not, we will leave and only come back when you are open. There can be no harm in that, right?" His wide grin was friendly and warm.

She was hesitant. "You know Matt?"

He nodded. "Yes, he is my friend. His office is just down the road. You can ask him if you would like. I assure you, you can trust me."

"What all can he paint?" she asked inquisitively.

"Whatever you want. Please, hand Jinhai some brushes and give him one hour to paint anything you request on whatever piece of pottery you want to test him on."

Lucille tilted her head in consideration while looking at the old man. He was shorter than most men, thin with silver hair in a long queue. His narrow thin face was clean of any facial hair, and he had aging, dark brown eyes that showed a lifetime of labor and hardness and yet, still kind and wise. "Okay, come in. I have a vase that he can use. How about a picture of a hummingbird feeding on a yellow rose? Can he paint that?"

Wu-Pen spoke in Chinese and Jinhai answered shortly with a gentle smile. "He says he can. Give him the supplies and then let's talk. I would love to meet your husband and children. I enjoy meeting new people."

An hour later, Lucille stood in the shop looking at the vase in amazement. The paint was still wet, but the hummingbird and yellow rose were flawless. The yellow rose was vibrant with what appeared to be texture on the rose petals. The green stem, leaves and thorns were the best artwork she had ever seen. The hummingbird was not finished, but it was designed perfectly. The rose's shadow on the breast of the bird was enough to know the soft touch of the paint brush was the best Lucille had ever seen. She prided herself on her skills with a brush, but there was no doubt that the old man could teach her much more than she knew. A seventy-five-cent gray vase had just become a five-dollar work of art. Jinhai's artistic ability was stunning.

"Do you like it?" Wu-Pen asked. He had talked with Lucille and Lawrence for the past hour and liked the young couple a lot.

"I'm speechless. I love it!"

"Then you would like Jin to work for you?"

"Yes," Lucille stated quickly, "I would. But how can I tell him what I want him to do?"

"Let him do what he wants, and you won't be disappointed. But if you want him to do something, you can tell me, and I will translate for him. You can write a list for the following day, and I will copy the list in Chinese. He will work each day until he is done. But he must leave before dark. Once you trust him, you can give him a key to the shop so he can start work as the sun rises. He will not do you wrong." Wu-Pen went to a shelf where six gray plates the same color as the vase were set on top of each other. "How about for the remainder of today he paints these plates with hummingbirds to match the vase? If you add teacups, tea plates and bowls you will have a whole set."

Lucille grinned. "I love that idea."

"Very good. I will tell Jinhai what the plan is to get him started. He is very excited."

Wu-Pen left the pottery shop with his two guards, Bing Jue and Uang Yang. He enjoyed meeting the young couple and their children. He would do what he could to help the young couple succeed in their business. Wu-Pen had no remorse for Dragon's Fire or the deaths and tragedies like Lawrence losing his leg that it caused. It only created more opportunities to step in and do good things. Karma, every bad deed could be undone by a good deed, or at least that was how he thought of it. Offering Jinhai was another brick in his foundation to change how the community looked at the Chinese people. Destroy, help rebuild and gain admiration. He had the Fasana Furniture and Mortuary burned down to hide any evidence of poisoning Oscar Belding. The old building was burned to the ground and now, he had made a deal with Solomon Fasana to clean up the debris and construct a two-story brick building with Chinese labor. One by one, the bricks would raise the Chinese Benevolence

Society upwards to be one of the most respected societies in the community. The title was nothing more than a cover for Wu-Pen and his greed for riches and power. Jinhai Zhang was merely a pawn placed on a community chessboard.

2

Matt Bannister looked at Jimmy Donnelly with a bit of pride. Jimmy was a young man facing prison time for repeated theft charges. In an attempt to avoid prison, he had escaped out of the Branson jail. Matt located and arrested him and then spoke with Judge Jacoby to suspend all charges on the condition that Jimmy stayed in Matt's jail and labored three days for every family he had stolen from after he returned their possessions. It had been a humbling experience for Jimmy. Still, every day he brought a note from the homeowner stating that Jimmy had accomplished eight hours of labor to the satisfaction of the homeowner's expectations. If expectations were not met, another day or two of free work was given.

Jimmy's gray long-sleeved V-neck shirt was sweat-stained and dirty from laboring in the warm spring sun. He handed Matt a paper note signed by one such homeowner satisfied with his three days of building a fence around their yard. Matt read it and nodded approvingly. "Well done, Jimmy. You have completed all that was asked of you. Jimmy, you are free to go. I'll warn you that if you pick up those lock picking tools again, the past will come back to haunt you and it will be an immediate prison sentence. Remember the deal we agreed on."

Jimmy's lips raised just a bit. "I'll never steal again after three weeks of being here and working for people like a slave. I want to say thank you. It was hard, but I know you did me a huge favor. I'm grateful."

Matt gripped his hand firmly. "It's been my pleasure." Matt was in his mid-thirties, stood near six foot tall and had broad shoulders that matched his muscular build. His handsome square face was partly covered with a well-groomed dark beard and mustache. His dark straight hair was long and usually kept in a tight ponytail.

Jimmy laughed. "I *know* it's been your pleasure to work me to death! What did you do, go to every house I jotted down and tell them to kill me?"

Matt gave a brief laugh. "Close. Everyone you have stolen from labored for what they have, and then some worthless rat turd comes in and steals it. The thief has no idea the value because some things are far more sentimental than money can replace. I don't think sitting in jail is enough deterrent; hard labor and learning how to work for something, in your case, freedom, might change the way you see things in this world. I hope so. You're young and have a life to live. Live it to the best of your integrity and achieve something of value. You've done well, Jimmy. Good luck to you."

"Thank you, Matt. And thank you for helping me find a job. Starting tomorrow morning. I'll be slinging bags of flour."

"It's honest work. Take pride in what you do and your supervisors will take notice of you. Sooner or later, you'll be promoted when they know you're dependable. Laziness does the opposite and gets around town too. You're young enough to make a career of the grist meal and with the railroad coming, it's a good time to get a foundation built there. You have a chance to start your life over again. Don't waste it, Jimmy."

"I won't," he said with sincere determination.

"As we've talked about, employment is only part of living. You've come to church with Phillip for three weeks. Do you think you'll keep coming? It's up to you now."

He shook his head with a growing grin. "It's funny. You made me go to church every week I was here and told me to read my Bible, but I never saw you at church one time."

Matt's smile faded to a saddened frown. "I know. I've been busier than usual," he explained. It wasn't true, his Bible hadn't left the kitchen counter since Reverend Ash's funeral, nor had he been to church. Whether he was depressed by the loss of the man or discouraged from not being able to save Reverend Ash, he didn't know. Perhaps it was both, but nonetheless, he had missed three straight Sunday church services. He wasn't busy and he wasn't sick;

he just didn't go. He added to Jimmy, "I hope you keep coming to church. I'll see you there one of these weekends."

Jimmy widened his eyes with emphasis. "After being stuck here for three weeks with nothing to do but read, and all there is to read is the Bible or the Chinese writing, which I can't read. Yeah, I think I'll keep coming."

Matt grinned in reaction and then furrowed his brow questionably. "What Chinese writing?"

"The Chinese writing on the board holding up the top bunk. The whole board is written on."

When Jimmy left, Matt went to the first jail cell where Jimmy had stayed and knelt to look at the bottom side of the top bunk. One of the cross boards had strange writing covering the board. It was pressed into the soft cedar by a thumb nail by the look of it. Matt knew it had been written by Izu Chee. He pulled the board down and carried it to his office.

"Broken board?" Phillip Forrester asked from his desk. He was a young deputy. He was a medium-height young man who kept his short brown hair combed neatly and his oblong face clean-shaven.

"No," Matt answered thoughtfully. "It appears Izu wrote something on it before we hung him. I don't know what it says, but I intend to find out. Tomorrow, measure another board and have the mill cut a replacement. I'll be leaving early to ride to Natoma. I'll stay tomorrow night at the Big Z and be back on Wednesday."

"You're not going to ask Wu-Pen or Ah See to read it?"

Matt shook his head slowly. "Not right now. Truet and Nate should be back tomorrow. Don't mention this board to them or anyone else until I come back. Not anyone, Phillip, and I mean it. You can tell them I'll be back on Wednesday and that's all you know. Understood?"

"Sure," he said hesitantly. "But why the secrecy?"

"I have my reasons." The sound of a cowbell ringing sounded as the door opening caught their attention. An older Indian man in his early to mid-sixties stepped inside the office, followed by a white woman near his age, perhaps a little younger. The man had long black hair with gray streaks that fell loose over his shoulders, and a weathered face pockmarked heavily by chicken pox in his youth. He was a good-sized man with broad shoulders and a thick, broad chest. The woman was heavy set with a round face and had long silver hair in a loose ponytail. They were followed inside by a much younger lady who appeared to be in her late teens. She had long black hair that was pulled into a ponytail. She was broad-shouldered and heavy set as well, but quite attractive. Her mouth dropped open when she saw Matt.

"Can I help you?" Matt asked curiously. He neared the three-foot partition separating the entry from the inner office.

The man did not appear friendly. "Are you Matt Bannister?"

"Yes, sir. I am," Matt answered. He put his hand

out to shake.

The man did not shake Matt's hand. "My name is Roman Crowe and this is my wife, Linda. That's our daughter, Mercy. Bo was our son."

Roman Crowe, much like his sons, was once a notorious outlaw with a cruel and bloody reputation that terrified the central and southeastern parts of Oregon. However, his sons picked up where Roman left off and created a reputation that equaled, if not, surpassed their father's brutality.

Matt was quickly wary of the man standing in front of him. "My sincere condolences to you and your family."

Linda Crowe spoke, "I wanted to thank you for staying with Bo while he passed and for killing the men responsible. We could not cross the mountain when he was killed. We went to Natoma and mourned our son. We are on our way back home now, but I wanted to thank you."

"You're welcome. I couldn't leave Bo," Matt said softly.

Roman sputtered, "What happened to Bo in your jail? Do you always beat up your unarmed prisoners?"

Matt sighed inwardly. Bo had been mistreated while in his custody and there was no denying it. He was hit in the face by Truet for threatening Matt's sister. That threat reached Matt's brothers Adam and Steven and they came to the jail with their cousin William Fasana, and Adam forced Bo's head between the iron bars, humiliating him. It never should have been allowed to happen, but Matt had no choice but to explain it as best as he could. "No, we don't normally mistreat our prisoners. Bo had made threats towards my sister, that deserved to be hit in the mouth. I am sure you would expect your sons to hit someone in the mouth if they heard someone make the same threats towards your daughter. My deputy hit Bo and then my brothers came and made sure even a threat wouldn't go unpunished. I wasn't here at the time to stop it."

Roman's eyes narrowed revealing the coldness that once terrorized a large region around the Ochoco Mountains. "You have no idea what we'd do if someone threatened my daughter. My wife wanted to thank you for staying with Bo. I think you would have killed him if the other man had not. I came to tell you we are staying the night in your town and leaving in the morning. We'll be camped outside to the west. I told all of my boys to behave, but if they cause any trouble, come get me, and I will take care of it."

Matt could not afford to be told how to enforce the law by a man who was used to intimidating the law south of the Blue Mountains. "If your boys break the law, they'll pay the consequences for it. Tell them that's a promise and maybe they won't find any trouble." Matt finished with a shrug. "Again, my sincere condolences for Bo."

Roman spoke curtly, "Linda, let's go."

She held out her hand out and took hold of Matt's. "Thank you. The boys will behave themselves."

"Nice to meet you, Missus Crowe. You folks have a good trip back home."

"Bye," Mercy said with a shy smile before she followed her parents out the door.

Matt watched them walk away before saying, "Phillip, go let Tim and the boys at the sheriff's office know the Crowe brothers are in town. If there is any trouble tonight, I want to know about it. I feel old Roman Crowe thinks he can throw his weight around here like he can down in Prairieville. And if he tries, he needs to know he's wrong."

3

Billy Jo Fasana admired the diamond ring on her finger. It had a square diamond with four tiny red rubies on each side of the diamond. The ring was worth far more than the forty dollars Joe Thorn paid to buy it from Matt Bannister. Matt had bought it for thirty dollars from the Natoma stage stop. Knowing Joe Thorn had won a hundred dollars in a drawing at the Spring Fling Dance and wanted to buy her a wedding ring, Matt sold the ring to Joe. The ring on her finger was a promise of a wedding and a lifelong commitment to her first and only love. It hadn't always been a good relationship, but the past two months had been wonderful. Joe was a changed man after a near-death experience in the mine. He had quit drinking and become a loving father to his boys. It was paradise, even though they lived in a two-room cabin in the slums of Slater's Mile.

Dinner was made, the cabin was clean, and she made the effort to look nice when he came home from work, with her blonde hair brushed back and held out of her eyes with a hair comb. Billy Jo looked nice and cared more about how she appeared than she had in a very long time. It was good to watch Joe take an active role in the lives of their two sons and enjoy being with them. Life was better than it had ever been, and it was bound only to get better.

The door was open to let some fresh air in when Joe entered the cabin. He paused in the doorway with an angry scowl on his rugged face.

Billy Jo's brow narrowed with concern. It was a fearful thing to recognize the hostility behind his eyes, waiting for the right moment to explode. She had not seen that scowl on his face since he had changed his life. She immediately feared he had found out about her short-lived romance with Wes Wasson. "What wrong?" she asked anxiously.

Joe's expression softened just slightly. "Jeremy Isaacson fell a hundred and fifty feet straight down a shaft today because the damn cable snapped when they were pulling him up. They knew the cable was frayed, but they never replaced it! They just kept hauling ore carts out of that shaft until it finally snapped."

"Is he okay?" she asked, horrified. Jeremy was a new employee that lived with two other young men in Slater's Mile. He was twenty years old and on the job for less than a month.

"No, he died!" Joe shouted. "That's a stupid question, Billy Jo. It was a hundred-and-fifty-foot fall onto the rock. He was almost at the top when the cable snapped. Do you think he survived?"

"No. I'm sorry. I'm just stunned," she replied honestly.

Joe stepped inside with his dirty boots and clothes and sat down on the davenport, still holding his lunch pail. "They didn't sound the alarm or anything. They let the rest of us work without saying a word. They pulled him up and took him to the funeral parlor. I didn't find out he fell until after work. They kept it quiet. The young man's dead, and the mine keeps working full steam ahead. We don't matter to them, and I've been saying that for a long time now. Billy Jo, I don't want to disappoint you or make you mad, but I'm going to town with a bunch of the men tonight. It's time we seriously talk about a strike."

Billy Jo sat beside him and took hold of his hand. The word *strike* sent a chill of fear down most wives' spines when it came to the Slater Silver Mine. "Joe, you remember what Mister Slater said about anyone who strikes. We'll be kicked out of this place, and you'll lose your job. We would be okay because I have my house in town and my father could hire you. But everyone else around here would have no place to go."

Joe groaned. "They can hold that threat over our heads forever and more of us are going to die, because we're too scared of losing what little we have. We deserve more money, more time off and safer working conditions. I've already been trapped in the mine once, and I don't want to do it again. Since we hit that vein of gold, we're searched before we go into the mine and searched when we come out.

We're pushed harder for longer hours and our pay remains the same while the mine makes millions. But they won't replace an unsafe cable for the lift, and Jeremy is dead. Last week Edgar broke his ankle, Tim's hand was nearly cut off by one of the frayed wires on that cable, and Luke Simpson could have been killed when a chunk of the ceiling broke off from an unexpected explosion in the stope. They're pushing us hard, Billy Jo, and people are getting hurt." He paused before continuing, "That's what the other men and I are going out to talk about tonight. Billy Jo, I told you I wasn't going to drink anymore, but I am tonight. One or two won't hurt."

Billy Jo nodded uneasily. "There's warm water on the counter if you want to clean up first. Just promise me you won't drink too much and come home mean." Her concern was readily noticed in her expression.

"I promise. I won't do that to you, Billy Jo."

4

Joe Thorn sat with a group of eight men at two tables pushed together not far from the door to the Thirsty Toad Saloon to talk business. Joe held a pencil in his hand and listed every complaint the men could think of about working at the Slater Silver Mine. The complaints varied between equipment safety, operating conditions and hours, lack of pay raises while hiring Chinese at a lower wage. The lack of compensation for the families of injured or killed on the job employees, and again, the low pay that made living month to month in the Slater company housing a lifestyle instead of prospering.

"I'll add the degradation of being searched by security before we enter the mine and then again when we leave the mine," Joe said as he wrote it down on the paper. "I think our list of concerns is about complete. Now we need to narrow it down to a list of demands."

Alan Rosso stated plainly, "That's your fault. If

your woman had kept her mouth shut, we could all be high-grading ore to this day."

Joe's head rolled back as he laid the pencil down. "I know. Okay, that's another complaint. What's that word for hiring family members?"

"Nepotism."

"Yeah, that. That's a complaint we need to list."

"Joe, here's your drink," Ritchie said, setting a glass of whiskey down in front of Joe. "It's nice to have you back with our little gang. The men's gang."

Joe shook his head. "I'm not back in the gang. We're talking business and that's the only reason I'm here. I have a good thing with my family, and I don't want to ruin it. But I suppose one more won't hurt."

Two hours and multiple drinks later, most of the men who had to come to discuss business had gone home, leaving Joe and Ritchie Thorn, Bobby Alper and Bruce Ellison to enjoy the night. Newt Collins had taken the list of demands to mail to William Slater and now that talking business was done, it was time to drink and enjoy the moment.

The words, 'One more won't hurt' had opened a gateway to drunkenness and Joe was feeling good enough to stand and holler, "Vince! Jack! How are you?" when Vince and Jack Sperry walked into the Thirsty Toad. They were followed in by four young men ranging in ages from twenty to thirty. All four of the men looked similar and had long loose black hair flowing over their shoulders and appeared to be of mixed Indian blood. A young lady wearing blue jeans and a cotton plaid shirt with her neck exposed followed them inside. Her long black hair was braided and fell to her lower back. Her brown eyes were filled with the excitement of exploring a larger city that she had never visited before.

Jack Sperry raised his palms upwards questionably as he joked at his friend. "What's this, Joe? I haven't seen you around in a while. I hear you're domesticated and church-going now."

Joe grinned as he shook the two brother's hands. "Not quite. We met here to declare war on our bossman. It looks like you brought us the warriors," he laughed, while looking at the Crowe brothers. "And a cute little squaw too!" he added as his attention fell on Mercy Crowe.

"Hey!" One of the four brothers shouted with his finger pointed at Joe. The cold expression on his face was merciless. "Call my sister that again and I will cut your throat!"

Joe was taken back by the sudden fury of the stranger, but then a tiny twitch of his lips brought the corners of Joe's lips upwards into a challenging smirk. "That might be a little harder than you can do, Geronimo."

"Try me!" the man said and stepped forward to reach Joe.

Vince Sperry stepped in between them. He spoke urgently, "Knock it off! Joe is my friend, Tyee. Okay? He's drunk. He didn't mean anything by it." Vince turned his attention to Joe. "This is my cousin, Tyee Crowe. I suggest you sit down and shut up because he's no one to play with. These are his brothers, Adrian, Corbin and Lorenzo and their little sister,

Mercy. Now that you know who they are, I suggest you apologize and go home." He turned back to his cousin, Tyee. "This is my pal, Joe Thorn. He's drunk. Let's move on over to the other side of the saloon." He waved his arm to direct his cousins across the saloon towards an empty table. Vince watched his cousins follow Jack to the table and turned to his friends. He exhaled with an expression of relief. "Ritchie, take Joe home before he gets himself hurt. Jack and I can restrain ourselves when we drink; my cousins don't."

"Mer-cyy!" Joe spat out, prolonging the pronunciation while he watched her and her brothers walk away. "Mer-cyy me in blue jeans! Please, Mer-cyy me." He laughed.

She stopped and glanced back at him with an uncomfortable and hurt expression on her round, attractive face. She was seventeen years old and shorter and heavier than her brothers. It was her first time in Branson and going out to a saloon with her brothers was an exciting moment, but her excitement turned to humiliation as her cheeks reddened. She was the only girl who dressed like a boy most of the time and most recently, the young man she had her hopes set on had told her she was too fat for him to be attracted to her. It had broken her gentle heart and she now feared the man making fun of her name was poking at her weight too. It showed in her hurt expression. "Mer-cyy," Joe shouted. He paused when he made eye contact and recognized the hurt that showed in her sensitive eyes. He lowered his voice and spoke directly to her, "You're a very pretty girl. I truly mean no disrespect to you."

"Thank you," she said, bashfully.

Joe took notice of the four brothers, each one eyeing him severely. His attention went to Tyee, who wore a rabbit fur vest over a bare muscular chest. He wore a rawhide necklace with a bear claw held in place by bead work. "No disrespect, Mercy, I think you're a beautiful young lady. And almost as pretty as your brother in the fancy fur vest." He laughed mockingly and took a drink of his whiskey.

Tyee Crow's chest lifted and fell with agitation. He approached Joe quickly but was stopped by Vince putting a hand on his chest. Tyee nodded towards the saloon door that was in the middle of the building. He spoke to Joe, "Step outside with me!" Tyee was the second eldest in the family in his late twenties. He was an average height and shoulder-width but had a muscular body that was quite noticeable under his vest. Tyee kept his triangular face clean-shaven and was a handsome man, but he also had the quickest temper in the Crowe family. He could back his temper up with his gun, knife or hand fighting, and had on many occasions. A drunk fool insulting his sister and mocking him was not going to be tolerated, no matter what his parents had told him about staying out of trouble. Their mother insisted the boys leave their weapons in the wagon if they were taking their sister out on the town. Although they respected their mother, their father had the final say and no one argued with Roman Crowe. Tyee didn't need his weapons though, his hands and feet were the only weapons he needed to shut up a forty-year-old drunk man.

Joe gave a friendly laugh, while he stood with a slight sway and holding his drink in hand. "I don't want to fight. I'm just messing with you, boys. Heck, let me buy you a drink."

Tyee grimaced with distaste. "I'll touch nothing you buy! Watch your back," he warned and allowed his older brother, Adrian, to guide him back to their section of the saloon.

Vince Sperry warned, "You don't want no trouble with them. Trust me." He spoke to Ritchie Thorn, "Take him home before he gets hurt. I mean it."

Bobby Alper asked. "Are they the actual Crowe Brothers?"

Vince lifted his eyebrows, emphasizing the seriousness of his warning. "Yes! Just take him home."

Joe grinned. "What's the young chap's name wearing fur?"

Vince was hesitant to say. He had been around Joe many times before when he had way too much to drink. "Tyee. Joe, he is not someone to play with."

Joe's grin grew wide with a thought. He began to shout, "Tyee! Tyee Crowe. That sounds like a war cry, doesn't it?" he asked Ritchie. "That's probably the last thing Custer heard, Tyee Crowe!" He and Ritchie both laughed.

"Joe, shut up!" Bruce Ellison said nervously. "Are you stupid?"

"You better be quiet," Bobby suggested. "You're going to get us all killed."

"No, he'll get himself killed," Jack Sperry corrected suddenly as he approached their table. There was not one bit of humor on his face as he emphasized to Joe, "But that's on you. I'm warning you now." He glanced at Ritchie Thorn. "Get him out of here or keep him quiet."

Ritchie stopped laughing but grinned widely. He was having a good time having his brother drinking with him again. "Relax. They're not wearing gun belts nor have any weapons. I think we are safe enough. We'll have one more drink and call it a night. We do have to work tomorrow."

The four friends were preparing to leave the saloon to make the two-mile walk back to Slater's Mile when Wes Wasson entered the Saloon. He was dressed in a tan suit and a brown derby hat and appeared as professional and respected as any businessman in town. His sister encouraged him to wear a new gentleman's look to earn more respect within town than his usual transient roaming from town-to-town wear. Wes carried a cane but didn't necessarily need it for walking; it added a touch of mystic to his presence. Though his sister disapproved, he wore his gun belt around his waist in case he needed it. He was surprised to see Joe Thorn sitting at a table, already quite intoxicated. It brought a small pleasing smile to his lips. If there was one thing he knew, it was a man of bad character can only change his ways for so long before he returns to his natural ways. To see Joe intoxicated meant it was only a matter of time before Billy Jo left him and returned to Wes.

"How are you, Joe?" Wes asked while faking a friendly smile. In truth, he despised Joe.

"Wes!" Joe shouted. "Wes Wasson. Wes Wasson, Wes Wasson," he laughed heartedly. "Say that three times fast and you sound like a slurring kid choking on a mouth full of drool, doesn't it?" he asked Ritchie. "Westh Wassthon!" He slurred the name intentionally. "You look like a want-to-be banker nowadays, Westh. Mer-cyy me!" he shouted and looked across the saloon where the Sperry brothers sat with their cousins.

Ritchie laughed. "We were just leaving, Wes. Joe's been drinking quite a bit and trying to pick a fight with the Crowe brothers over there. I need to get him home before he does."

"The Crowe Brothers? The gang?" Wes asked with interest.

"Yeah," Ritchie chuckled,

"Well, don't run off. Let me buy you all one more drink before you go. I haven't got to drink with Joe in a long time." He called to the bartender, "Hey, Briggs, another round for the table here."

Joe focused his eyes on Wes as best he could; he was starting to see double. "You got a woman to dress you now? You're like a brand-new dapper boy."

Wes removed the derby hat and set it on the table as he sat down in an empty chair. "I did. I fell in love with a young lady, and she was falling in love with me too, but she left me for another man. The man she left me for is a waste of flesh, in my opinion. He's just going to hurt her again, but I figure she'll come back to me sooner or later."

"Oh yeah?" Joe asked with a slightly troubled expression. "I have to pee. What's her name? Because I've known a lot of women here and Mer-cyy," he shouted, "is over there!" He laughed with a glance towards the other side of the saloon.

Wes grinned slowly. "Her name is Billy Jo."

Bruce Ellison's eyes lifted in surprise that his uncle Wes would openly state Billy Jo's name. Bruce and his family were the only people that knew Billy Jo had started a relationship with Wes. It was a secret Bruce had been keeping from his friends.

Ritchie and Bobby both laughed.

"Huh?" Joe asked with a confused expression.

"You know, your Billy Jo."

"What?" Joe asked. There was no humor in his tone.

"He's joking, Joe," Ritchie said.

Wes laughingly murmured, "Relax, I'm joking. Her name was Ethel Bur-bonnet."

"Ethel, who?" Bobby Alper asked. The only Ethel he knew was a friend of his mother's.

"She was in California," Wes answered quickly. "Drink that up. Let's have another one."

"I still have to pee," Joe stated and stood on wobbly legs. "I'll be back. Save my drink because I'm not done yet." He made it to the door and stepped outside and braced his arm against the exterior wall along the covered boardwalk to keep his balance. He worked his way to the edge of the building, where a narrow alley three feet wide separated the saloon from the next building. Joe leaned his shoulder against the establishment and unbuttoned his pants to relieve himself.

Inside, Wes Wasson, who sat at the table facing the door, watched Tyee Crowe follow Joe outside. None of the others at the table appeared to notice and Wes wasn't going to mention a word about it. Five minutes later, Tyee came back inside and had a bit of smeared blood on his hands. Wes continued his conversation with the others just as if he had not seen Tyee return. He would wait for Joe to be discovered dead or alive by someone else and react accordingly.

The door opened part way and Joe's bloody hand clung to the door jamb as he leaned his body inside the saloon. "Ritchie," he said and fell to the floor unconscious. His face was covered with blood.

"Joe!" Ritchie shouted in alarm and quickly attended his brother. There was a deep gash across his right eyebrow and his top lip was split open as well. His left eye was swelling. "Who did this?" he yelled. Ritchie stood up and turned towards Tyee Crowe. "Did you do this?"

Tyee calmly took a drink. "I did. Count him lucky to be left breathing. I wouldn't push any further if I were you."

Ritchie turned towards his friends. "Did any of you see him follow Joe outside?" he shouted.

They all shook their heads.

"I didn't notice anything," Wes said innocently.

"Bobby, let's take him home," Ritchie said to his roommate.

Once they had left, Wes and Bruce Ellison went over to talk to Jack and Vince Sperry and were introduced to the others.

Adrian Crowe was the eldest brother at thirty years old. He was the leader of the gang and perhaps the cruelest of them all. His empty eyes revealed nothing except cold blackness that cared little for anyone except his family. "I know you watched Tyee follow him outside. Why did you say you didn't, or go help your friend when you could?"

Wes answered honestly, "He's not my friend. I don't like him." He looked at Tyee. "You would have done me a favor if you killed him."

"I still may if we pass the same roads again. We're not very forgiving."

5

Billy Jo Fasana tried to comfort her growing anxiety as she peeked at a pocket watch she kept on a wooden shelf. Time became an essential factor to know when an abusive man could potentially become explosive. The time he had to be woken up for work and when his lunch break was because he could come home. When he was getting off work and the time supper needed be ready to keep him content for the day. Time mattered. What made Billy Jo nervous was Joe's time at the saloon with his brother and co-workers. He had been gone all night and missed dinner, and that much time drinking brought back plenty of fearful memories of Joe coming home and terrorizing her and their children. Their home had been a wonderful place for two months and she prayed it would remain so, but she feared Joe would come home enraged by the alcohol and beat on her. She thought back to the many times the boys were woken up by

Joe's drunken tantrums and hiding under the covers, visibly shaken by their father beating on and throwing their mother around. It wasn't supposed to be like that, and it hadn't been since Joe quit drinking. She breathed in slowly, praying that the boys would not be woken up by such a traumatic scene again. Historically though, the odds were he was coming home drunk and he'd either go to bed or find a reason to raise his voice and then hit her.

The door flung open unexpectedly as Ritchie Thorn and Bobby Alper carried Joe inside, each held one of Joe's arms over their shoulders. Joe's face was covered with dry and thickening blood from his wounds. His shirt as well was saturated with blood. He was barely conscious and unable to stand on his own. His stomach heaved, and a consistent flow of blackish-colored liquid projected out of his mouth like a punctured pipe, across the floor and then ran down his chin, neck and soiled his shirt, mixing with the blood.

"What happened?" she asked with alarm. She jumped off the davenport and pointed at it. "Put him down there! What happened?" Her only concern was the blood. The vomit she had dealt with before.

The two men were sweat covered from laboring to carry him for over two miles. Ritchie explained, "He had too much to drink and got a bit lippy with one of the Crowe brothers. We didn't see him follow Joe outside. If I had, this wouldn't have happened."

She put her attention on the gash above Joe's eye. "Bobby, will you get me a bucket of water from outside, please? I have to clean his face before I can stitch that eye up."

"Yes, Ma'am," he said and carried the water bucket from the kitchen outside to the community hand pump.

"You should have told him to shut up!" she snapped at Ritchie.

"We all did, but he was having too much fun. You know Joe, he likes to aggravate people."

"Well, someone didn't like to be aggravated, now did they, Ritchie?" she asked in a raised voice. "You know he quit drinking. He shouldn't have been there in the first place."

"That's where our meeting was, and it was Joe's idea. So don't blame me. He's a grown man and older than me. I don't babysit," Ritchie spoke irritably. He continued in a more remorseful tone, "We planned on bringing him home before he was hurt, but Wes came in and bought us more drinks. I suppose you'll be sewing Joe up like you did, Wes. Huh?"

She bit her lip as a wave of anxiety rolled through her at the sound of Wes's name being mentioned. She calmed herself, remembering her last conversation with Wes at the Spring Fling Dance was short, but he was surrendering to her desire to marry Joe and content with being friends. "Yes. I'll stitch that gash closed and the lip should heal on its own. It's not too bad. He'll sleep through it, I'm sure."

"Will you need help?"

She was kneeling on the floor beside where Joe's head was. She looked up at her future brother-in-law and gave a sad smile of appreciation to his offer. "No. I'll take care of him and then clean up his mess." She nodded to the vomited alcohol and bile on the floor. "You go on home and get some sleep. You all have to work tomorrow."

Joe's mouth opened and his stomach contracted, forcing what little liquid in his stomach out of his mouth onto the cushion of the davenport. A guttural choking sound of his body convulsing to get every drop of poison out his body and the stench of the whiskey and bile soaking into the cushion caused Billy Jo to shudder with disgust.

"Oh! I am so angry!" she kept her voice down to not wake her two sons, but the tone spoke loud enough.

Bobby carried the bucket of clean water inside and set it next to Billy Jo. "Do you want me to clean up his mess?" he asked.

"No. It's fine," she snapped, displeased. "Thank you for the water. I'll see you two tomorrow."

When the two men left, she used a cloth to wash Joe's face of the blood so she could see clearly to use her needle and thread to stitch the gash above his eye. He was out and other than flinching a bit, he never woke up once while she ran the needle through his flesh and tied the stitches tight. The occasional heaving of his stomach and his deep breathing were the only symptoms that he was alive. Billy Jo covered him with a blanket and then set to cleaning up the blackish liquid off the floor that had burst out of his mouth as they brought him inside.

She checked her pocket watch. It was near midnight. Joe would be in bad shape in the morning when it was time to get to work. One benefit to living in the Slater's Mile was every man watched out for one another and never let one of their own oversleep or miss work. Too many times, Joe and his group of friends had stayed at the saloon late, got a few hours of sleep and still went to work. The more responsible men at Slater's Mile that went to bed early were very much appreciated because it was not acceptable to miss work for any minor illness or injury. A man had to be deathly sick or hurt to get a day off from the mine.

In the morning, Joe would feel the aftereffects of his drinking. The sharp shrill sound of the hammer pounding on the rock drill would increase his headache all the more as it echoed in the confined space of the wince they were digging. Tomorrow would be a bad day. Joe would come home feeling sick, tired and in a foul mood. The Joe Thorn cure for a hangover was going back to the saloon with his friends and doing it over again. It was the first time Joe had fallen from his promise to quit drinking; it frightened Billy Jo. Life had become peaceful and enjoyable. She didn't want it to change.

Joe was a good man and had a good heart when he wasn't drinking. She leaned down and kissed him on the cheek while he slept. "I love you," she whispered.

6

Natoma was a twenty-five-mile ride to the far edge of Jessup Valley before the main road traveling west crossed over the Blue Mountains. It was a long ride and took most of the day. He had planned to ride over to Willow Falls and spend the night at the Big Z Ranch, but Matt didn't want to ride another nine miles, so he checked into the hotel and boarded his tired horse for the night. Natoma wasn't an exciting town. It was merely a small farming community along the main road traveling east and west and ideally situated for a stage stop between distant cities. The livery stable kept fresh horses for the stagecoaches. The hotel served as the stage stop, restaurant and supplied rooms for overnight layovers. Natoma was set against the beautiful Blue Mountains that towered over the town on the edge of a beautiful valley that was a farmer's paradise. The people were friendly, although the one saloon in town could be a bit rowdy. The hotel encouraged the travelers to unwind and not risk going to the saloon for their protection. Aside from the saloon being a threat to strangers, Natoma was a nice place to rest for the night. However, there was a certain stench that a person's nose might pick up on occasionally from the Heather Creek Tannery.

The tannery was a large building beside an artificial pond along Heather Creek created by a dam to provide a channel for the water wheel. The water wheel controlled the grinder for the oak bark needed for a chemical called tannin, an essential ingredient for the final product, leather. The tannery produced various grades of leather for multiple purposes and buyers. Their primary customer was the Natoma Glove Factory which made quality gloves not too far up the creek from the tannery.

Matt wrinkled his nose as he opened the office door of the tannery. The office was nothing more than a small room with a wood desk with stacks of papers and a single wooden chair behind it. Matt turned the knob of a door on the back wall that opened to a stairway going up or a short hallway leading to another door. He opened the door found it opened to a series of open pits dug in the ground filled with liquid soaking hides in one solution or another. Matt did not see anyone below he could question about finding Tillie. Upstairs was the main production area of the tannery. There were multiple large tubs anywhere from four to eight feet across built like wine barrels lined up in rows. A few tubs soaked the hides in milky white lime water. Others soaked hides in a dark brown liquid, and others appeared to be clean water. The atmosphere inside the building was well-lit by windows that allowed fresh air inside to keep the humidity down. Matt had not been inside the tannery before. He could not make heads or tails out of what appeared to be a very confusing and complicated business of soaking hides in one product or another for various lengths of time for whatever the purpose. Matt tried to speak to a middle-aged lady, but she merely pointed her finger at a thin older man with white curly hair who was bent over a vat of pink dye.

"Thank you. Enjoy your day," Matt said to the lady who had come across as quite rude. He approached the older man. "Excuse me. I'm looking for Tillie," Matt said, getting the man's attention.

"Oh!" he exclaimed, startled. He stared at the badge on Matt's blue shirt. "You're the marshal?"

"I am. You are?"

"Harry Yablonski. I own this place. Tillie is right over here. Follow me." He paused to dry his hands off on a multicolored stained towel. Harry tossed the towel on a table and asked, "Tillie's not in any trouble, is she?"

"No. She's not in any trouble at all. I need to ask her a question, is all."

Harry sighed with relief. "Good. I would hate to lose her. Tillie is one of my most valuable employees other than my two sons. She knows the whole process from start to finish. Do you know anything about tanning, Matt?"

"I only know enough to salt the skins and bring

them here."

Harry's face brightened with pride. "That's a good start. You bring them here and we get started by soaking the skins and hides to remove the salt and dirt. The next thing we do is scrape the extra flesh off the skins and hides. If you are wondering if there is a difference between skins and hides? There is. Deer and other small game are referred to as skins. Larger game, such as elk, along with cattle and horses, we refer to as hides. We end up splitting the hides into two pieces to make them easier to work with. Anyway, after we clean the salt and dirt, the next step is soaking them in lime to loosen the hair. That takes anywhere from three days to two weeks, depending on the hair. If you can take your hand and run it across the hair and it comes out smoothly. It's ready to unhair. And that is what we will find Tillie doing right now; beaming the hides. That is only the first few steps of what we do here. It's rather gross sometimes, very time-consuming and smelly, but we make a good product when it's done. Follow me and I'll take you to Tillie."

Tillie stood behind a twelve-inch-wide wooden beam that was flat and smooth and set at a forty-five-degree angle pointed down away from her. A hide was draped over the beam with the bottom top half already stripped of hair and tied in a knot to keep it off the ground. Tillie held a fleshing knife, which was similar to a carpenter's drawing knife with two handles and a twelve-inch blade, except it was very dull and used to push away

41

from one's body and not pulled towards them. She quickly scraped the hair free from the hide in long downward strokes down the beam. The hair being removed left a smooth white skin behind every down stroke.

"Tillie, the marshal is here to talk to you," Harry said.

In her sixties, Tillie was a petite Chinese lady with a square-shaped wrinkled face and wore a cotton headscarf over her hair.. She wore a long leather apron to protect her clothing, and a home-made black pullover loose-fitting shirt. Sweat beaded on her brow. She paused just long enough to wipe her brow with her sleeve and glance at Matt before pulling the skin up the beam to keep stripping the hair off the hide.

"Hello, Tillie. Can I borrow you for a few minutes?" Matt asked, holding the board from the bunkbed.

She shook her head vigorously. She answered in a high-pitched voice, "I'm working. Come back at five o'clock."

"Tillie, you can talk to him," Harry said, offering his permission for her to speak to Matt.

"No. I'm working until five when I go home. He can talk to me then. Come to my house at five o'clock."

"All I need is for you to read this board for me. It's written in Chinese," Matt explained. He didn't want to wait until five.

"Leave it here and I will read it on my way home at five o'clock."

"No, I'm not leaving it here. If you don't want to read it now, then I'll be at your place at five o'clock," Matt said with a hint of annoyance.

"Yes. I'm working. Come then."

It was twenty minutes after five o'clock and Matt was dumbfounded. He stared at Tillie in disbelief. "You want two dollars to translate the writing on that board?"

Tillie held the board in her hand and met Matt's gaze evenly. "Yes. Two dollars, please."

"A few weeks ago, you charged me twenty cents to bandage my head, but you want two dollars to read that?"

"Yes. Do you have someone else who can read it to you?" Tillie asked, extending the board out for him to take back.

"No."

"Then two dollars, please."

Matt fished for two one-dollar coins and handed them to Tillie. "You have mastered the art of supply and demand, haven't you? Is that why you didn't read it earlier today?"

Tillie wasn't fazed by his apparent irritation. "I get paid to do my work. They do not pay me to read this for you. You pay me to read this to you. So please, sit down and you can write as I read if you want. A nickel for the paper and ink, please."

Matt grinned. "Sure." He gave her a nickel. He sat on a wooden chair, and she gave him a cutting board to set across his lap along with a piece of paper, inkbottle and quill.

She began to translate:

"Beautiful Pearl..."

"Beautiful Pearl? Is it a poem or something?" Matt asked, surprised by the first words he was writing down.

Tillie gave him an indignant gaze. "Meizhen, is her name. In English, it means beautiful pearl. Please hush and let me read."

Matt snickered. "Okay, go ahead."

"Beautiful Pearl – I would write a letter, but I know it would never leave Wu-Pen's hands. He controls the mail to and from our homeland. Any letter I wrote would be burned. I know this will never reach you, but perhaps others who lay where I am will read and understand that neither Wang nor I am guilty of the crimes Wu-Pen says we committed. My dear brother Wang will be left motionless if I do not do as Wu-Pen says, and I could not live with that. I do not know how this will end, but if Wang can be spared that fate, all will be worth whatever happens to me. Ah See said today that Wang and I will be released, and Wu-Pen will be in an American prison or hung for his crimes. I hope so. The Americans do not understand our words. Only Wu-Pen and Ah See can speak their language. I do not know if the Americans hear my words. My Beautiful Pearl, I dream of coming home to you. I once dreamed of returning rich with money to buy a home for you and me. Now, I only dream of returning to you. I may never return home. My heart is filled with regret for leaving you. I hoped you would wait for me, but if I do not make it home,

44

my beautiful pearl. Do know I lived every day of my life for the one hope of spending the rest of my living years loving you. Your, Izu."

Matt finished writing what Tillie read and blew on the ink to help it dry. "He was married?" Matt asked, recalling that Wu-Pen had told him Izu was not married.

"It appears so. Where is Izu now?" Tillie asked.

Matt hesitated. It had become clear that his stomach and instincts at the time were right. He had hung two innocent men. Matt took a deep breath. "Dead. He and his brother were hung for crimes they were innocent of." Matt shook his head with a sickening feeling boiling in his gut. "I knew it. I knew something wasn't right." He bit his bottom lip to keep from cursing. "Thank you for reading this."

She opened the door held it open. "It is what I was paid to do. You must go. I have to work in my garden, cook supper and go to sleep."

Matt smiled sadly and stood. "Thank you, again. Can I ask you something? What did Izu mean by his brother Wang being left motionless? Is that death?"

Her eyes met his with a seriousness that he hadn't noticed before. "Chinese torture is ruthless. It could mean many things, but there is one worse than death. That is what he means. It is something you do not want. It would be better to die than suffer what these men threatened. One thing before you go." She paused to make sure he was listening. "If these men threatened Izu's brother, then they will do it. Chinese do not make threats that they

45

do not intend to keep. Sir, I suggest you stay away from them for your own good."

Matt pressed his lips together. "I'm afraid I can't do that. What kind of torture are they talking about exactly?"

Tillie gasped and closed her eyes emotionally. When she opened her eyes, they were filled with rare tears that she refused to let fall. She took a deep breath and fanned her cheeks with her hand while her other hand closed the door. "Please sit." She sat back down. "I have not spoken of it since coming to America and no one here knows, but I will tell you, so it does not happen to you. Before my husband and I fled China, my brother committed a bad crime with our village head's daughter. They caught him and left him motionless. He could not move his arms or legs and never would again. That punishment wasn't enough; they came to kill all of his relatives. We fled, but the rest of my family were killed." A single tear slowly escaped her eyes and rolled along her cheek. "My brother was placed on the village street for everyone to see but could not help him. They would not let him die, though. Death was too easy. They wanted him to suffer, and he may be alive today, all these years later, as a warning to others. I do not know." She wiped her eyes. Matt could see her hands were shaking with the painful memory. "Now you know why we came here to America and why this is my home. The man named Wu-Pen sounds as bad as our village leader many years ago. Do not trust him or the other man, Ah See, for your own good."

"I don't trust them," Matt said quietly. He was troubled by the story he had heard. "Wu-Pen controls the Chinese Benevolence Society and because of that, apparently Chinatown. Wu-Pen and Ah See are the only ones that speak English. That's why I came to you."

"Others speak it too, but they may be afraid to if Wu-Pen wants control of his people. I've seen that before in California. There are good and bad men that want to control the Chinese people, but my husband and I trusted none of them. We stayed here far away from Chinese communities."

"What did they do to your brother?"

Tears misted her brown eyes. She swallowed noticeably before speaking. "You can move your limbs freely because of muscle and tendons. When those are cut, you can never heal them."

A chill ran down Matt's spine. It was the vilest thing he had ever heard, and he wasn't prepared to hear of such evil. "Wu-Pen threatened to do that to Wang if Izu didn't do as he instructed?"

"It seems so. The Chinese have many ways to torture and yes, that is what motionless means. But there are many ways to say it and many more painful things they can do. Luckily, we survived to come to America because China is not like America. I suggest you let the Chinese take care of the Chinese and worry about your American people."

"He's killing Americans too. I can't look the other way. Thank you, Tillie."

"Does Wu-Pen have men with him? Protectors?"

"Yes, he does."

"Before you confront a leader of a tong like that, remember to not turn your back on them or I may never see you again. That goes for your wife and family members too. Learn that lesson from what happened to my family because of my brother's sin. Most Chinese people you will meet are good people who want to help their families, but those who seek power over others and can accuse someone else of their crimes are always dangerous. Very evil, some of them."

7

Matt returned to Branson late the next afternoon and carried the board into the marshal's office where he was questioned immediately by Truet Davis.

"Where did you go? Some people don't like you around here and when you disappear like that, we don't know if you're on business, pleasure or dead." Truet had returned from delivering tax and court notices in the mountain town of Galt the night before and Matt was nowhere to be found. Truet didn't know if Matt was missing or not.

Matt yawned. "Phillip and Christine knew where I went, but I told them not to tell anyone. It's nice to know I can trust you, Phillip."

"Thank you," Phillip replied.

"You lied to me?" Truet asked Phillip. "You let me worry and be concerned for nothing?"

He grinned. "I was given strict instructions. I couldn't tell you."

Nate Robertson leaned back in his desk chair

and said, "I wasn't worried about you, Matt."

"Good. Let's all have a seat at the table," Matt said with an all-business tone to his voice.

"So, where were you?" Truet asked.

"Come have a seat at the table and I'll tell you." He laid the board on the table. "What do you fellas notice about this board?"

"It looks like cedar," Nate replied, taking a seat at a large table near the woodstove where the coffee pot sat. The table had six chairs around it. "It would make good kindling."

"Look closer." Matt sat in his usual place against the far wall.

Nate picked the board up and flipped it over. "It's got writing on it. Chinese, Hebrew, Egyptian, I don't know what. Did you buy it in Chinatown? What's special about it?" he asked with a shrug.

Matt explained, "Our former guest Jimmy Donnelly told me about this board, which I took from under the top bunk in his cell. That means Izu Chee pressed those Chinese words into the wood with his thumbnail. I wasn't about to guess what he wrote, so I went to Natoma and had Tillie read it. I wrote what she read." He pulled a folded piece of paper from his shirt pocket, slowly unfolded it, and handed it to Truet to read. "That's what the board says."

Truet exhaled and handed the paper to Phillip to read. "They were innocent?"

Matt nodded to affirm quietly.

"How?" Truet asked, perplexed. "Izu and Wang both answered the questions the same through two

50

different interpreters. How could they possibly be innocent? The story never changed."

"I intend on finding out. I can't tell you gentlemen how troubled I was to learn that I had hung innocent men. That is not acceptable. I relied on two men to translate honestly, and it appears they did not. I don't know how Wu-Pen and Ah See gave the same answers for Izu and Wang, but I will find out. Tomorrow, we arrest Wu-Pen Tseng and his two guards for the multiple counts of murder and everything else I can think of listing. I will ask Sheriff Wright to join us in the arrest for extra guns because I've seen what those two guards can do and how fast they can do it. There will be no chances taken tomorrow because I don't know how many more guards he has, if any."

Nate stared at Matt in disbelief. "So...you're saying those two brothers did not blow up the mine. Was it Wu-Pen? How do you know what Izu wrote is the truth?"

Matt took a breath before answering. "Who gained from it?" he asked simply. "Think about it. The mine is sabotaged and a few hours later, who was prepared to be there? Who shined and was praised by the local paper? Wu-Pen. Oscar Belding died of a sudden heart attack half an hour after arriving for work and drinking a cup of coffee. I spoke to him as he drank it. Who was there that day handing out coffee? Didn't I warn Wu-Pen just a month before that nothing strange had better happen to Oscar? I told Wu-Pen I would have an autopsy done on Oscar because it was a little too fishy to me, and then just so happens, the mortuary burns to the ground that night. Who gained something from burning the mortuary down? It wasn't my uncle Solomon. Wu-Pen gained from it because I believe he poisoned Oscar. And just so happens, who do you think is being paid to clear the rubble from that fire and hired to construct the new building? Wu-Pen."

"You think he planned to blow up the mine and then take care of the families?" Nate asked.

"I do. I believe Wu-Pen welcomed, comforted and fed the families of the very men he had planned to kill. That is the kind of man we are dealing with, and it pisses me off! Tomorrow, we will deal with him, and I won't be nice about it. You can bet your asses on that." Matt's eyes had grown harder the more he had spoken.

Truet spoke, "It's going to take more than a board to prove all that in the court of law. We already hung the two men convicted of sabotaging the mine and the murders of Leroy Haywood and Roger Lavigne. You have no evidence other than a letter scratched into a board. What you're implying is almost unimaginable that anyone could be that cold-blooded."

"Really?" Matt asked. "Do you fellas ever study history? Evil just like that has been around forever. Way back in 60 A.D., when Apostle Paul was sitting in prison writing the epistles, the Roman emperor Nero wanted to build a great palace and villas for himself in a certain section of Rome. I'm sure it would have been an amazing location for a palace, but thousands of people lived where he wanted to build. A large portion of the population living there was poor; we might call it a big city slum in our modern society. Nero wanted to tear that community down and build his palace, but the Roman senate wouldn't let him. In July, he left town while his thugs lit a fire and physically forbade anyone from trying to put it out upon torture and death. The fire burned for six days and burned a large section of Rome to the ground, killing hundreds and leaving thousands homeless. When the fire was out, Nero came back and welcomed all those poor homeless people to stay in public buildings, stadiums and even built temporary structures for them to stay in. He fed those people and cared for them while making plans to build his palace and gardens right where their homes once stood."

"That's kind of like what Wu-Pen did," Nate stated thoughtfully.

"There's more," Matt added. "Nero didn't want his name stained, so he blamed the fire on a group of innocent people known as Christians. Nero had a plan and that accusation allowed him to start crucifying, torturing, beheading and feeding Christians to the lions in the colosseum, while people happily cheered him on. Nero was so cold-blooded that he tied hides of animals around Christians and chained them to stone poles, covered them with inches of pitch and lit them on fire to be streetlamps to see at night while he rode through the pillars of fire on his chariot, listening to the sound of the Christians screaming. Don't forget; it was Nero who had Apostle Paul beheaded as well."

He paused and added, "That evil is still around, but Wu-Pen is not an emperor nor blamed Christians; he accused two innocent brothers. It's the very same tactic, though. You have a motive and a plan. You strike hard, come to the victim's rescue, and then cast the blame on someone else to suffer the consequences while you reap the benefits. So, I ask, who has gained from it? That is who you become suspicious of. Nero wasn't helping all those homeless folks. He was merely trying to stay in their good graces and appear honorable while he built his palace where they once lived. And Nero could rid the world of Christians without the population uprising because they hated the Christians now too. He pitted the people of Rome against them with a lie. Sound familiar?"

Phillip spoke softly, "The same thing happened here. Those people at the hanging hated Izu and Wang. Remember?"

Matt nodded his head slowly. "I remember. I'm sure Nero is not the first person ever to use that tactic nor is he the last. So, I ask again, who has gained from everything that has happened around here?"

Nate answered, "Wu-Pen. I remember you saying at the time that you didn't believe Izu or Wang were guilty. They didn't act like guilty men."

Matt crossed his arms and rubbed his beard. "Well, what's done is done."

"You still don't have proof," Truet repeated.

It was very seldom that Matt got irritated with his friend, but Truet was getting on his nerves by repeating the same fact that Matt already knew. "I will have proof tomorrow. Until we make an arrest, not one word about this to anyone. I'll put it to you all this way, if anyone finds out that we are arresting Wu-Pen and Ah See before we do, that person who spoke will be fired. I don't care who it is. Understood?" His eyes roamed over his deputies.

"Yes, sir."

"Understood?" he asked Truet.

Truet nodded quietly in agreement.

Matt stood up. "Gentlemen, I am calling it a day. I'll talk to Sheriff Wright in the morning, or everyone in town will know what we're doing tomorrow. Remember, keep it quiet. I'm not joking; your jobs are on the line."

8

Christine Knapp could feel the slight burn of her shoulders as she moved the mop handle from side to side across the dance floor. The men that came into the dance hall were encouraged to wipe their boots on a rug in the entry before entering the ballroom, but mud, dirt and dust were tracked in no matter the season. Drinks were spilled and undoubtedly, there was a man or two who took to spitting on the floor. Of all the chores that needed to be done, mopping was the least desired. Every lady employed at the dance hall had a chore schedule and it was Christine's turn to mop. No one mopped too often to save the ladies from receiving blisters or calluses on their hands. A lady needed soft hands that were more pleasurable for the gentlemen to hold while they danced. Mopping was hard work and beads of sweat gathered on Christine's forehead below the plain light green headscarf tied around her hair.

Her time was getting short to be employed at

Bella's Dance Hall. It was April and the sun was out and shining bright on most days with flowers blossoming on the trees and flower beds around town. It was a beautiful time of year in Branson, and in just over a month, she would become Missus Matt Bannister. She had chosen her wedding dress and veil; the church was reserved, and invitations were being sent out to family and friends. Unfortunately, Christine didn't have any family other than her grandmother, and she didn't know where her grandmother was or if she was even alive after nearly four years since she had seen her. There was no address to send her letters, nor did Christine know where to begin to look for her. After her grandfather died, her grandmother had sold their small farm and moved to her sister's home somewhere in Indiana. If her grandmother had given her an address, Christine had long since lost it. The money from the farm sale was given to Christine with a strong encouragement to move west. Her grandparents were devout Christians and believed they would all be together again someday in heaven. There was a sad goodbye with many tears when Christine watched the stage take her grandmother away. It weighed heavily on her heart as she pulled the mop from side to side cleaning the floor. One good thing about mopping a large area is it gave a lady time to think.

Rose Blanchard came out of the kitchen, followed closely by the newest dancer, Sherry Stewart. They had become good friends and snickered while they stopped and watched Christine.

"Would you look at that? The great beauty Christine Knapp *does* do work around here. I was thinking you were too special to do any real work," Rose said with a touch of bitterness in her voice. It was Christine's first time mopping the ballroom floor since being shot by Martin Ballenger.

Christine paused the mop handle and glanced at the two ladies with a flicker of irritation. "I've mopped dance floors for a lot longer than you, Rose."

Rose smirked. "Well, it's good to see you working up a sweat. I was almost convinced you never sweat. You are such a perfect lady and all."

Christine gave a fake smile and began moving the mop to the left and the right while ignoring Rose.

Sherry held a glass of sun tea and took a sip. "I don't know, Rose. Christine's getting married next month and then she'll be mopping every day of her life. Calluses will grow on her hands like conks on a tree and Matt will miss the feel of a lady's soft hands and come back to us. Christine will be waiting at home like all of the other unhappy and lonesome wives."

Rose snickered. "I will be the top money earner of this place and the highest last dance bid winner once you're gone. I give it six months and Matt will back bidding for my hand. Marriage never lasts, you know. You'll be back here."

Christine held the mop and took a deep breath to try to answer calmly. Rose and Sherry seemed to feed off one another to discourage her from marrying Matt and belittle her as well. There appeared to be a bit of jealousy the closer her wedding day came. "I hope both of you meet a man as good and honorable as Matt when you two fall in love with someone. And you will. You're both too beautiful not to draw men like bees to a beautiful flower." It was wiser to answer with kindness than anger. There was also a bit of an underlying insult in there if they had heard Bella's analogy of the Birds and the Bees that she had told Edith Williams when Martin Ballenger was courting her.

Rose's full lips pursed into a pout. "Don't forget to rinse out the mop bucket when you're done." She turned towards the stairs.

Sherry flicked her wrist and emptied the remaining half glass of tea onto part of the floor Christine had already mopped. "You missed a spot." She turned and followed Rose out of the ballroom.

Christine was irritated. Since a late-night talk, Sherry Stewart had become embittered at Christine for criticizing Sherry's unfaithfulness to her husband, Hiram. Hiram had caught her with another man and kicked her out of the hotel, which brought Sherry to Bella's Dance Hall in the first place. Since then, Hiram had no contact with Sherry and went back home to Ohio without her.

Sherry stopped at the bottom of the stairs near the entrance door. "Oh, Christine," she called nicely with a pleasant smile. She held Matt Bannister's arm as she guided him to the ballroom. "Your fiancé is here." She patted Matt's bicep to get his attention off Christine. "You see, Matt, she isn't always so beautiful."

"Oh, yes, she is," Matt replied. Christine wore

a typical brown dress and a light green headscarf. "She's more beautiful every time I see her."

Christine grinned and nearly skipped over to him before giving him a loving kiss to intentionally show Sherry that her discouraging words mattered none whatsoever. "I'm sure I'm not looking my best right now but thank you. How was your trip?"

"Good. I thought I would come to visit with you for a couple of hours before you start working. Can I help you mop?"

"You're so sweet. If you wouldn't mind, sure. Sherry spilled her tea over there where I already mopped," she said with a knowing glance at Sherry. She turned away and began walking up the stairs leaving Matt and Christine alone. Christine continued, "If you could mop that up and just this half of the floor, that would be great. Wu-Pen brought me a robe-type thing a couple of hours ago. I forget what he called it, but it's beautiful. I want to put it on and show you,"

"Wu-Pen came here. Why?"

"He brought me a gift. I don't know why. He insisted I take it. It is beautiful though and probably expensive. It's silk. Let me change into it and show you."

"Christine, did he make you feel uncomfortable at all?" Matt asked curiously. A women's intuition was often a good evaluator of a man's character and intentions.

She was hesitant. "Kind of. I was surprised to see him here. When Chusi gave me his wife's dress I was honored. And I know it meant a lot to Chusi when I told him I'd wear it at our wedding, but since he's not here, it wouldn't be wrong if I wore a white dress, would it?"

Matt could feel a touch of irritation sizzling within him. "No. How did Wu-Pen make you feel uncomfortable?" A slight furrow in his brow let her know he was concerned for reasons she did not know.

"I was caught off guard. Wu-Pen showed up unexpectedly with his two guards and gifting me with the robe. I don't know why, and he didn't give a reason when I asked. He just insisted I have it. Friendship," she said with a casual shrug of her shoulders.

"Do me a favor; don't trust him. I don't know why he would give you that either, but he seems to want to help people around here and I suspect he'll want a favor in return at some point. I doubt he'll be back, but if so, don't be alone with him. Promise me that." He wanted to say more, but he couldn't risk one of the ladies overhearing him. Bella's Dance Hall was a rumor mill and one story coming in meant ten going out.

Christine added, "He did say he stopped by your office to ask for your permission to give it to me, but you weren't there. Is there something I should know?" she asked, reading Matt's expression correctly.

"No. Did you tell him where I went?"

"I told him you went to Natoma but would be back today."

Matt gave a frustrated sigh.

"Why? What are you not telling me?" she asked with concern. "Are you mad at me?"

Matt shook his head. "No. I didn't want anyone

to know I was going there. I don't think it matters much." He looked at Christine hesitantly and then said with emphasis, "Just don't trust him. And don't go anywhere with him if he asks you to."

"I wouldn't. Trust me, I learned my lesson about trusting strange men asking me to go with them back in December."

Matt grinned. "Let me help get your floor mopped and then we can visit for a while."

9

Wu-Pen Tseng was troubled. He didn't know why he felt an uncanny sense of trouble on the horizon. It was most uncommon to feel troubled over nothing at all. Crime, they say, has a way of making a person weary from the worry of being caught. He had covered his crimes perfectly with no ties to him, yet he was feeling anxious. The nervous mannerism of deputy Phillip Forester when Wu-Pen went to the marshal's office made Wu-Pen feel uneasy. Phillip lied about where Matt was and there was no reason for Phillip to lie unless it had something to do with him. More than just the lie, the expression on Phillip's face revealed there was a secret he knew about Wu-Pen that he would not speak, but his anxiousness displayed. It made Wu-Pen curious to know what the young deputy was hiding.

Wu-Pen picked out his favorite hanfu, a loose-fitting silk robe with wide sleeves that closed with a silk belt tied in the front. The hanfu belonged to his consort and loyal partner, Ling Tseng. It was bright red with a gold ornamental design of flowers and interconnected profiles of female lions. It was one that he found irresistible when Ling wore it. Wu-Pen folded it neatly and approached the dance hall to give it to Christine as a gift of friendship. To ease the awkwardness of receiving a gift, he stated to her that he had stopped by the marshal's office to get Matt's approval, but Matt was not there. Casually, he inquired where Matt had gone, and Christine fell into the trap like a flea jumping on a passing dog. Christine was honest when she said she did not know why he went to Natoma.

The town of Natoma meant nothing to Wu-Pen. He recalled Matt had recently lost his deputy Jed Clark there a few months back and killed a man near there in recent weeks. Wu-Pen was confident Matt's business did not concern him, yet he could not explain why the deputy Phillip was anxious and quick to lie. That alone concerned him and the mystery of it made him uneasy. Phillip and himself had been on friendly terms, but now Wu-Pen had been misled by a friend. It troubled him.

Ling Tseng approached him and knelt in front of him to hand him a plate of food. "Why do you appear troubled?" she asked with concern.

Wu-Pen sat in his favorite plush chair in his home above the temple. He usually would be in his office taking care of business in one form or another, but he wanted to be alone without his two security guards. Wu-Pen had come to Branson and inserted himself as the community leader using the Chinese Benevolence Society as his throne of power. New rules had to have consequences the people feared. Wu-Pen's two guards, and the others from his caravan to get to Branson, wasted no time breaking the spirit of the pawns of Chinatown and demanding strict obedience. Yet, to meddle in people's lives, it was a good idea to be protected as well. Bing and Uang were with Wu-Pen whenever he left the safety of the apartment that he called home. Wu-Pen wrinkled his nose thoughtfully. "I do not know why Matt's deputy would lie to me. I can think of no reason why he would be skittish and lie. He was hiding something, and I cannot think of what there is to hide."

Ling Tseng rested her weight on her heels. She wore a white robe with an intricate black floral design. Everyday Wu-Pen could say she never looked prettier, and it would not be a lie. Ling was a stunning young woman he bought for a purpose, but he had come to love her and honored her with his last name.

She suggested, "Perhaps he was afraid of getting in trouble if he told anyone and not just you. The town the lawman went to seems to be trouble for him. Perhaps you are worried about nothing that concerns you? Maybe he has a woman consort there and does not want his fiancée to know."

He briefly laughed at the thought. "No. Another woman is not his way. But I believe you are right; whatever his business there is, it does not concern me." He frowned. "I am so close to achieving what we set out to accomplish here. I am right on the edge of succeeding and do not want anything to interfere with my plans. The only loose end and threat to me is Ah See. He must be silenced for soon."

"Do you wish for Bing Jue to silence him tonight?" Ling asked.

"No," he answered softly. "Ah See is inscribing proverbs on a granite pillar for the temple. When that is done and brought here, he will no longer have a purpose. But we must be wise on how he is silenced because Ah See has been here for a long time and knows many people. On that day, I will have you bring Ah See and his sister to my office to reward him for his good service. I will keep my promise and send him back home with much wealth." He smiled devilishly. "Or he'll think and say his goodbyes and leave this community with excitement and end up buried in the mountains where he'll never be found. His sister, Meili, will come back here and live her days underground in the pleasure room. Your thoughts?"

Ling smiled. "You are very wise. However, you should be aware that Bing Jue is quite fond of Meili, and she would make him a good consort. It might be unwise to anger your devoted servant in such a way."

Wu-Pen lowered his brow. Meili would make him a profit, which appealed to him far more than allowing his guard Bing to have a woman to cater to him. He did not respond.

To petition the city of Branson for permission to build a six-block extension of Chinatown to accommodate the coming influx of Chinese working on the railroad, Wu-Pen agreed to supply the soil and labor to fill the ruts and holes on the city streets. The soil used, he explained, would come from digging six inches of soil and building a stone pathway all along Chinatown. It was an excellent way to get rid of the excess dirt the Chinese were digging for underground tunnels. The tunnels and rooms underground were nearly complete. It was hard to believe that not one American had figured out there was more wagon loads of dirt being hauled onto the city streets than what could possibly come from the walking path. It proved the Americans paid no attention to what was happening under their feet in Chinatown or for that matter, right in front of their noses.

It took supplies to frame the walls and secure the ceiling of the tunnels to keep them from caving in. River rocks were easily collected along the rivers and streams. The wagon loads of rock were shrugged off by the Americans as stones for Chinatown's pathway. Lumber, bricks and mortar were easily accessible as Chinese labor was constructing the new three-story brick building that would become the Fasana Furniture Store and Mortuary. A wagonload of boards would be ordered for the construction and then taken to Chinatown and unloaded. The bill would be sent to Solomon Fasana for the structure of his new business. Most everything needed was found, collected or purchased in such ways. The tunnel work was laborious and continuous twenty-four hours a day, with sixty-four men assigned to the workforce. Seven men leveled the streets and hauled the soil while ten men labored to build the new mortuary. Wu-Pen only offered ten men to slow the process down so more supplies could be whittled from Solomon's finances. When Solomon received a bill for twice the lumber and bricks needed, there would be an issue, but Wu-Pen could raise his hands innocently and claim there must be a mistake. There would be no evidence of extra lumber, bricks or mortar anywhere except for the new furniture store and mortuary.

The life Wu-Pen envisioned was one of wealth, respect and accepted as an equal by the Americans. He wanted Chinatown to be an attractive and thriving above-ground community serving the Americans for many of their needs and taking their money. But underground, hidden away in the tunnels, was a world hidden from the whites above. A world where every Chinese man could gamble, drink, laugh and find a woman to hold. The main tunnel was nearly complete and there were businesses already down there taking men's money. Every Chinese man in Chinatown swore an oath of secrecy to keep the knowledge of the tunnels among Chinese only. A simple security system was set in place if an American ever encroached on their secret world.

Above ground and in the public Wu-Pen would be a respected businessman known for his charity and friendly smile. Underground was where Wu-Pen could fulfill all his sordid plans without them ever being known. Chinese women were smuggled into America and transported to where the most money could be made from buyers like himself.

Wu-Pen had another idea with less expense, what if a beautiful American lady disappeared? The marshal and all those frantically searching for her would never know she was right under their feet. But the dividends would be excessive as a Chinese man of some wealth would give it all to own an American lady. Wu-Pen's plans were being played out and the first American woman he had chosen to take underground was Lucille Barton. Until the day she disappeared, he would play a game of chess with the lives of her family, using Jinhai Zhang as a game piece.

10

The smell of stale whiskey was strong on Joe's breath the next morning and it took Ritchie Thorn to come over and throw a cup of water on Joe's face to get him up. Joe dressed wordlessly, grabbed his lunch pail, and left for work without saying a gentle word to anyone or a kiss goodbye. Other than a harsh glare filled with hostility, he had ignored her altogether. It was an expressive glare that Billy Jo knew all too well. When Joe drank whiskey, he would often come home with a feral look in his eyes and a fury that could quickly turn violent. It didn't take whiskey for him to hit her, but it was always worse after drinking whiskey. The glare he gave her sent a wave of dread down her spine. Joe had done so well not drinking and being a loving fiancé to her and a wonderful father to their two boys for long enough that she honestly believed their future would always be as good as their life had become. Now she wasn't so sure, and it worried her.

Billy Jo made eight-year-old Wyatt's lunch and sent him to school with the other kids from Slater's Mile. She had been agitated all day not knowing what mood he would be in when he came home from work. She had worried and prayed consistently that Joe would not go back to his old ways and make a habit of drinking again. In the meantime, to not give him a reason to want to fight, she scrubbed the davenport where he slept, washed his shirt, cleaned the cabin and walked to town with her younger son and charged a roast on her father's account. She cooked Joe's favorite meal to make sure he had everything he could want when he came home. He had gone to work still partly drunk and would be hungover most of the day until he sweat the alcohol out of his body and then he'd feel weak, tired and sick. Despite her efforts to make his home perfect and a good meal to come home to, she still expected the worst. She heated a bucket of water for him to wash up with and placed some clean clothes on the bed for him to change into. Shortly before she expected him home, she sent the two boys outside to play in the woods with some other boys, not knowing what to expect. Her anxiety heightened.

Joe Thorn opened the door and stepped into his small cabin to the aroma of a roast in the cookpot. The scent of the tender meat caused his stomach to growl. He had eaten his lunch, but it didn't settle, and he vomited it up soon after going back to work. He was sick, lethargic and had a headache for most of the day. Every swing of his sledgehammer sent a vibration through his body that felt like it was pulling the stitches out above his eye. The high-pitched clinging of the hammer's head slamming against the blunt steel of the rock drill, rang like a church bell, increasing the throbbing in his head. He would have loved to come home saying he was sick, but his job and his housing depended on him being able to work. Being hungover from a night of drinking was not a good reason to lose his job. It had been one of the longest days of his life. The ten-hour day crept along slower than the twenty-four-hour nightmare he experienced being trapped in the mine.

He stood inside looking like a haggard man who had not slept in a week. He held his lunch pail silently while staring at Billy Jo by the cookstove. He was too tired and sick to care about many things, and all he wanted to do was wash up and get some sleep. It was not hard to recognize the worry and skittish, nervous expression in her eyes as soon as he looked at her. He hung his head shamefully and finally set his lunch pail on a shelf by the door.

He stepped near her. "I am sorry. I drank too much, and I don't remember coming home last night. Was I mean to you? Did I hit you?"

A slow smile came to her lips. The anxiousness was replaced with relief, and she exhaled with a deep breath that lowered her tense shoulders. "No. You were passed out." She waved towards the cookstove. "I got the water warm to wash with. I know you must be exhausted."

"Very exhausted. I still don't feel good. Thank you for stitching up my eye. I don't remember anything after I was attacked."

"I was too worried about you to listen to what Ritchie was saying last night. Who attacked you?"

"It doesn't matter. I won't be going back there and if I do for other meetings, I'm taking you so that I won't drink so much. Billy Jo, I feel like I let you down and I want you to know I'm sorry. Yesterday I was angry that another good man died from something the company should have fixed. The other men and I wrote a list of demands and sent it to William Slater. I hope he meets us halfway at least and we don't have to strike. But we will if we must." He yawned. "I don't want to lose what I have with you and the boys. So, if there is a next time, because I'm one of the organizers of this potential strike, I'll want you to go with me and keep me from drinking more than I should." He shrugged shamefully. "I'm just glad I didn't mistreat you or the boys."

Billy Jo wanted to hug him, but his clothes were filthy, and she didn't want to get the rock dust and mud on her clean clothes. "How about you wash up and change your clothes and come eat? I made your favorite supper."

"It smells great. I'll do that."

When he was washed up and dressed in clean clothes, she wrapped her arms around him and kissed him. "Thank you for caring enough to ask if you hurt me. I'm falling deeper in love with you all the time," she said with confidence for the future that she didn't have earlier.

"Me too. How about you cut me a slab of that roast? I couldn't keep my lunch down and I am starving." There was an unexpected knock on the door. "I'll get the door if you make me a plate."

"Deal. Tell Ritchie he is welcome to stay for dinner. I got a big roast." She giggled and went to the kitchen, assuming it was Ritchie Thorn at the door.

Joe opened the door and was surprised to see Wes Wasson standing there holding a bottle of bourbon in his hand. His horse was tethered to a hitching post not far from their home. "Wes? What are you doing here?"

Wes was dressed in blue denim work jeans with his gun belt around his waist and a gray and white pinstriped pullover shirt with the three buttons left open, exposing his hairy chest. He removed his worn and sweat-stained Stetson. "I came by to see you. You were in bad shape last night and I wanted to make sure you were okay."

"I'm fine. Come in. Are you hungry? Billy Jo made a pot roast and there should be plenty."

In the kitchen, Billy Jo's back stiffened with a sincere hope that Wes would decline and leave.

"I am hungry, heck yeah. I brought a bottle to help with that hangover. I brought the good stuff too." He looked at Billy Jo with a slight nod. "Evening, Billy Jo."

"Hello," she said, sounding as stagnant as a bitter pond.

Joe looked at the bottle of bourbon and held his palms outward. "I'm afraid that's the last thing I want. But you go ahead."

"Maybe Billy Jo will have a drink with me over dinner?" Wes suggested.

She shook her head, faking a polite smile for Joe's sake. "No thanks. I prefer sober company."

Wes gave a gruff laugh, ignoring her cold uneasiness. "That's fine. It looks like Billy Joe sewed your head as well as she did my nose. She's getting enough experience between you and me that she could open up her own sewing business in town. Huh?"

Joe grinned. "Yeah. She does all right at it."

"What do you remember about last night?" Wes asked. "You were having a lot of fun harassing those half breeds. I tried to talk to them a little bit, but they didn't like me either. If I had noticed Tyee follow you outside, I would have stepped out and broken his skull open. That attack on you was an act of war and I don't tolerate that, especially by half-breed outlaws."

Joe took his plate and sat at the small table barely big enough to have four chairs around it. "Have a seat. I don't remember anything after having my head slammed into the corner post of the porch. It was the one with a fur vest, right?"

Wes affirmed, "Yes. Tyee Crowe. The Sperry brothers said you were lucky to be left alive. I hear they are a bad bunch, but they just looked like rats that need to be exterminated to me. Speaking of which, I saw a big rat run across the road as I rode in here. You folks seem to have a rat problem if you see one in the daylight. It's not what most folks would call high living around here, is it?" he laughed mockingly with a glance towards Billy Jo. She set a plate of roast and vegetables in front of Wes. "Thank you. It looks and smells delicious."

"Thank you," she replied as an obligation of courtesy.

"Rats, mice. Yeah, that's why it's called the Slater's slum of shacks and rats. But it's where we live for now. What have you been up to?" Joe asked to change the subject.

"I'm doing good. I'm working at the Seven Timber sawmill and making pretty good money. I come home in a good mood and nothing to complain about. I haven't ridden my horse in a while and figured I better get a ride in." He took a bite of his meal and nodded pleasantly. "That's delicious." He longed to have Billy Jo cooking supper for him someday. "Do you have a glass? I didn't intend on having supper with you folks, but I'm thankful because I believe I brought the right bottle. Are you sure you don't want some?" he asked Joe as he opened his bottle.

Joe shook his head politely declining. "No. I plan on going to bed right after supper. I'm beat."

He took a bite with his fork and chewed quickly. "I came on a wrong day, didn't I?" Wes asked before taking another bite. "I should have come on a day when you felt like drinking with me."

Billy Jo sat down with a plate of food. "Joe doesn't drink anymore."

"Last night must have been an exception?" he asked with a slight chuckle.

"It was," Joe answered honestly. "It won't happen again."

"Then I won't encourage you," Wes said while pouring himself a glass of bourbon. "Where are your boys?"

Billy Jo answered, "Outside playing. They'll come in soon enough." She wished he'd finish his meal and leave.

Wes took a sip of his glass. "Mmm, I tell you, there's nothing finer. Now that my foot is healed and I can walk on it, I've been working and getting out of the house more often. It feels great. I'm telling you, there is nothing worse than being unable to roam outside and experience life. I've even started courting a young lady recently, but we're not committed yet. I'll tell you about her in a minute. I came out here to check on you and see if Ritchie and Bobby wanted to go to the dance hall tonight. I hear they have a new dancer who is taking the hearts of the young men in town by storm. The great thing about being a bachelor and not committed to the young lady I'm courting is I can still meet all these young women and find out which one I like the best." He paused to eye Joe momentarily. "You wouldn't know about that, though, would you, Joe? I heard you and your amazing lady here have been together for a long time now."

Billy Jo set her fork down and gave Wes a warning within her gaze. "Ten years and we are very happy together."

"I wasn't implying you weren't," he answered quickly in his defense. "I am forty-nine and have never found a woman I loved near enough to commit myself to. Well, except one. But she left me for another man some time back. I'll tell you, Joe, I think it was the biggest mistake she ever will make.

I think the man she left me for is a..." He paused to smile at Billy Jo. "Well, there's a lady present, so I'll watch my language. You get the idea, though."

Billy Jo kept her face down towards her plate while she ate. The anxiety building within her reddened her cheeks. She knew Wes was talking about her and the man he referred to was sitting with them.

Joe swallowed his food and shrugged a shoulder uncaringly. "It happens. You're not the first man to fall for a woman that doesn't love him back. Heartbreak is just a part of life."

"Have you ever had your heart broken, Joe?" Wes asked.

"Nope. Billy Jo is the only woman I've ever loved."

"Well, it's a little late for me to say that, but I hope to," he said while his eyes moved over to Billy Jo. "You know with Viola. That's the young lady I've been courting. She is from here. Viola Goddard."

"I know Viola," Billy Jo said with interest. "She used to be a good friend of mine. How is she?"

"Good. Viola's working at Ugly John's Saloon and raising her six-year-old daughter, Bonnie. You had ought to know that though, she's your daughter too, isn't she, Joe?" Wes asked innocently.

Wes had met a new friend at the sawmill named Bart Goddard. He was an older man in his fifties and when Joe Thorn's name came up in conversation, Bart told Wes an interesting story. Bart had married a widowed woman named Ellie years before that had a six-year-old daughter named Viola. Bart loved her like she was his own daughter and raised Viola with the same affection and adoration that he had for the next three daughters that he and Ellie brought into the world. Their home was a peaceful one, with church on Sundays and prayer before meals and bedtime. Viola had grown up to be a wonderful young lady with high values and she made her parents proud. Unfortunately, Viola had become friends with Billy Jo Fasana, and she introduced Viola to Joe Thorn. It was common knowledge that Joe was a no-good thug who lived out of wedlock with Billy Jo and had a child together. Billy Jo would invite Viola to do things with her frequently because they were best friends. Bart always considered Billy Jo a nice girl that had been corrupted by Joe Thorn. He was most troubled to discover that the sewer rat, Joe Thorn, was coming over to see Viola without Billy Jo. Bart wasn't a fool and knew what Joe was doing and confronted him, but Viola was twenty years old and argued she could be friends with whoever she wanted to be friends with. Bart wanted the best for Viola and when she started coming home with alcohol on her breath and hungover from drinking with her so-called friends, hostilities began to take the place of the peace and trust between the parents and the adult daughter. It was Bart and Ellie's home, and they would not allow, let alone support Viola if she did not abide by their rules. One night Ellie and Bart forbade her to leave with Joe, after a hostile argument she left the house angrily and they watched her walk away with Joe. Viola came home late, quiet and troubled, but swore nothing was wrong. Ironically, Joe Thorn never came over again and when Billy Jo did come over, Viola wasn't interested in going anywhere with her, and their friendship faded. Viola was never quite the same person, and the reason was discovered a few months later when she could no longer hide her pregnancy. Being confronted by two angry parents, Viola claimed through a torrent of tears that Joe had forced himself upon her at his cabin at Slater's Mile and the rape was not by choice. Bart and his wife had caught Viola on other occasions flirtatiously talking to boys and even kissing one young suiter with his hands on the thigh of her dress. Bart didn't believe Joe had to force her and the outrage of having his daughter become an unmarried mother of a Joe Thorn baby brought nothing except shame to his respected family name. Bart and Ella had three younger daughters to raise, and they didn't want them corrupted by Viola and her loose ways. Though, Viola claimed to be a virgin and innocent of any wrongdoing of her own will, Bart and Ellie forced her out of their house and told her never to come back. It had been seven years, and even though they lived in the same small city, neither Bart nor Ellie had spoken to her since then.

Wes asked questions around town and discovered Viola Goddard worked at Ugly John's Saloon. She and six-year-old Bonnie lived in an apartment at the Dogwood Shacks on 2nd and Dogwood Street. Wes went to Ugly John's Saloon to introduce himself to her but discovered the owner, Big John Pederson, did not like him and Wes would be looking for trouble if he ever came back to Ugly John's. It seemed Big John was friends with Chusi Yellowbear and blamed Wes for the heathen's death. Nonetheless, Wes made it a point to meet Viola and with a motive or two of his own, he began courting her.

Sitting at the table, he already knew Billy Jo had been friends with Viola and the truth of what had happened. Billy Jo was about to be shocked, and it may not end well. Wes knew it would be an emotional conversation and one that could quickly turn violent when Joe was confronted. Wes was no stranger to violence and wore his gun belt just in case.

"What?" Joe stated with a perplexed expression.

"Isn't Bonnie your daughter?" Wes repeated.

Joe scowled. "No! The two boys are the only kids I have."

"Joe doesn't have any other children," Billy Jo added with a condescending tone.

Wes raised the glass to his lips after taking another bite. He hated to cut the delicious meal short, but he knew he would be asked to leave in a minute. He looked Joe in the eyes. "Viola said Bonnie is your daughter. She says you raped her right in there about seven years ago," he said, pointing at the bedroom door. "While Billy Jo was gone."

Joe's eyes widened in alarm and then hardened angrily. "Get out of my house! Now!" he shouted and stood up to force Wes outside.

"Hey, okay. I'm going. I just thought I'd ask," Wes said with a sly smile as he stood. He had noticed the shocked blank expression come over Billy Jo's face.

"Now!" Joe grabbed Wes and pushed him away

from the table towards the door.

Wes spun around, pushed him back, and quickly rested his hand on his revolver's grip, threatening to pull his gun. He grunted forcefully, "Don't ever try manhandling me, Joe! I'm sorry to ruin your nice dinner, but I won't be manhandled by anyone."

"She said that little girl is Joe's?" Billy Jo asked with a bewildered expression.

Wes spoke with a touch of empathy to his voice, "She did. You were out of town for a week or so visiting with your family in July, about seven years ago. Viola said she could never face you after Joe raped her."

It was beginning to make sense why Viola didn't want to be her friend anymore. She looked at Joe with tears forming. "Joe, is that true?"

"No!" Joe answered sharply. "It is not. I don't know what he's talking about!"

Wes chuckled lightly while keeping his hand on the revolver's grip. "Sure, you do. You told her you'd hurt her if she ever told Billy Jo. Viola told you she was pregnant with your child and had nowhere to go after her family threw her out onto the street. You told her, and I'll use nicer words, to get lost." He spoke to Billy Jo, "That's why Viola didn't want to be friends with you anymore. Joe raped her."

Tears magnified her blue eyes to the size of silver dollars as she stared at Wes wordlessly.

"That's a lie!" Joe's angry voice boomed suddenly. "Get out of my house before I force you to use that gun, but I'll kill you before I die!"

Wes's lips curved upwards into a humored smirk.

"I'm not a man you should try to threaten. Unlike you, I have killed many men and it's nothing new. Well, keep the bourbon, and thanks for dinner." He put his old Stetson on and left their cabin, closing the door behind him. His job was done, and he would let the debris fall where it would. He expected Joe and her to argue and ruin the peace they had found. It was a cold thing to do, but his love for Billy Jo would suffer the hostility she would have towards him presently, but she would thank him later. He would let them fight but would stay near if it got physical where he could become her hero.

"Joe...?" she asked hesitantly. Her mind swam in a slurry of memories that came flooding back that never made much sense until now.

His lips twisted into a bitter sneer. "He's lying!" he shouted. "For crying out loud, Billy Jo, she was your friend. Who did she tell you the father was?" His eyes bore into her as abrasively as the tone of his voice. His cheeks reddened.

Billy Jo's brow furrowed. She tried to think back to when she first learned Viola was pregnant. She was younger than Billy Jo and a good Christian girl who was saving herself for marriage. Billy Jo remembered being shocked to hear Viola was pregnant. Thinking back, Billy Jo answered him hesitantly, "She never said who the father was. She always avoided the question." Her eyes raised to meet Joe's. "You did it, didn't you? I went to the Big Z for a week for a family get-together. I remember Wyatt was just a baby. Viola never talked to me after I came back home." Her expression grew darker.

"You invited my friend here and...in our bed? Tell me the truth, Joe."

Joe grunted and grabbed the bottle of bourbon off the table and took a long drink.

"Tell me the truth!" she demanded.

He gazed at her wordlessly, turned his back to her and went outside, slamming the door closed behind him.

She opened the door and followed quickly. She pushed him while he guzzled a long pull on the bottle. "You raped my friend? Is that what you did? Joe, is that true? How many other children do you have?"

"Stop!" he shouted, before turning to face her. "I didn't do anything."

She read the agitation on his face and knew the allegation was true. "I don't believe you. Viola was my friend!" Billy Jo pulled the ring off her finger and threw it at him. "I don't want your ring. I'm moving back to town!" Her tears were immediate.

Joe ordered, "Pick the ring up and put it on."

"No! Give it to the next woman you bring home."

"You don't want it?" he asked bitterly and took another drink.

"No, I do not. Not from you!"

"Fine!" he screamed. He scooped up the diamond ring and walked towards the privy.

"What are you doing?" she asked and began following him.

"You don't want it? Fine. I don't either."

"Joe? Joe, what are you doing?" she asked as he opened a privy door and stood over the seat above the pit of excrement.

"If you want it, go get it!" He threw the diamond ring with four rubies into the privy's pit.

"That's my wedding ring!" she screamed, suddenly realizing she'd never see it again.

"Oh, now you want it? Then go in and get it!" He grabbed her by her blonde hair and dragged her towards the privy while she screamed. "You want it? Get your fat ass down there and get it!" He forced her head towards the hole while lifting her leg up, trying to force her headfirst into the pit below. She was holding onto the sides of the seat, fighting him while crying out in horror. "It's where you belong, Billy Jo!" he exclaimed with the fury of an obsessed madman.

Wes Wasson ran his horse to the privy and jumped out of the saddle. He grabbed Joe and yanked him backward to the ground. Wes glanced at Billy Jo's horrified face as she stepped quickly out of the privy, visibly shaken and sobbing.

Joe cursed at Wes. "I'm going to bust your head open!" He raised his fists to fight.

Wes was furious to see the lady he loved treated in such a way. He knew Joe was physically stronger and in better physical condition to fight. If he could outrage Joe to the point of grabbing a weapon of any kind, even a simple rock off the ground, Wes could shoot him in self-defense and be done with him. Wes held his hands up to defend himself and said, "She was leaving you to be with me before the mine accident. I doubt Billy Jo will want to go back to you now. She's a good kisser, isn't she? I know I've been missing those lips." Wes snickered intently to rile

Joe even more. "Joe, I'm going to raise your boys as my own two sons. I may even change their name to Wasson. How would that be, Joe? Wyatt Wasson…"

"Wes!" Billy Jo shouted emotionally and collapsed to her knees in anguish. She knew the truth was out in the open and her relationship with Joe was over for good now.

Joe could feel his chest expanding making it harder to breathe as the words cut his heart open like a knife slicing a doe's liver. He watched Billy Jo respond to Wes's comments and it left no doubt that the words were true. A low growl of fury came from deep within and it came out like a shout of rage. He ran forward to tackle Wes to the ground, but Wes spun as he fell to his left and rolled Joe to his back as they landed. Wes threw a right fist that skimmed Joe's cheek. Joe kept his left arm extended on Wes's collar bone to keep him at a distance to limit the contact of his swings.

Wes swung another right, but his arm wasn't long enough to connect with a solid blow, with Joe holding his shoulders at a distance. He swung again and realized he was wasting his energy with his right fist. Extending his left fingers straight, Wes jabbed his left hand down, driving his fingernails into the stitches of Joe's head wound.

Joe cried out and released his grip on Wes's collarbone and covered his now opened gash with his hand.

Wes lowered his center of gravity and swung a hard right that connected with Joe's cheek and then plowed down another right followed by another.

Ritchie Thorn came running to save his bleeding brother and dove on Wes, forcing him off Joe. Ritchie and Wes rolled on the ground, trying to get the better position on one another but ended coming up to their feet. Knowing he was fighting two brothers and surrounded by their friends who were quickly gathering and cheering Ritchie on, Wes drew his revolver and pulled the hammer back with the barrel pointed at Ritchie. Wes had a slightly bloody lip from butting heads with Ritchie.

"Back off!" Wes shouted while he tried to catch his breath. Fighting hard rock miners was a bad idea because their strength and endurance far outmatched his own. Joe nor Ritchie were out of breath like he already was. He looked at Joe, who approached Billy Jo. "If you hit her, I'll kill your brother," Wes warned with his chest heaving with his breaths.

Joe looked at Wes with blood flowing freely down his face from the reopened wound. He turned his attention to Billy Jo. He shouted, "You kissed him?"

"It was before you changed…" she tried to explain.

"Get your clothes and get out! Don't come back, Billy Jo, we're done." He picked up the half-drained bottle of bourbon off the ground and took a long drink while Billy Jo sobbed uncontrollably. "You can come to get the boys tomorrow. But I want you gone now!"

Wes spoke softly to her, "Come on, Billy Jo. I'll take you to your Pa's or wherever you want to go."

She pushed Wes away and cried out through her tears, "Stay away from me! You ruined everything!

I told you I don't love you. Just go away."

Joe spoke uncaringly, "You can get your stuff tomorrow when I'm gone. You might as well hop on your lover's horse because you're not welcome here. We are done! I'll tell the boys and I'll let them know it's your damn fault."

"It's not worse than what you did!" she cried out.

Joe scoffed with disgust. "We had something good, and you let this guy ruin it. Marrying you now would be like digging the ring out of the crapper. Fittingly, that's your worth!"

"I'm not leaving without my sons!"

Joe's words were hard as firm as stone, "Yes, you are! You can take them tomorrow, as I said. But do not be here when I get home or I will hurt you! Now go and stay away from me." He looked at Wes coldly. "She's yours." He went into his cabin, followed by Ritchie and a few others curious about what had happened.

"Thank you," Wes hollered with a slight chuckle. He reached his hand out to Billy Jo gently. "Come on, I'll give you a ride."

She slapped him with a stinging right hand. "Get away from me! Just go away." She collapsed to the ground and bawled.

11

Luther Fasana enjoyed quiet evenings as the sun laid low over the western horizon. He sat on his bench swing watching the sunset while drinking a room-temperature glass of sun tea. He didn't have any ice to keep it cold, but it was wet and tasted fine. He wondered when his brother Joel was going to come back to Branson. Joel retired from the granite quarry the summer before and decided to visit their sister in Astoria on the Oregon coast for a month. It had been nine months now and Joel had yet to come back home. Joel was staying in a cottage overlooking the Pacific Ocean. He was enjoying his time fishing, crabbing, clamming and whittling pieces of driftwood into animals in his spare time. Luther had received letters inviting him to join his brother, and it was tempting as he had never seen the ocean. He was fortunate enough to retire if he wanted to, but the fact was he enjoyed working too much to want to stop. Luther's life was a simple one and it didn't take much to make him happy but sometimes the simplest people suffer the most for some reason.

Years ago, when the city was still young, he married the first woman that showed him some attention, named Courtney. They had two sons together and eventually she ran away with a gambler leaving him to raise the boys alone. Luther eventually fell in love with a younger blonde beauty named Lisa, who he would say was the love of his life. They married and tragically, Lisa died while giving birth to Billy Jo. It was a horrific loss to him, and it still broke his heart when he thought about her. He was given no choice but to raise Billy Jo as a single father. The two boys helped, but years later a single letter from the boys' mother invited the two young men to California to work in a business her late husband left to her that she could not run alone. Anxious to get out of Branson and the family business at the quarry, the two boys left him for sunny California and hadn't been back. Luther was a hard man, especially in his younger years, but hindsight is far more recognizable than foresight. He had pushed his boys so hard that they wanted out of the granite business and in general, to get away from him.

Billy Jo was all he had left. Often, he wondered what she would be like if her mother had survived to raise her. It would have been nice to sit on the bench swing and watch the sun set with Lisa beside him. Perhaps he would be more interested in retiring and exploring the shores of the Pacific Ocean if he had someone to share the experience with.

He didn't have anyone to love, and he would never again. Those days of romance and love were long past him now. Kids dream of the future, young men struggle to make those dreams come true, and old men reminisce about the glory of youth and wish they could experience it all over again. The changes Luther would make if he knew then what he knows now. He loved his sons and his daughter, but if he could do it all over again, he would not marry Courtney and would not have any children with Lisa. His heart was full of empty spaces where the people he loved should have been. Even on the most beautiful evenings, the quiet of his home could feel far too lonely for a man who enjoyed being alone. There was a vast difference between loneliness, being alone and feeling alone. Luther knew the difference because he had known them all.

He sipped his glass of sun tea and watched the sun dip a little more on the horizon. He reached down and stroked the neck and back of his red dog. The red dog had become a constant friend and he was glad to have it. He was trying to teach the dog to retrieve ducks, pheasants, or other game birds he hunted, but the dog would rather grab a stick. The dog's head lifted, and he growled before barking at a horse and rider that was nearing the granite hitching post that had the name *Fasana* professionally engraved down both sides.

"Hush," he said gently to his dog that he simply called Red. He knew immediately by Billy Jo's expression that something was wrong. He stood up and watched Billy Jo slide off the saddle in her usual jeans and come quickly towards the porch, clearly upset. She wrapped her arms around her father and began sobbing. He held her and let her sob while his eyes slowly filled with moisture. He hated to hear his baby girl cry. His attention went to the man that hitched his horse and slowly neared the porch, cautious of Red, who let out a deep growl, warning him not to approach.

"I wouldn't come any closer. My dog does not like you," Luther said with little friendliness in his tone. The one belief that he staked his soul on was that Jesus Christ was the son of God and died for our sins. Salvation was found in that sacrifice and God's forgiveness and grace alone. Another belief just as firmly ingrained in his heart was that dogs were the best judge of a person's character and if his dog did not like someone, he would never trust them.

"I see that," Wes said.

"What's going on? Where are my grandsons?" Luther asked Wes.

Wes pointed at Billy Jo, indicating for him to ask her.

Luther held his daughter lovingly in his large arms. "What is it, Sweetheart?"

"Joe and I broke up," she said through her tears and her face pressed against his chest.

Luther rolled his eyes, having heard those words a dozen times before. He would have tried to comfort or at least sympathize with her if he wasn't glad to hear it. The problem was it never lasted more than a month or two at most. He remained silent and just held her until she broke the hug and wiped her cheeks dry.

"The boys are with Joe," she answered.

"Why?" Luther asked with concern. He never thought Joe could be a good influence on them. "Red, go lay down!" he pointed at a blanket beside his bench swing. The dog's angry barking was becoming annoying. "Red!" his deep voice boomed to shut the dog up. "Go in the house." He opened the door and forced the dog inside before closing the door. He motioned towards Wes. "Who is this?" he asked Billy Jo.

"Wes. He brought me here."

"Wes Wasson," he introduced himself, reaching out his hand to shake Luther's. "I'm a friend of your daughter."

Luther kept his hand at his side with a scowl. "Wes Wasson. Isn't that the name of the man that Matt said was harassing Chusi and eventually got him killed?"

Wes was not expecting such a blunt question. "Ah...he and I had some issues," he answered slowly.

"Like what? Him being an Indian is what I heard."

"Pa, please," Billy Jo tried to intervene.

"No, Billy Jo," Luther continued irritably. "What kind of issues did you have with Chusi? I want to hear them."

Wes grinned uncomfortably. He had hoped to make a good impression on her father. "I was part of the soldiers that attacked his camp on Bear River."

"That's not what I heard. Let me tell you, right now, I am half Indian and Billy Jo is quarter blood. I have nothing more to say to you, except Chusi was my friend and no wonder Red doesn't like you. You can leave and don't come back around my daughter again."

"Pa..." she whined. She knew her father well enough to know he wasn't going to change his mind.

"Just go, Wes," Billy Jo said sounding frustrated.

"Okay. I'm leaving," Wes said and walked back to his horse.

Billy Jo turned to her father, angry. "Pa, you are so rude!" She watched Wes ride away.

Luther answered just as heatedly, "What's ruder, kicking someone you don't like off your property, or hating a man for the color of his skin? That man hates Indians just because they're Indians, Chinese because they're Chinese and blacks because they're black. I won't have that kind of man around my house. Red hates him and I know why." He took a breath. "Anyway, what happened to you and Joe?"

Billy Jo hesitated. "We better sit down. I don't know what you're going to say when I tell you." Billy Jo explained what had happened with Wes before the mine explosion and how she intended to leave Joe. She continued to tell him what happened earlier that day between Joe and Wes.

Luther listened and if Joe Thorn were standing in Luther's front yard, he would not hesitate to snap Joe's neck for trying to throw his daughter in the privy. It infuriated him. Luther learned to listen and keep his opinion quiet over the years until Billy Jo was finished with her story and asked for his opinion. He wasn't always successful at it, but he listened and bit his lip to keep quiet.

"Tomorrow, can you take me to the cabin and help me get the boy's and my things and bring them here?" she asked to finish the explanation.

"Of course."

"Aren't you going to say anything else?" She was surprised he was being so calm and not raising his voice.

He smiled sadly. "Yeah. Billy Jo, I wish your mother was here to teach you how to find men worth knowing. I bought you a house to get you away from Joe, but you kept going back. Now there's Wes Wasson." He hesitated thoughtfully. "How about I take you and the boys to Astoria for a month or so to see the ocean and visit with your Aunt Eleanor? Would you like that?"

"The ocean? Yeah."

"Good. I think it would be good for you to take some time in a new location and get away from here. I'll make plans and we'll leave next week. Until then, just stay away from both of those men. Neither one is any good." Luther hoped a month or so in the company of his sister, Eleanor, would leave a vast impression on Billy Jo. If nothing else, she would learn there is a whole other breed of people in the world than rough necks and thugs. Some people live far above the filth and grime of the granite quarry or the silver mine, which were all Billy Jo and her two boys knew. Though he wouldn't say so, he hoped Eleanor could teach his daughter how to be a lady.

12

Matt followed the old Chinese priest in an orange robe down a narrow hallway with four closed doors on the right, and two on the left as he was led to the door at the end of the hallway, which was Wu-Pen's office. He held the board with Izu's writing on it in his left hand as he and Truet walked to the office overlooking Flower Lane. The old priest held the door for them to enter the office with a smile.

Wu-Pen came around his wide desk with a friendly smile on his face and extended his hand to shake. "Marshal Bannister and Truet. Welcome, welcome. What do I owe this honor?" His head tilted. "Please tell me this is a friendly visit and not business." His two guards, Bing Jue and Uang Yang stepped closer, suspicious of the board in Matt's hand. Both men were ready to move in quickly if necessary to protect Wu-Pen.

Matt smiled politely, but his attention went to the opened curtains on the two windows overlooking the street. To Matt's angst, one of the windows was opened to let the fresh spring air inside. In about ten minutes, Deputy Nate Robertson and the Branson Sheriff and his deputies would come into the building and come upstairs to make the arrest. Matt had emphasized the need to enter quietly, and the opened window threatened to ruin any surprise if they made any noise at all.

"A little of both," Matt answered while shaking Wu-Pen's hand. He offered a friendly nod at the two guards with a casual smile. Uang Yang's touch of a smile appeared more of a challenge than his usually content smirk. His eyes darted to the board then back to Matt.

"Have a seat, my friends and let's talk," Wu-Pen invited as he went to sit behind his desk. "Would you like some tea or anything to eat?"

"No, thank you," Matt answered as he and Truet sat in the two chairs in front of the desk. The two guards stepped back to their familiar places behind the desk near the windows.

Wu-Pen waved both of his hands towards Matt with emphases. "Please do tell me that you are not upset with me for giving Miss Christine a beautiful hanfu as a gift. A robe, if you will in English. Did she tell you about that?" he asked with mock concern. His curiosity had shifted to the board a few times, but he waited politely for Matt to mention it if it pertained to him. "I did come by your office to ask your permission to give it to her, but you were not there. I hope I did not cross a line?"

"No. Christine told me about it. She said it was

beautiful."

"I am delighted to hear that," he said with a pleased grin. It faded as he asked, "Are you angry with me? You seem more tense than usual." He observed Matt's eyes nervously bouncing between Bing and Uang suspiciously. Truet's lips were tighter than usual, like a snake coiled before it struck. It made Wu-Pen nervous, and the pending feeling of doom he had been experiencing rose through his chest into his throat.

"Not at all," Matt answered. "The reason we are here is that one of my prisoners found this above where Izu slept in my jail. Izu wrote on it, but I don't read Chinese," Matt explained with a coy smile and handed it to Wu-Pen. "I was hoping you would read it and tell me what it says."

Wu-Pen took the board and looked at the markings pressed into the soft wood. "Yes, I see." For a fleeting moment, his expression couldn't hide the concern as he read it. He was taken by surprise, and his heart began to beat faster as he laid the board on his desk and looked at Matt with a forced smile. He knew Matt was a clever man, but he never expected to be cornered in an unexpected trap. If Matt wanted to trap him, it would have been easy to have Ah See translate the board before coming to see him. Wu-Pen had made it clear to Ah See that if Matt ever spoke to him about anything, Ah See was to let Wu-Pen know immediately, but he wouldn't be able to if Ah See was at work in the granite quarry before Matt came to the office. Wu-Pen's intuition brought a sense of caution. Wu-Pen glanced at Uang Yang and picked up the board with a humored smile. He spoke in Chinese, "Laugh and glance outside. Are there horses?"

"No horses," Uang responded with short laugh.

Wu-Pen explained to Matt, "I was just telling Uang that Izu is trying to blame me for his crimes in a love letter." By the slight raising of Matt's lips, it had become clear that he already knew what was written on the board. Ah See had translated it at some point, but not that morning or their horses would be outside. Wu-Pen decided he would play the game. "It is a letter to his woman, who I was not aware he had. I will read it." He read the letter correctly. He gave a fake lazy laugh. "I assure you Marshal, a man so evil as Izu has no trouble lying. This board means nothing except a lasting reminder of a desperate last chance to cause trouble for me. I turned him over to you, and he was filled with hate."

"Hate?" Matt asked skeptically. "He never appeared hateful to me. You?" he asked Truet.

"No," Truet answered plainly. "Except for when he looked at Wu-Pen."

Wu-Pen laughed, easily humored by Truet. "Of course. I am to blame for his arrest, or so he thought. I am sure your prisoners are angry when they are arrested. Yes?" He continued, "He was an evil man. Certainly, Ah See would have said so when you showed him this."

"Evil all right," Matt agreed.

"Yes. I'm glad justice was done."

"Me too," Matt said, looking at his pocket watch that was attached to his vest pocket. It occurred to

Wu-Pen that Matt never wore a vest nor carried a pocket watch in view. Matt put the timepiece back in his vest pocket and stood. "Can you do me a favor, Wu-Pen?"

"Certainly, my friend. What can I do for you?" he asked as Truet stood as well.

"Tell your guards to remain still because I'd hate to kill them." Matt pulled his revolver and aimed it at Uang Yang. Truet, a second behind, drew his and aimed steadily at Bing Jue. Uang's eyes turned deadly as his brow lowered. He slowly stepped forward, fearlessly. "Now, Wu-Pen!" Matt warned as he pulled the hammer back until it clicked. Truet followed Matt's lead.

Wu-Pen spoke in Chinese, "Stay back! Do not fight them."

"He is threatening you! Let us kill them now!" Bing Jue snapped back at Wu-Pen with his fierce glare burning into Truet.

"Hush!" Wu-Pen ordered sharply in Chinese. He spoke to Matt calmly in English, "Why would you threaten to kill my friends? Am I being arrested for something? Please, explain."

"You are under arrest."

"For what, if I may ask? Writing on a board by a condemned criminal does not make me guilty of a crime," Wu-Pen stated with a questionable grin.

The sound of a bell ringing outside alerted Bing and Uang as both men turned their heads to look out the window. The voices of the Branson Sheriff Tim Wright and his deputy, Bob Ewing, could be heard commanding the other deputies to be quiet and have their weapons at the ready as they entered the temple.

Wu-Pen's features hardened. "Are you going to tell me why I'm being arrested before your friends come uninvited through our temple? Have I entered your home uninvited for no cause? You are irritating me, Matt. What did Ah See say to you to make you decide to invade my home?"

Matt could hear the men's approaching footsteps walking down the hallway and the metallic clinging of three pairs each of wrist and ankle shackles that deputy Phillip Forrester was carrying. He answered Wu-Pen, "I haven't spoken to Ah See yet, but once you and those two are in jail, I will be going to the granite quarry to do just that. I'll get to the bottom of how you two translated the same stories, and if we made a mistake hanging Izu and Wang, which I believe we did, then you will be tried for their deaths as well."

Wu-Pen looked at Matt with the fierceness of a wild predator. "As well? Are you implying I have done wrong?"

"Yes, I am," Matt stated with ease.

The office door opened, and Tim Wright carried a shotgun into the room, followed by his deputies, Bob Ewing, Alan Garrison, and Mark Theisen, who had shotguns. Nate Robertson had a Winchester.

Tim spoke loudly, "Don't move! Turn around and put your hands behind your backs. Shackle their hands and feet, boys."

"They don't speak English, Tim," Matt said. He spoke to Wu-Pen, "Tell Bing and Uang to turn around and get on their knees. Any resistance, and we will not hesitate to kill them."

Wu-Pen had labored too long and hard to create the paradise he had made in the Branson Chinatown to lose it now. What had seemed like a harmless game turned into a threat that could ruin all he had created. If the coward Ah See told Matt the truth, it would condemn Wu-Pen to death on the gallows. In Chinese, he spoke to his guards, "Bing, turn around and get on your knees without resisting. Uang, you are faster. Turn towards the window and begin to kneel, but then jump through the window and kill Ah See at the quarry. He must die today. We will kill these men later."

Bing Jue turned around and knelt to surrender. Uang turned towards the window, bent his knees, then suddenly burst forward, covered his face with his arms as he dove headfirst out of the second-story window. He fell six feet onto the tight canvas awning over the door to the store below them. The canopy slowed his fall enough for him to roll across the canvas as the awning tore loose from it anchors and fell to the ground allowing Uang to land on his feet unharmed seven feet below where the awning once was mounted. The canopy laid on the ground while Uang quickly ran away.

Matt hurried to the window to shoot Uang, but only for an instant did he catch a glimpse of his black shirt and pants before he disappeared. "Where's he going?" Matt demanded to know from Wu-pen.

"I don't know. I told Uang to do just as you requested. I am shocked. He has never disobeyed me before," Wu-Pen said with mock surprise.

It was turning into Matt's worst fear. He knew how dangerous Uang could be without a weapon. "Shackle them and put them in different cells. Nate, leave the shackles on and stay out of the jail until I get back. Stay with Phillip and keep your shotgun handy. If Uang walks in the door, shoot him! Do not let him get close to you! Truet, come with me. We have to find Uang!"

"What about us? Do you want us to help?" Tim asked.

"Once those two are secured in jail, come back and help us search every building in Chinatown until we find Uang."

The corners of Wu-Pen's lips curled upwards. It pleased him to know that the marshal and the others would be wasting their time searching for Uang in Chinatown, leaving Uang free to kill Ah See. Without a witness, the marshal had no evidence of Wu-Pen's guilt. It was checkmate. Wu-Pen would be free very soon.

13

Uang Yang hurried out of town and cut across the valley on foot, avoiding the farms and roads towards the granite quarry two miles north of town. Like a bullet fired from a gun, he had a mission to kill a target, and no obstacle would get in his way. His service to Wu-Pen was total allegiance no matter the cost to himself. Uang was a very straightforward man and never understood the games Wu-Pen liked to play. Uang was given a very clear command, and it would be done, but he had to be wiser than an inanimate object such as a bullet. He would lead Ah See away from any witnesses and kill him in the remote wilderness on the way back to Chinatown. Soon, Wu-Pen would be released, and they would continue to rule over Chinatown through the Chinese Benevolence Society.

The Fasana Granite Quarry was an interesting place. A large and deep pit with granite walls continuously grew broader as the employees, a mixture of Americans and Chinese, worked together to cut the granite blocks out of the earth. Blocks of granite ranging in size from a few feet to twenty feet long were lifted out of the pit with donkey engines and large derricks before being moved to several buildings where they were cut, shaped, smoothed and or engraved to meet whatever purpose they were being sold. Ah See worked in the engraving building and had gained much respect for his work ethic and skill. He was also an interpreter for the other Chinese that worked there. Uang had no fondness for the Americans as a rule, but he did have a certain respect for the Americans that treated his people well. The men who owned the quarry treated all their employees as equals and paid them fairly, whether they were Chinese or not. The Americans that did not treat the Chinese well were the ones Uang was pleased to kill.

He passed the quarry pit, listening to the sound of hammers, steam-powered donkey engines and a few shouted orders above the crack of a large block breaking away from the earth. Uang walked past unfinished granite blocks separated by boards, and peeked into the first long single-story building. He saw a huge, muscular man with short yellow hair wearing bib overalls and a sweat-stained green V neck shirt underneath with sleeves cut off at the shoulders revealing arms larger than Uang's legs. Uang decided it would be easier to have Ah See brought to him than trying to find him on his own. He approached the giant of a man and spoke in Chinese.

"What?" Saul Wolf asked. "You're going to have to speak English."

Uang spoke again in Chinese.

Saul raised his hands questionably. "I don't know." He went back to work, ignoring Uang.

Uang raised his voice a bit but could only speak in Chinese. He held his hands upwards with a shrug of his shoulders to indicate a question. He pointed at Saul, then himself and motioned towards the door.

Saul frowned. "Go ask, Ah See. I don't speak your language, little man. Do you need a hammer or what?"

Uang repeated the hand motions of leaving the building.

"No. It would help if you communicated through Ah See because I don't speak sign language either. Come on, let's go find Ah See and see what the heck you want." He waved his hand for Uang to follow him. Saul led him to another building where they found Ah See bent over a block of granite, polishing the top.

"Ah See, I don't know what this new hire wants but take care of him. If I'm supposed to train him, he'll need to learn a few words," Saul said, slightly agitated.

Uang offered a fake smile of appreciation to Saul and then spoke in Chinese, "Ah See. Please tell this man thank you for leading me to you."

Ah See turned around and was surprised to see Uang. He noticed a stream of dried blood that had rolled down Uang's arm from the window cutting him. The slight wound's blood trail stopped at the tip of his finger, where the blood dripped off his hand. Ah See spoke in Chinese, "Uang, what are you doing here?"

"Please do as I asked."

When Saul left, Ah See asked cautiously, "What are you doing here?" He was growing uneasy by Uang's presence.

Uang's expression was as emotionless as any stone along a riverbank. "Wu-Pen would like to discuss a future opportunity with you. I am here to take you back to see him."

Ah See choked out with a lump in his throat, "But I am working. I cannot leave until the workday is through. Sorry. I will come to see him then."

"Wu-Pen insists. It is most urgent. We must go," Uang persisted.

Ah See was growing more nervous. If there was anything he had learned in recent times, it was not to trust Wu-Pen or his guards. "I cannot leave, or I may lose my job. I must get permission before I can leave. We are very busy."

Uang was annoyed not to be obeyed immediately. "Then do so! Do not keep Wu-Pen waiting," Uang spoke with authority.

"I dare not. Wait, I will ask if I can leave."

"You will leave!" Uang exclaimed loudly with harshness penetrating his cold eyes.

Uang's voice drew the attention of Rufus Daily, one of the longtime employees. Rufus was in his forties, bald with short hair above his ears and around the back of his head. He had strong facial features and kept his face clean-shaven. Rufus was a kind man but could be quite firm. "Hey!" he shouted with a stern look at Uang. "Is everything okay, Ah See?"

"Yes, sir."

"Your friend needs to leave."

"Yes, sir."

"Does he speak English?" Rufus asked.

"No."

"Then tell him to leave. We have work to do."

"Yes, sir." Ah See turned his head to Uang. "He says you have to leave. I'll come to see Wu-Pen when my workday is over."

Uang's patience had reached its end. A snarl slowly appeared on his lips as his head lowered with his wicked eyes glaring dangerously into Ah See. "Let's go now," he growled in Chinese as a final warning.

Ah See backed away, seeing the murderous intention in Uang's expression. "I...I have to work," he stuttered, petrified of Uang.

Rufus Daily stepped forward between Uang and Ah See. He grabbed Uang's bicep to escort the man off the company's property. "Let's..."

Uang's right hand struck quickly, grabbing Rufus by the throat for a moment to gaze into the bald man's face, tempted to crush the man's windpipe. Ah See sprinted out of the building leaving Uang no choice but to shove Rufus out of his way and give chase. Rufus fell to the ground and rubbed his throat, surprised to have been attacked by a Chinese man.

"Rufus, are you alright?" Wade Marks asked, surprised by what he had seen as well. The other Chinese in the building stood with the most uneasy and frightened expressions Rufus had ever seen them have.

"I think so." He stood to follow Ah See. Wade Marks went with him, picking up a spacer board four feet long and two inches thick to use as a weapon if necessary.

Ah See ran towards the company office, a small three-room building at the front of the quarry off the main road. It was the safest place he could think of going, where the company owners were. The office was within twenty yards when he glanced back and saw Uang not far behind him. "Robert! Luther! Help me! Help!" he yelled as he got closer to the office.

The office door opened, and Luther Fasana stepped out of the doorway when he saw one of his best employees running towards him, appearing terrified. A Chinese man dressed in black chasing him did not seem friendly at the least. Luther waved Ah See past him into the office door and then put his hand out to stop the stranger. "Hold up, buddy," Luther said to end the quarrel between the two.

Uang approached quickly noticing Luther's left foot was planted flat on the ground and drove his heel straight into Luther's leg just above his knee hyperextending the knee. Luther collapsed as hard as a granite slab to the ground groaning in agony while holding his knee. Uang stepped over Luther without concern and kicked the closed door to bust the lock. When it didn't open, he kicked it again, but the door refused to open. He shouted in Chinese, "Ah See! Open this door right now. Open the door!"

Rufus and Wade, along with a couple of other

concerned men, ran to help Luther. Rufus let the other men comfort Luther while he approached the Chinese from behind and wrapped his arms around Uang's chest while driving him into the door. Uang threw his head back, connecting with Rufus's forehead, which jarred him. Uang pushed back against Rufus and then quickly lifted both legs and braced them against the door to push himself backward, forcing Rufus and himself to fall towards the ground. Rufus kept his hands locked around Uang as he hit the ground and squeezed Uang tighter to keep the squirrely man in his grip.

Uang's arms were useless as they were in the grip of a more muscular man. He fought to position his right leg and then brought a hard heel kick downward into Rufus's groin. Uang did not wait to see if Rufus would let him go, he immediately threw his head back into Rufus's forehead, followed by another hard heel kick. Rufus let go and rolled to his stomach, gasping to breathe after the shots to his groin.

Uang stood with fierce eyes focused on Wade, who held the board. Wade waited until Uang turned towards the door and then ran towards him with the board lifting behind him to hit the stranger over the head. Uang glanced over his shoulder and then jumped up and spun his body while raising his right leg perfectly timed to kick the side of Wade's head as he came forward. Wade hit the ground already unconscious at the same time that Uang landed on his feet. He glared at the other men to see if any of them wanted to challenge him. When no one showed any desire to do so, he turned towards the door, ran and jumped to kick the lock with his body weight and momentum coming downward.

The lock bolt burst through the doorjamb, and the door flew open with a loud bang against the wall. Uang stepped inside with ferocious determination and found Ah See standing against the far wall of Robert Fasana's office with a terrified expression on his face. Robert stood in front of Ah See, dressed in a clean suit holding his palms outward in a surrendering position.

Robert spoke intentionally in a soft voice to calm the angry man, "Hey, we don't want any trouble. Okay? Money? Do you want money?" He held out eighty dollars in paper money as an offering to Uang.

Uang's fierce glare looked through Robert to Ah See like a lion fixated on a cornered gazelle. His voice hissed in Chinese through a cold sneer, "Come with me, or I will kill you and the American right now!"

Ah See did not know why Wu-Pen wanted him dead, but he had sent Uang to kill him and there was nothing he could do about it. There were no weapons in the office and Robert was no match for Uang, Ah See wanted to tell Robert to get out of the way, but he choked on his words and Uang was moving towards them quickly.

Uang unexpectedly jabbed Robert in the throat and he fell backward into Ah See while grasping at his neck and fell to the floor gasping for air. Uang's hand grabbed Ah See by the throat and held him against the wall while applying pressure to his windpipe. He spoke through his sneered lips, "You are a weak man. Your life is about to end, and you choose to run? Fight!" Uang shouted and removed his hand.

Ah See trembled and began to weep in desperation. "I did nothing wrong. I just came to America to work and now I'm to die? Why? I've done everything I was told to do. There is no reason for me to die," he wept.

Uang's lips turned upwards slightly. "I will tell you the truth. If you can kill me, you'll be free of Wu-Pen forever. That is why you must die."

"What?" Ah See asked, confused.

Robert lying on the floor, got his first deep breath and began breathing normally aside from the tightness in his throat. He couldn't lie still and do nothing while his employee was hurt; he kicked Uang in the leg. The kick was unexpected and annoying but did not harm Uang. In an instant, Uang turned and planted a heel in Robert's face that left him with a broken nose that bled profusely. Robert cupped his hands over his nose and got to his feet to leave the office but was shoved to the ground by Uang.

Ah See took advantage of the diversion and tried to run, but Uang's right hand grabbed him by the chin and fiercely threw him back against the wall. "Please, Uang. I am no one," he pleaded.

"You hold secrets that cannot be told. You must die now."

Ah See shook his head desperately. "If you kill me here, you will be arrested and hung, like Izu and Wang. There are too many witnesses, and these men are relations to the marshal," Ah See tried to persuade Uang to spare him with a bit of reasoning.

Uang grimaced. "I am dead if you live, but Wu-Pen will live if you die. The talk is over." He curled his knuckles to create a solid straight blade with his right hand, intending to drive it through Ah See's windpipe and crush it.

"Saul, help me!" Ah See cried out desperately when Saul Wolf came storming into the office like a furious wild-eyed bull looking for a man to run through.

Saul had been summoned by of his co-workers and told Luther was hurt. He ran to the office and found Luther unable to stand, Wade barely coming to consciousness and Rufus still on his knees. His three friends being hurt and the other men afraid to face the little Chinese man in black, was more than Saul could stand. He had sworn never to fight again, but sometimes a man deserves the beating he gets. "Hey!" Saul shouted with a deep voice of authority as he came into the office.

Uang waited and listened to the heavy footsteps drawing close behind him. Quickly, he turned and released a straight right knuckle punch into the chest of the man behind him. He expected his punch to sink into the sternum of the man and leave him on the ground writhing in pain, but his punch was absorbed by a tight muscle mass that was much thicker than he had ever experienced before. It may have hurt the big man, but he stood unfazed. For a second, Uang was surprised to see him standing. He had put one hundred and fifty pounds of his weight all into the punch, and no one had ever absorbed a punch like that without falling before.

The yellow-haired giant's big hand grabbed his shirt and yanked Uang forward. Expecting the big man to swing a wide right hook to his head as most American's did, Uang raised his left arm to block the anticipated blow. Once it was blocked, Uang planned to knee the groin, gouge the eyes with a finger jab, hit the groin again with his shin bone, and watch the big man drop to his knees and whimper like a child. The right hook didn't come, but a right uppercut straight up between them connected with the bottom of Uang's chin with more power than Uang had ever felt. The power of a three-hundred-and-fifty-pound man was comparable to falling from a three-story building and slamming his chin on a steel bar three-quarters of the way down. His teeth slammed together, shooting sharp pains through his jaw as his front teeth broke and others were jarred out of position and loosened from the impact. Barely conscious but realizing he was hurt, Uang made a weary effort to look at the angry giant and then the right cross came that connected with the force of being kicked by a horse. It drove Uang to the floor unconscious.

Saul watched Uang fall and then rubbed his sternum. "That hit hurt." He helped Robert to his feet. "He broke your nose, boss. I'll take you and Luther both to the doctor. Ah See, grab some rope and we'll hogtie this little fella up good and tight and take him to Matt. He hurt Luther's knee."

Ah See stared dumbfounded at Saul. "You beat him."

Saul nodded proudly. "Yeah. I hit him pretty good. I hope I didn't hurt him too bad, but he shouldn't have hurt my friends. How'd you make him mad?"

Ah See shook his head innocently. "I didn't. He came to kill me. Can I go with you to Matt's? If I stay here, Bing Jue may come next."

Saul grimaced. "Why did he come to kill you?"

"I don't know."

"How was he going to kill you?" Saul asked, searching for a knife or gun that might have been dropped.

"His hands and feet. He is a weapon."

Saul chortled. "He's not much of a weapon. Two hits and he's out cold, bleeding on the floor. I mean, for being a weapon, just look at those broken teeth, and his cheek is swelling up like a horse's bladder. I felt kind of bad, but now that I know he was coming here to kill you, I don't feel so bad." He bent over to get a closer look at Uang's teeth.

"Saul," Robert said with his face covered. Blood dripped between his fingers and his eye were swelling closed and turning dark. "How about you tie him up before he wakes up?"

"You don't want to go a round or two with the so-called weapon?" he asked Robert with a humored grin. "All right, Boss. Rufus, go get some rope, and I'll tie him up so tight his cheek pops like a pimple."

"I could have taken him," Rufus Daily said from the office doorway.

"I know you could have," Saul agreed. "Thanks for letting me have a shot. It feels good to fight again. I forgot how good it feels," Saul said while looking at his bear sized fist.

14

Wu-Pen had been in jail for a few hours when Matt sat on the bench across from the jail cell where Wu-Pen was seated on the bottom bunk contently. "We searched Chinatown and Uang's not there. Where did you send him?" Matt asked to hear what Wu-Pen would say.

Wu-Pen gave a fake heavy sigh. "I told him to surrender, but he disobeyed me. I do not know where he is or what he is doing. Did you find anything interesting in Chinatown?" He was curious if Matt had discovered the tunnels.

"Yeah," Matt admitted. "I discovered there are a few women there. Are they not allowed to leave the kitchen or restaurant or whatever that place was where they were cooking?"

The right side of Wu-Pen's lips rose in a spiteful smirk. Matt had not found the tunnels, or he would have discovered the girls in the bordello and the opium den, among other things, kept hidden from the Americans. "No. To keep our ladies safe from Americans, they must stay out of view and not step out of Chinatown. Where you saw them is a restaurant. The same restaurant I had once invited you and Christine to share a meal with Ling and me. It's not too late; we could still eat a good meal as friends. This," he waved around at the jail cell, "is an honest mistake. Yes?"

"I hope so. I would hate to think you are capable of doing the things that I suspect you have."

"Such as?" Wu-Pen asked. "I still do not know why Bing and I are here. Or why you would invade my home with guns drawn on me. The lovesick poem of a condemned murderer pressed into a board is hardly a reason to arrest a friend."

Matt hesitated before answering. "I'll let you know when I find Ah See. Whether you are to be hung or set free depends on what he tells me." Matt shrugged and stood. "You don't know where Uang went?"

"No. Uang's purpose is to protect me, but he betrayed me and ran like a coward."

"Betrayed?" Matt questioned slowly. "Does that mean he is no longer in your favor?"

"He is not."

"I'm curious. If I'm wrong and end up apologizing to you and let you go home, when Uang comes back, what are you going to do to him? Would you give his job back to him, or no?" Matt asked.

Wu-Pen's brow narrowed in contemplation. He had backed himself into a corner by having Uang go out the window to kill Ah See. He knew Uang was smart enough to kill Ah See quietly and stay hidden until Wu-Pen and Bing Jue were released from jail. Wu-Pen had not considered what would happen after Ah See was dead. Uang would be accused of murder and have to leave the area to evade the law. Wu-Pen honored loyalty and would not betray either of his loyal guards unless it served him more to do so. Uang was a great asset and trustworthy friend who would lay his life down to protect him. It irritated Wu-Pen to lose Uang's presence, but there was no other way for him to stay once Ah See was dead.

"Hard to decide?" Matt asked. "If one of my deputies betrayed me like that, I'd fire him. And we'd have nothing to say to each other again. Period."

Wu-Pen took a deep breath. "I'd cut his queue off and send him back to China as a prisoner. He'd be killed upon arrival, but he'd have a long journey home to think about it."

"What would you say to him if we had found him?"

Wu-Pen lifted his head and leaned back across the bed to look at the boards supporting the bunk above him. "I would call him a coward."

Matt asked carefully, "What did you tell him right before he dove out the window?"

"I told you, I told him to surrender and let you bind him. Just as I did Bing Jue."

"I find it odd he can jump out a window and not cut himself. We searched Chinatown and found nothing. I mean, there were a few drops of blood that led to the restaurant I mentioned, but it stopped. Not another drop of blood to find anywhere. We searched and found nothing. Finding no other sign, it occurred to me that your people are hiding him or perhaps we couldn't find him because you might've sent him to kill Ah See."

Wu-Pen turned his head towards Matt and sat up straight. He grinned with a mock chuckle. "Ah See is my good friend. I would never wish him any harm."

"I didn't think you would. But we rode out to the quarry, and Ah See was fine. He'll be here pretty soon to talk to me on his way home. I'm glad I was wrong about you and Uang, though."

Wu-Pen hid the annoyance and surprise of Matt's words. Uang was given an order, and he never failed to be faithful. He was made for killing and had not failed Wu-Pen yet. How could he fail him now when it was most important? "Yes," Wu-Pen answered, sounding troubled. "Me too. If my friend Ah See arrives, maybe you could allow me a moment to speak with him?"

"Sure, when I'm done talking to him." Matt walked to the steel door that separated the jail cells from the office. He pushed it open and said, "Bring him in."

Truet and Nate carried an unconscious Uang Yang into the jail. His hands and feet were bound by rope. Wu-Pen was horrified to see the left side of Uang's face was swollen and black and blue. His mouth was ajar revealing his front top and bottom teeth were missing. Blood covered his lips and dripped freely down his chin.

Wu-Pen stood with alarm. "What have you done to him?" He glanced at Matt, dumbfounded to see

Uang in such an unimaginable condition. "You lied to me?"

Matt unlocked the cell door and held it open for them to carry Uang into the cell. "How's it feel, Wu-Pen?" he asked pointedly.

Wu-Pen scoffed. "I have not lied to you once. What did you do? Beat him after you tied his hands and feet? He needs a doctor. Take him to the temple and let Ling treat him," he suggested while the two deputies carried him into the cell and laid him on the bottom bunk. Neither deputy wore a weapon, but Matt had his, if needed.

Matt held up a hand to answer Wu-Pen's concern. "I asked Doctor Ryland to look at him. He said I needed to take him to a dentist, but Doctor Ryland thinks Uang's facial bone is fractured. Maybe severely fractured. The dentist couldn't do anything except pull out several of his teeth. They were broken or ripped out of the jawbone."

"Who did this to him, you?" Wu-Pen accused with growing hostility.

Matt shook his head. "No, I didn't. But your friend got whipped by a much better man."

"Who?" he demanded.

"Let's just say he stepped into a small corral with the wrong bull. He'll tell you about it when he wakes up."

Truet laughed as he left the jail cell. "Yeah, if you can understand him."

Matt closed the cell door and locked it. "Your friend broke my cousin's nose and hurt my uncle's knee. Let Uang know he's not that tough after all.

120

I have a small jar of teeth from the dentist to prove that. I saved the teeth for you as a souvenir because they are the same teeth Uang used to tell Ah See that you wanted him dead. Ah See is alive and well. He's sitting in the office waiting to talk right now." Matt shrugged empathetically. "I don't think he's feeling very loyal to you anymore."

Alarm comes in many levels, but for the first time, Wu-Pen felt a chill run up his spine. He turned towards the opened steel door and yelled loudly in Chinese, "Ah See! If you say one word, your sister will suffer! You will be left to rot beside her bed in the dungeon as a footstool for her customers! Say nothing, and you will be rewarded greatly. I'll send you and Meili back to China immediately with more gold than you can carry. You have my word for safe passage. The choice is yours! Remember, Ling will seek vengeance if anything happens to me; remember that! Suffering or reward, you can choose to live!"

Wu-Pen spoke to Matt calmly in English, "You don't want to ruin our friendship, Matt. Trust me." He raised his eyebrows to emphasize the warning.

Matt's lips raised slowly. "As I said before, if I'm wrong, I'll apologize. If not, you will stay here until you are hung. You can trust me on that. Friendship has nothing to do with the law."

A tight trembling sneer fought the fake smile that Wu-Pen forced upon his lips. "Let us go, before there is no turning back."

Matt chuckled. "If unspecified threats scared me, Wu-Pen, I would have turned in my badge years ago."

Wu-Pen smiled as he watched Matt walk out of the jail cell and close the steel door behind him. "Bing, the marshal is now an enemy. We will deal with him soon."

"I will kill him when we are free," Bing Jue said as a matter of unquestionable fact.

"No," Wu-Pen answered, "I want him to suffer first. I want to see him beg while he cries. I want to break him down so low to the ground that he never stands upright again."

Wu-Pen's threat sent a wave of foreboding through Ah See. Wu-Pen could not be trusted. The only reward Wu-Pen would give him was death, no matter what he told Matt. Ah See's sister would never go back to their parents and become one of Wu-Pen's ladies of pleasure in the bordello that was moved underground. Ah See had come to America voluntarily to labor and support his parents and younger siblings back in China. He worked hard to learn English and labored without complaint in many gold fields before he migrated to Branson and found employment at the granite quarry. He was finally making good money as the quarry paid the *man*, not the nationality. Ah See was a gifted craftsman and could shape and engrave the granite stone almost as well as Luther Fasana could. As his skill improved, his pay increased, and when they hired more Chinese, his importance for communication means also increased.

He was treated well, and life was good until

Wu-Pen arrived with thirty-some other Chinese men. They came with skills of their own and soon the temple was built, and the Chinese Benevolence Society came into existence, fully sanctioned by the San Francisco Six Companies. No one voted for Wu-Pen to become the iron-fisted community leader; Wu-Pen had taken the position by force. Any resistance to his mandated rules was met with brutality. One of his first actions was a mandate requiring an official census of all Chinese living in Chinatown. It was very detailed beyond the primary name, age, sex, family and employment. They had to list each family member and where they lived in China. It was an innocent offering of information, so Wu-Pen could notify the family if anything happened to any of them. Many questions were asked, but it was supposedly an official census, but Ah See would learn it had a much darker purpose.

The first rule Wu-Pen enforced was no other Chinese man was to speak English other than him, to the Americans. Painful punishments strictly enforced the new law, and if someone continued to speak in English it could become a death sentence. Several Chinese men were banished from the area, or so it was stated, but Ah See had reason to believe they were long since dead and buried all too quietly. Ah See spoke English every day as an interpreter for his countrymen when they needed one. Wu-Pen could not banish Ah See without appearing like a controlling overlord to the Americans and that would be bad for the image he desired to portray. If Wu-Pen was the only Chinese who could speak to the Americans, he could control Chinatown and every business deal and employment between his countrymen and the outside world. He knew every agreement between a man and his employer, right down to the penny. He knew everything being said and being done in his community because he was the only source of communication. There was only one other man that spoke fluent English and that was Ah See. No one knew the power Wu-Pen had until the day Ah See's youngest sister named, Mei-li, had been kidnapped from China and brought overseas to Branson with her honor still intact. Meili was fourteen years old and lived with Ah See. Wu-Pen had her brought to Branson for the single purpose of having leverage over Ah See's actions and the threat of hurting Meili if Ah See did not conform to Wu-Pen's authority in every way.

One cold November morning, Ah See and his two friends went to work and were attacked by three Americans. Chee Yick and Kot-Kho-Not were thrown over the edge of the granite quarry pit to their deaths. Ah See was scourged with a customized whip with bone, metal, and glass pieces pressed through the leather. The three attackers worked for the Slater Silver Mine and the company covered up the crime by showing work records that proved the men were at work that morning. Wu-Pen refused to accept that injustice and murdered the three men one by one over time and then sabotaged the silver mine with explosives, which killed several men and injured others. Crimes are investigated, and when Marshal Matt Bannister started to question Wu-

Pen, a plan was formed to accuse two brothers, Izu and Wang Chee, of Wu-Pen's crimes. To his great shame, Ah See was complicit in sending his two innocent friends to their graves instead of holding Wu-Pen responsible for his crimes. It was a heavy burden to bear. At the time, Meili's life depended upon translating Izu and Wang's anxious and honest pleas of innocence into proud confessions of guilt. To look at his friend in the eye and say, 'I know you're innocent' and then turn to look at the marshal in the eyes and say, 'He's guilty' had taken a heavy toll. Ah See wanted to be free of the burden, but he could not without losing his baby sister. For a few hours, he intended to unload the burden knowing Wu-Pen was in jail, but now after hearing the threat from Wu-Pen, he changed his mind.

Matt could be trusted to keep his word, but Wu-Pen's reach with an evil arm stretched much further than Matt's integrity allowed. Wu-Pen had placed his loyal servants in businesses around the community for a reason. Part of the reason was to gain information, share information and act where it benefitted his schemes. There was no safe place for Ah See. If he told the truth and condemned Wu-Pen and his devilish guards, he would still be tortured or dead before the day was through. Meili would never see the sunlight or her parents again.

For those who knew what Wu-Pen was like, it was fear that kept them subservient. For those who didn't, they served in quiet and blind obedience. Wu-Pen and the Chinese Benevolence Society was nothing more than a virtuous idea that was a cancer intent on enslaving the lives of the Chinese while they not only served but paid Wu-Pen to lead them.

Ah See was sitting at the table by the woodstove, feeling his world coming to an end. He had not only heard Wu-Pen's threat from his view at the table, but he had also made eye contact and felt the evil that was going to destroy him. It wasn't a matter of justice as much as a matter of mercy. If he condemned Wu-Pen, his torture would be slow and agonizing with unspeakable implications. If he lied and Wu-Pen was released, maybe Wu-Pen would send Meili back home as a reward and kill him quickly. He needed to ask Wu-Pen if that could be agreed upon, but Wu-Pen could not be trusted even if it was promised. Meili was a beautiful young lady, and to Wu-Pen, that meant pleasure and profit.

Matt sat across the table from Ah See and handed him the board to read. Ah See felt his mouth slowly fall open as he read Izu's writing to his beloved. He read the letter and laid the board on the table. To be named in the letter and referred to as a trusted friend and knowingly betrayed Izu; it felt like the floor supporting the weight of his heart and lungs collapsed. There was nothing left except hollowness within him.

Matt asked, "Is what Izu wrote true? Did Wu-Pen commit those crimes?"

"I don't know," Ah See stuttered.

"What do you mean, you don't know?" Matt asked with a hardening tone. "You and him were the only two who could talk to Izu and Wang. Did they say they did it, or not?" He glanced at Truet with frustration. "Get me that notebook."

Ah See could feel the vacuum of a deep whirlpool sucking his mind and soul out of his conscious state and into a dark world of the unknown. Fear gripped his chest like the teeth of a dragon's bite clenching down and shaking him around to tear him in two. He was terrified of Wu-Pen, and not even the lawmen in the town could bring an end to that.

"Ah See," Matt said firmly to get his attention. "It's a simple question, did they say they were guilty or not? It shouldn't take very long to answer because it's not that hard!" The frustration in Matt was evident.

"I...I can't say because I wasn't there. I don't know who did it," he answered nervously.

"For crying out loud!" Matt shouted angrily. "What did Wu-Pen say?" He had noted the sudden change in Ah See's demeanor since Wu-Pen had yelled in the jail.

"Nothing," Ah See said, frightened. His anxiety increased when he saw the same notebook that Wu-Pen had forced him to memorize. He was filled with a wave of panic that urged him to leave.

Matt took the notebook from Truet and laid it on the table. "Obviously, he said something. Wu-Pen sent a man to kill you today, Ah See. You'd be dead right now if it weren't for Saul, and you're going to sit here and tell me that you don't know if Izu said he was innocent or not?" He paused. "How about I make it even easier. I'll read what you asked Izu and read the answer you gave us. You tell me if that was a true answer or a false one."

"I don't feel good," he said faintly. "I must go," he stood up to leave quickly.

"You're not going anywhere until I have some answers!" Matt shouted leaving his seat to grab Ah See's arm. He yanked Ah See back to his chair and sat him down like a disobedient child.

Panic, terror, emotional tears that were nearly ready to burst into sobs all appeared in his eyes. "I have to go. Please! Nervous stomach. I must use the outhouse!"

"Go!" Matt shouted irritably. He watched Ah See scurry away like a jackrabbit after a hunter's missed shot.

"Wu-Pen's got him scared," Truet offered. "Do you think he'll come back?"

Matt had a cold scowl on his face. "No."

"Do you want me to get him?"

"No."

"Do we need to let them go?" Truet waved towards the jail cell.

"I'm not letting them go, yet." Matt walked to the steel door and opened it. Truet followed him into the jail.

Wu-Pen was leaning over Uang, looking at his wounds. He faced Matt with a concerned expression. "I need to get Uang to our doctor to help him. Your American doctors do not know Chinese medicine. You should not have pulled his teeth." His bottom lip quivered with indignation.

"What did you say to Ah See?" Matt asked bluntly.

"Learn Chinese, and you'll know. Until then, it's a private matter. I'll assume he is not speaking

128

the way you want. Good! You can let us out of here now. Yes?"

"No. You'll be here for a little while. I'm not quite done with Ah See."

Wu-Pen scoffed skeptically. "We are no longer friends, Marshal Bannister. I will have retribution for what you have done to my friend and for keeping us here. Don't keep us locked up long. You may regret it."

Matt laughed mockingly. "Are you going to kill me with black widows?"

Wu-Pen opened his mouth to answer and almost fell into the trap. He grinned, appreciative of the effort. "Izu Chee had strange ideas, but I kind of like them. No, I never said I was going to kill you. I am not a murderer. I am a simple businessman."

"Ah See and me are going to have a talk. Have a good night."

"Oh, Matt," Wu-Pen said as Matt stepped away, "tell Christine hello for me. I'd love to see her in the hanfu I gave her," Wu-Pen said with a coldness in his eyes that made them much darker than usual.

"I bet you would," Matt said as he closed the steel door and locked it behind him.

Wu-Pen watched the steel door close and heard the lock secure the door for the night. "Oh, Marshal Bannister, I will," he said quietly. "That is a promise."

15

Ah See hurried out the marshal's office as quickly as he could with no destination in mind. He didn't need to use the privy, but he was too afraid to answer Matt's questions and too afraid to go back to Chinatown. He didn't know where to go or what he could do, he only knew he had to get away. Two blocks ahead, a small group of people were standing outside of the new pottery shop that would be opening soon. Ah See recognized his friend Jinhai Zhang standing within the small group. Jinhai's smile was broad and sincere while a lovely young lady with long curly dark hair put an arm around his shoulders as they gazed at the new sign above the shop. Red, white and blue banners meant to draw the public's attention were draped under the new store sign that said in large spanning letters, *Barton's* with smaller print underneath, *Pottery Shop*.

"Don't you love it?" Lucille Barton asked her oldest son, five-year-old Michael. Her face beamed with excitement. The building had been painted a lighter shade of gray with dark gray trim around the windows and the freshly painted bright red door. The sign was the same light gray color with bright red letters outlined by a thin line of dark gray. Lucille was not excited when her landlord, Lee Bannister, said he would paint the building gray, but little did she know it was being done in unison with the sign that Albert and Mellissa Bannister had made for the business. It was an unexpected gift that brought great joy to Lucille's heart as she stared at the store front.

Five-year-old Michael was not nearly as impressed as his parents. He was still upset about being pulled away from playing with his neighbor just to look at a sign. "Can I go play with Robbie?" he asked his mother.

"Yes, go play," Lucille excused Michael. She turned to Jinhai fondly. She could not say any words that he would understand, but he was undoubtedly the most incredible artist she had ever known and perhaps the hardest working man. Her gratitude for him and his quiet and consistent work ethic was far more than she could communicate in words. Appreciation was universal, though, and she put her arm around his shoulders and quickly kissed the old man on the cheek. "Thank you," she said with sincerity. He grinned a pleasing smile and nodded. He did not need to know English to understand her appreciation.

Albert Bannister stood with his hands on his hips, admiring his handy work proudly. He and one of his employees had brought ladders, mounted the sign, and then hung the banners that morning before they allowed Lucille and Lawrence to step outside to see it. Albert glanced at Lawrence and shook his head with mock disappointment. "Pottery is a good business to get into, but I still kind of wish you would have gone with my idea of a peep show. A coin slot would have been easier to make."

Lawrence laughed. "Shut up. Seriously, thank you for everything you and Mellissa have done for us. I don't know how to say it, but Lucille and I can't thank you enough. You changed our lives when we had nothing but hopelessness. We'll never be able to repay you."

Albert waved the idea off. "A pencil holder, that's all I wanted out of the deal. We're even."

Lawrence scoffed. "No, we're not. Just know we thank the Lord for you and your brothers."

"You're welcome." He lowered his voice just a bit, "How's the China man working out?"

"Great," Lawrence answered. "Jin is an amazing artist and works hard. I think he will make a big difference in the business. His clay work and paintings are both stunning. I was worried about the pottery shop failing, but I'm more confident it will be okay since Jin started. Wu-Pen said we could sell pieces in his store in Chinatown too."

Albert nodded approvingly. "That's good. I have a gifted China man working in my blacksmith shop too. His name's Bo-Dinka Dong, but we just call him Grant. It's easier to say one syllable than it is three or four," he explained.

"We call Jinhai, Jin. He's a nice man. We like him."

Albert smirked with a twinkle in his eyes. "Jen is short for Jennifer, isn't it? You should give him a manly nickname like Garth. You can't mistake a name for being feminine if it starts with a capital G like Grant, Garth, Glen, Gus, or Greg. Just stay away from the full Gregory, and you'll be fine. One syllable is all you want for a boy's name. The women like to say anything beyond one syllable with a whine in their voice, Greg-ory, Gio-vanni, Gab-ri-el. It's irritating just thinking about it. But then you have to worry about the whining names causing a boy to want to sew and cook with the women rather than hunt with the men. Greg hunts, Greg-ory sews," Albert said while raising his eyebrows and nodding to emphasize his point.

Lawrence furrowed his brow for a moment, followed by a hesitant, "I see."

Albert continued, "You can trust that because it's in the Bible. Esau, one syllable. Esau hunted. Jacob, a two-syllable name, sewed and cooked with the women. Go figure." He shrugged as if the argument was settled. "Our boys are named Joshua, Jason and Tony. I learned my lesson with our firstborn, no more three-syllable names. We tried two syllables with Jason. Forget it. We're down to one syllable from here on out if we have any more children at all. If we ever have a daughter, her name is going to be Gill. It will be short for Gillian or some multi-syllable name that we'll never call her." He lowered his voice, "I said no more kids because I'm afraid we'd have a girl and Mellissa would always be wanting to whine, 'Gil-li-an.' A man can only take so much whining, you know?"

Lawrence chuckled. "Yeah, I know."

Mellissa Bannister overheard her husband and moved over to hook her arm around Albert's forearm lovingly. "What are you men talking about?" she asked, already knowing.

"Names?" Albert asked more than stated.

"Oh. That seems like an odd subject for two men to talking about. Shouldn't two men as rough and tough as you be talking about bolts, steam engines or guns?"

Albert's upper cheeks turned slightly red above his beard. "He brought it up."

Lawrence grinned. "No. I was thanking him for you all helping us. It means a lot to us."

Mellissa released Albert's arm and hugged Lawrence gently. "You are most welcome. We will see you on Monday at the grand opening. I can't wait!" she said with excitement. "Well, Al-bert," she whined his name in a prolonged pronunciation, "and I have an appointment to get to." She led Albert by the arm as they casually walked towards their home.

"We don't have any appointments," Albert corrected her. "You just wanted to get away from there and used me as an excuse. You're always using me for one thing or another."

"No," she snickered. "I thought I would save you the embarrassment of him correcting you. The name Esau has two syllables."

"No, it does not?" he asked with a growing grin. "E-sau."

134

"It figures you'd whine it. At least I was half right."

"You are such an ass," she laughed. "Do you think Lawrence will ever figure out that you were suggesting baby names when Lucille tells him she is pregnant?"

Albert laughed. "No. But I love that goofy expression he gets when I'm talking to him sometimes."

Mellissa smiled. "He thinks you're serious about everything. You should smile more when you're teasing. You love to tease him, though, don't you?"

Albert grinned. "I like to leave him a bit dumbfounded, yeah. His sense of humor is a bit too narrow. I feel it's my duty as his friend to expand it." He shrugged. "Even if it's just me that finds something funny."

"How did you start talking about names to begin with? You didn't hint that Lucille was pregnant, did you?" she asked earnestly.

"No. I wouldn't ruin that for Lucille. I told him I had a Chinese man working for me named Bo-Dinka Dong, but we call him Grant."

"You don't have any Chinese people working for you."

"You know that, but he doesn't. Besides, I wanted to suggest a good baby name or two. I like talking about baby names. Next time we'll cover pretty girl names."

"Like Gill?"

"I couldn't back track on the whole one-syllable thing, now, could I? I'll let Lawrence know it's the complete opposite for girls. Girls need to have two or three syllables in their name, or they'll grow up spitting spit wads of paper on the reverend during church and we can't have that going on. Not in church anyway."

Ah See had stood around the corner of a building across the street, waiting for the small group to disperse. Ah See had nowhere else to go without the fear of being stabbed, his neck broken or attacked by anyone in Chinatown with the knowledge that Wu-Pen wanted him dead. Bing Jue and Uang Yang were not the only men that were loyal to Wu-Pen and if any devoted laborer killed Ah See, they would elevate themselves in Wu-Pen's eyes and be rewarded. Jinhai was a friend before Wu-Pen arrived, and Ah See knew he could trust him. Jinhai had recently told Ah See that he was now working at the pottery shop and was excited to be doing what he loved and not laboring along a creek bed for gold. There were no other Chinese at the pottery shop and no one to overhear what Ah See had to say. There was little privacy in Chinatown and there were always ears listening through the thin walls to gain any sound of treason or discontent that could be sold. Wu-Pen's woman, Ling, made daily rounds with her lovely smile and a reward in her pocket for any information that she found interesting through the human trait that spanned the globe known as gossip.

Once the group had dispersed, Ah See crossed Main Street and went through the bright red door into a room filled with pottery on the shelves of multiple sizes and colors. One plate was set on a wrought iron display stand on the purchase counter near the cash register. The plate was a beautiful work of art with faint green vines and leaves with pink lotus flowers gently floating on a still black pond at night. Dewdrops on the leaves and flowers reflected the moon's light from the sky above. It was an incredible work of art that Ah See couldn't take his attention off once he noticed it.

Lucille Barton wasn't sure how she was going to communicate with the Chinese man that entered her store, but she said, "I'm sorry, we don't open until Monday at noon. That's our grand opening."

"Oh," Ah See said, taking his eyes off the plate. "I'm here to speak with Jinhai if that is okay?" he asked anxiously in English.

"You speak English? Wonderful. That is a beautiful plate, isn't it?" she asked, directing his attention back to the plate.

He nodded in agreement. "Very."

"Jin painted it. The man is amazing. I just don't know how he can paint something like that with a brush and make it look so real. I thought I could paint well, but no," she said, shaking her head. "What is your name?"

Ah See liked her immediately. "My name is Ah See. I am a friend of Jinhai's. He is a very gifted man."

"My name is Lucille. Well, never mind me, I'll be over here working and leave you two alone."

Ah See spoke to Jinhai in their native tongue, "I need to talk to you. Wu-Pen tried to have Uang Yang kill me. I am in trouble and may soon be dead. Can I hide Meili in your room? I cannot go back to

Chinatown, or I may never be seen again. Wu-Pen, Bing and Uang are in the marshal's jail for now, but I left, and they will be let out soon." He had sputtered and revealed the panic in his expression. "I must hide Meili and get her out of this town or she'll be taken down to the harlot's palace. Please, can you take her to your room and hide her?"

Jinhai grimaced, not knowing what Ah See was talking about. "What is happening? Why is Wu-Pen in jail? Explain."

Ah See took a deep breath to calm himself and took the time to explain from the beginning all that had happened in the past several months and why Wu-Pen was in jail and why he wanted Ah See dead. When Ah See had finished explaining, he asked, "Will you hide Meili for me?"

Jinhai stared at the floor, hesitant to speak. "Wu-Pen took me from a creek bed and gave me this job. These are good people he is trying to help with my being here. Izu and Wang are the reason her husband is missing his leg. Are you telling me Izu and Wang were innocent and that Wu-Pen is guilty of that crime?" he asked skeptically. "Weren't our people feeding the miners? Wu-Pen comforted Lucille himself during that time? Can a man kill and comfort at the same time?"

"A man like you or me, no. But a man with a twisted mind, yes. My life is in danger, but I care for my sister more. I am scared, Jinhai. I need someone to trust. Please help me because my options are limited."

"I can't hide Meili for long. She will be found

within two days. My room is small with a shelf on one wall and my mat on the other. What can I do to keep her safe? I do not believe Wu-Pen is a bad man. He helps many of us and Americans too. You must be mistaken."

Ah See's tone grew harder, "He does not help anyone without a reason. His bringing Meili here was not an act of kindness, Jinhai. You know that. You must know that! She is used as a tool to keep me quiet and not cause a problem for him. Wu-Pen will hurt Meili. Please, will you protect her for a day or two? I only need time to think and arrange to leave here with her. I will talk to Luther and ask him to help me."

Jinhai grimaced. "Certainly, you can talk to Wu-Pen and be forgiven for any wrongs. He is a reasonable man."

"Jinhai, can you just hide my sister for the night?" he asked desperately.

"She can stay in my room for a day or two."

Ah See spoke with emphasis, "Do not let her go to work. She must remain hidden."

"Fine," Jinhai said with little concern. He didn't understand what was wrong with his friend, but he was sure Ah See was mistaken and worrying about nothing. "I must get back to work before the paint dries."

Ah See was relieved for the moment, knowing Meili would be safe at least for the night if she stayed with Jinhai. "Thank you, my friend." He turned to Lucille, who quietly set a small vase on a display table in front of two bay windows. "Thank you, Miss."

"Can I ask you for a favor," Lucille asked. "Will you translate for me so I can talk with Jin?"

He was anxious to leave before Wu-Pen came into the shop to see Jinhai, but he found it hard to decline the beautiful young lady who treated him well.

140

16

Matt left the office to talk with District Attorney
Jackson Weathers about arresting Wu-Pen for
crimes they had already condemned and hung two
innocent men for. The only authentic witness that
could prove Wu-Pen's guilt had fled, but Matt was
convinced Ah See would be found before too long.
It was unlawful to keep a man in jail for mere speculation, but Matt refused to let Wu-Pen out of jail
until Ah See could be questioned again. The supposed order for Uang to kill Ah See was enough of
a threat to hold Wu-Pen and Bing Jue in jail for now.
Matt could charge Uang Yang with four counts of
Aggravated Assault, but Uang had not hurt Ah See,
so he could not file attempted murder charges. The
question of *intent* could easily be argued since only
Ah See claimed Uang had gone to the quarry to kill
him. No one else spoke Chinese or knew what was
said between them in the quarry office. It was one
man's word against another, and it could be argued

that if Uang had intended to kill Ah See, why didn't he at least strike him to do so? An arrest needed evidence beyond speculation and hearsay. Matt had questions without answers and many assumptions that he believed were the truth, but the unverifiable beliefs and hearsay couldn't hold Wu-Pen and Bing in jail for long.

The red, white and blue banners below the new sign for Barton's Pottery Shop caught Matt's attention; he crossed the street to congratulate Lawrence and Lucille. He stepped inside and found Ah See translating a conversation between Lucille and Jinhai.

"Matt," Lucille spoke with a friendly smile. "How do you like the new sign? Albert put it up this morning."

"It looks great," he answered. He noticed Ah See's body grow tense with the urgency to leave. He motioned a finger towards Ah See to stay put. He could read the intent to run in Ah See's expression.

"Have you met Ah See?" Lucille asked quickly, noticing Matt's finger. "I discovered he speaks English when he came in to talk to Jinhai. He was nice enough to translate so I can talk to Jin."

"Yes, I've met Ah See. He's supposed to be talking to me right now," Matt's tone had grown harsher. "Lucille, would you mind if I interrupted your conversation? I need Ah See to come with me."

"No, that's fine," she answered slowly. She was curious what kind of crime Ah See may have done to have Matt eyeing him with such a cross expression.

Ah See's breathing became more rapid, and his

forehead began to bead with sweat. He spoke nervously, "I told you, I have no more to say."

Matt's tone had become as sharp as a honed knife's edge. "I have questions that I need to be answered, and you are the only person that can answer them. And you will answer them whether you want to or not. Let's go back to the office," Matt said pointedly.

Ah See's chest tightened while his heart pounded. His trembling hands turned into tight fists while his eyes darted between Matt and the door. The intention to flee was written across his face as boldly as a newspaper's headline. There was only one thing he could do, and that was to run. It was merely an arrest for Matt, but for Ah See, answering questions meant life or death for him and his little sister. In desperation, he grabbed an unfinished vase off the shelf and threw it at Matt and sprinted for the door.

Matt dodged the vase and moved quickly to grab Ah See from behind as he reached for the door and yanked Ah See backward. Matt spun him around as easily as twirling a child in a circle and drove him forcefully into the purchase counter. Ah See's forearm hit the plate with the lotus flowers on a dark pond that was on display and hurled it off the counter. Matt lifted Ah See by the waist and slammed him face down to the floor and dropped his right knee on Ah See's upper back to keep him there. Matt hooked Ah See's left arm with his own and cupped Ah See's elbow with his hand to keep it extended straight. He lifted Ah See's arm, putting pressure on the shoulder with enough force to make Ah See cry out with a painful grimace.

"I will dislocate your shoulder if you don't start answering me!" Matt shouted without a hint of mercy to his voice. "Were Izu and Wang guilty?" He lifted the arm higher, creating more force on the shoulder. Matt was tired of wondering and was determined to know if he had helped sentence innocent men, to their death or not. It had haunted him like the scent of smoke on a man's clothes that doesn't fade away. "Were they guilty?" he demanded to know with a loud voice while he raised the arm a bit higher to create more pain. The snarl on Matt's lips and the ferocity of his tone startled Lucille, who stood back watching with alarm.

"No!" Ah See cried out loudly and began to sob while his right hand pounded on the floor in an attempt to relieve the pain of his shoulder.

The answer felt like an ax blade breaking through Matt's sternum and cutting into his heart. It was hard to breathe for a moment while a wave of moisture filled Matt's eyes. He relieved some of the pressure on the shoulder as the truth hit him harder than he expected, and his arm lowered. He had condemned innocent men. His voice was softer, "You lied to me? You lied about what they said?"

"May God forgive me, yes." Ah See sobbed bitterly. The agony of knowing he could have saved his two friends but lied to condemned them was more profound than a man should ever know. It was a burden that he could not share with anyone for as long as he lived, and the weight was uncompromising. Now that the truth was known, the shame, agony and remorse all poured out of him in tears.

Matt kept some tension on the arm. "Why did you lie? I thought they were your friends?" Matt asked, more perplexed by the question than curious. How a man could translate a lie for the truth and know his words would condemn his friends to death was something Matt could not comprehend.

Ah See rubbed the tip of his nose across the floor as he shook his head. "I had no choice."

"Because Wu-Pen threatened to kill you?" Matt guessed with disgust while raising the arm to create more pressure on the shoulder.

"No, my sister!" Ah See shouted quickly with a grimace. "He was going to hurt my sister. I had no choice!" He sobbed bitterly.

Matt lowered the arm as he asked, "Your sister?" Matt was surprised by the answer. "I didn't know you had a sister. Why didn't you just tell me that then?" Matt watched Ah See sob bitterly while snot bubbled out of his nose. Matt asked more compassionately, "Wu-Pen committed all the crimes we charged Izu and Wang with, didn't he?"

Ah See's eyes opened wide as he shouted, "If I say anything, I will be killed, and my sister will suffer!"

Matt pulled the arm upwards, sharply increasing the pain. He shouted furiously, "And if you don't answer, I will snap your arm out of the socket and throw you in jail with Bing Jue!" He lowered his head closer to Ah See's ear and spoke with a cold sneer, "Listen to me. You're not an American citizen, and no one around here cares what happens in Chinatown or about a dead Chinese man or girl, except for me! Your only hope of survival is me, and you telling me the damn truth! If you don't, I have to let Wu-Pen and Bing Jue go free. But they won't ever be free again if you can find the spine to be a man for a minute and talk to me. Wu-Pen is nothing more than a man. Now, answer my question! Did Wu-Pen and his guards commit those crimes or not?" Matt was convinced they had, but he needed some evidence to prove it.

"Yes!" Ah See shouted through a painful grimace. "Izu and Wang did nothing wrong." His face deformed as he wept painfully. "They were good men. I'm sorry. Lord, I'm so sorry." He sobbed.

Matt alertly glanced at Lawrence Barton as he entered the shop with concern about the shouting. He rested a crutch against a shelf while he put a protective arm around Lucille. She reached up to place her hand on his. Matt's attention went to Lawrence's missing leg and felt a swell of anger pass through him. Finally, there would be justice done, including the injustice done to Izu and Wang Chee. "And the silver mine?" Matt asked.

Ah See continued, "Wu-Pen planned it all. I had no choice. Izu and Wang had no choice. Wu-Pen gave us no choice, or those we love would suffer. All of us must follow orders, or our families will die, even in China. You do not know his power! He brought my sister here from China. Do you not understand? He is not just a man!" Ah See strained his neck to look at Matt. "If you keep Wu-Pen in your jail, those you love will suffer too! Do you understand? He has people who will die for him and friends more powerful than him. There is nothing you or we can do."

Matt lowered the arm and removed his knee, allowing Ah See to sit up and lean against the counter. Matt knelt to look into his eyes. "I could have helped you."

Ah See rubbed his shoulder to remove the aching. He frowned hopelessly. "You don't understand."

Lawrence Barton asked, "Are you saying it was Wu-Pen that sabotaged the mine and not those two Chinese men?"

Ah See lifted his head. "Yes."

"Oh, my Lord," Lucille gasped and covered her mouth with her hands. Her stomach churned while a bitter taste filled her mouth. She had invited the man that nearly killed her husband into their home and lives. She was appalled.

Lawrence was infuriated. "Jin!" He pointed towards the door. "Get out! Get out and don't ever come back!"

Jinhai did not understand why the American lawman was hurting Ah See or what they were saying. He certainly didn't understand why Lucille was near tears and covering her mouth or why Lawrence was suddenly angry at him.

"Go now!" Lawrence yelled again.

Ah See stood up and held a hand up to stop Lawrence. "No, please. Jinhai is not a part of it. He is innocent. Please, he is a good man and loves being here. Please hear me. I came here to ask Jinhai to protect my sister from Wu-Pen. Miss Lucille,

I came here because he is a good man and will keep my sister safe. Please do not blame Jinhai for Wu-Pen's crimes." He quickly spoke in Chinese to Jinhai, explaining what had been said.

Jinhai's jaw fell as he listened. He turned to the Barton's with a stunned expression and spoke sincerely.

Ah See translated, "He did not know and is sorry. He will leave if that is what you want, and he will understand." Ah See added, "That is what he said. But I know him. If you are wise, you will allow him to stay because he told me earlier that your family has won his heart."

Matt spoke to Lawrence, "I don't judge all Chinese by the acts of a few. Hopefully, you won't either. If the man is doing you good, then keep him."

"Wu-Pen brought him here to work for us!" Lawrence exclaimed. "How can I trust him around my family?"

"That's a good point," Matt agreed. "Here is what I do know, Wu-Pen sent someone to kill Ah See today. He's not Wu-Pen's friend, and if Ah See came here to ask him to protect his sister, then maybe you can trust him too."

Ah See added, "I asked him to keep my sister safe because my life and hers are both in danger. He agreed to risk his life to save her. He would do the same for you. Your family has won his heart."

Lucille gazed at Jinhai for a moment and answered, "I trust him."

Matt suggested, "How about you two go inside your home and talk about it over while I finish my

148

conversation with Ah See? Please."

Once Lucille and Lawrence had gone inside, Matt sat on the floor leaning against the purchase counter beside Ah See. "There is a lot I don't understand. How did you and Wu-Pen come up with the same answers for every question we asked? I trusted you, not Wu-Pen, but when you both gave the same answers, it sealed their conviction. How was that possible?"

"The book," Ah See replied simply. "I had to memorize the book."

"What book?" Matt questioned.

"The book Truet wrote the answers in. Wu-Pen took it."

"He couldn't have taken it."

"Yes, he did. He has a key to your office. Wu-Pen sent Uang to take it when no one was there and returned it before you arrived in the morning."

"What?" He was stunned. "How could he get a key?"

"I don't know how he got it, but he has one. You cannot keep him in your jail. He will get out and come after me and my sister for talking to you. He'll come after you or those you love too. He is not a good man. He is very evil."

"And your sister? Where is she now?" Matt asked.

"Working at our restaurant." He turned his head towards Matt anxiously. "I hope they have not taken her yet."

"Let's go get her," Matt said while standing upright from the floor. "Uncle Luther's knee is hurt, and he'll be needing some help around the house.

It sounds like a safe place for you and her to stay while you help him. Once we have your sister in a safe place, I need you to tell me everything. Are you okay with that?"

Ah See took a breath with a lighter weight on his chest. "I will. Yes."

Matt recalled a plate falling over the back edge of the counter when he slammed Ah See into it earlier. Being courteous, he picked up the broken pieces and carried them to the door of the Barton family home. It was only right to admit to breaking the plate and offer to pay for the damage.

Jinhai whistled and then spoke while inviting Matt to give him the pieces.

Ah See said, "He says he can fix it."

Matt handed the pieces to Jinhai and then knocked on the house door. When Lucille opened the door, he explained, "I broke one of your plates that was by the register. I gave it to Jinhai. He said he could fix it. But I am more than willing to pay for the plate."

Her face fell with profound disappointment. "Did it break? Let me see." She formed the pieces together to see if they could be glued, but chips and small fragments were missing, making it impossible to glue back together. She was irritated that the work of art was ruined. "It's garbage."

"How much do I owe you? I'll pay for it and the vase Ah See threw," Matt offered.

"It wasn't for sale. It was priceless to me," she said with moisture filling her eyes.

Ah See spoke, "Jinhai says he can fix it."

She smiled sadly at Jinhai and put her hand gently on his arm. "Some broken plates can't be fixed." She turned to Matt. "Bring Christine by on Monday, and we'll call it even, Matt." She picked up the five broken pieces and began to carry them towards the trash can.

Jinhai spoke, and Ah See translated quickly, "Jinhai says let him try to fix it. It couldn't hurt."

"Fine. Tell him he can try."

Jinhai grinned and took the broken pieces of the plate from her hands.

17

Matt was not expecting Ah See's sister to be a
fourteen-year-old child. He assumed she would be
older having experienced the horror of being taken
from her home and transported across the ocean
to a new land. It was unimaginable that someone
could have the authority to arrange a kidnapping a
world away and deliver a person halfway across the
world for the single purpose of blackmailing another person. It was incomprehensible to imagine
someone doing that to a young girl. After meeting
Meili, Matt looked forward to putting the noose
around Wu-Pen's neck himself.

Ah See explained such organization and power
to do such a crime didn't come from Wu-Pen alone,
but a well-planned and secret society of tongs
headed by some of the most powerful men within
the Six Companies Organization in San Francisco.
There were Chinatowns throughout the west with
organizations like the Chinese Benevolence Soci-

ety that helped the Chinese laborers but wielded the power to tax the people they were meant to help. For a fee, the more corrupt individuals within the Six Companies held enough power and had a network to various people and tong leaders capable to achieve what would seem impossible. The Chinese Exclusion Act of 1882 stopped importing Chinese and limited the power of the Six Companies trading of exports of goods to China. The importing of Chinese officially on paper stopped but smuggling young Chinese girls into America for prostitution became a lucrative business. Wu-Pen knew the corrupt men in power and gave them Meili's name and where she could be found, and they got him who he wanted. The expense of sending for Meili would be recouped by prostitution when her purpose was through, and that made money. Nothing meant more than money to some people.

Prostitution was a common means of survival for many women in the American west. Most prostitutes had no other means of surviving for various reasons. Each lady had a story to tell, but Matt would bet his life that not one grew up wanting to be a prostitute. The idea of forcing a child into prostitution was a different subject altogether; it was both appalling and infuriating. There was nothing a man could do that was lower and more evil than touching a child sexually. There was absolutely no compassion or mercy in Matt's mind for those who did. It was comforting to know justice is found at the judgment seat of Jesus Christ and those evilest of people will sooner or later, pay the consequences of their actions and their dark soulless hearts.

Matt took Ah See and Meili to Luther's home and found Luther in his rocking chair with his knee wrapped up tightly with two pieces of lath to keep his knee perfectly straight with the hopes that it would heal on its own. Doctor Ambrose told him to stay off his feet for at least two weeks. His daughter Billy Jo and her boys, Wyatt and Brice, were staying to take care of him. Matt explained what had transpired with Ah See and the threat he and Meili were facing. Luther agreed to let them stay at his house until the threat was over. Rules had to be set for Meili to understand she could not leave Luther's home. Meili could not go to work at the restaurant or go back to Chinatown for any reason. She was not to leave the house, and stay inside as much as possible. If she was spotted, Luther and his whole family could also be endangered. The same rules applied to Ah See until they knew it was safe to go back to normal living. When Matt was leaving, he watched Meili's face brighten as she and the two boys played with the dog, Red. She was just like any other fourteen-year-old girl.

Matt went back to his office about the time it closed for the day. He was troubled to hear that Wu-Pen had a key to the office and wasn't about to take a chance of Wu-Pen getting free by someone with the key.

"Matt, where have you been?" Phillip asked as Matt entered.

"Busy. Where is Truet and Nate?" he asked.

"They went home. Truet said he was going to the

carpenter's shop to work on some cabinets, and Nate was going with his Pa to split wood somewhere. You know, they're taking advantage of the sunshine."

"Go home and get some sleep. I'll need you to come back around midnight. I'll stay here until then. I talked to Ah See, and I don't want to leave these prisoners unsupervised overnight. They apparently have a key to the door lock."

"What? How?" Phillip asked.

"The only opportunity they had was when his people fixed the damage the miners caused when they tried to break Leroy out of jail. They installed the lock on the door."

Phillip had no desire to cut his night short and spend the night awake in the office. "Can't we change the door lock? They don't have a key to the jail, too, do they? They couldn't get the steel door open if you took the keys home." He hoped his suggestion would be heeded.

"I'll have Truet change the lock tomorrow. No, they couldn't get into the jail, but just the same, I don't want anyone sneaking in here and going through our stuff. But for tonight, we need to stay vigilant. Go on home. I'll be writing an arrest report until late, I'm sure. You can write a copy of it when you come in. I'll make sure there is coffee made when you get here."

Matt grabbed the jail keys and unlocked the steel door leading into the jail. He sat on the bench in front of the two cells. None of the men looked at him; they laid on their beds, staring upwards. Uang appeared to be sleeping on the top bunk.

Wu-Pen asked from the bottom bunk, "Did you come to release us?"

Matt hesitated to answer to get Wu-Pen's hopes up. When Wu-Pen lifted his head with anticipation, Matt replied, "No. I'm afraid Uang is under arrest for four counts of first-degree assault. The only place he will be going is in front of the judge."

Wu-Pen laughed at him. "Child's play. I'll have our lawyer come from Portland and prove it was self-defense."

"I didn't know you had a lawyer. Does he speak English, or should I notify the court to send for an interpreter now?"

"He's American. He helps us Chinese for a price."

"He must be paid well if he'll come all this way. That's good because you're going to need him too."

Wu-Pen groaned as he sat up and placed his feet on the floor. He grinned. "I'm still waiting to hear what crime I have committed to be here. Maybe you could enlighten me why Bing Jue and I are in your filthy jail? We've done nothing wrong. I doubt Ah See had anything to say. Tell me I am right?"

Matt's eyes remained fixed on Wu-Pen as a slow upwards curve pulled on his lips. It was curious how such a small and unassuming man could hold so much power over a community. Matt licked his dry lips. "You are under arrest, Wu-Pen. I could list all the multiple crimes and misdemeanors, but we might be here a good portion of the night. None of the small stuff matters compared to the thing that's going to get you and your two friends hung soon enough. You are under arrest for the murders of Leroy Haywood, Roger Levine, Oscar Belding, Lloyd Jensen, Eunice Zuwalski, Danny Rosso, Jason Collins, Fred Longley and Izu and Wang Chee, as well. That's ten counts of First-Degree Murder and a long list of everything else I can think of. I'm not good at math, but I believe it all totals up to the gallows. This time, I'll be putting the ropes around your necks because it won't bother me to watch you three hang. Not at all," he emphasized.

Wu-Pen's grin faded into a relaxed smile as if he had already beaten the charges. "You leave me no choice but to do what I did not want to do. My lawyer will get the trial moved to Portland, where we'll be set free. I will give you one chance to make this right and let us go without charges. You don't have to be my friend, but I will mind my business if you mind yours. I believe Chinatown is not in your jurisdiction and my lawyer will make that known. You cannot win, Matt."

"We'll see. I was told you have a key to my office. I won't be leaving tonight and when I am gone, someone else will be here. My instructions are simple, no visitors unless I am here with an interpreter, so I know everything that is being said. If any Chinese man or woman wants to see you after our closing time, the door is to remain locked. If they force themselves inside, my instructions are to shoot to kill, whether it is a man or a woman. I think a shotgun and a revolver on the desk should be handy enough. If any of my men are killed by chance, I won't stop the crowds that want to burn Chinatown to the ground and run you all out of here. I have no compassion for you or your men. You will remain in foot and wrist shackles until you are hung." Matt stood. "Your days are almost done. But you have a new board above you where you can write a death poem if you want, just like Izu had to."

Wu-Pen's eyes were hard and scornful. A slow forming wicked smirk took form on his face. His lips twitched lightly while he controlled his temper. "It's been a good chess match."

"Chess match?" Matt asked curiously.

"Yes. I have played you since the beginning, but you were too dumb to know it. I won't let you turn the table over and ruin what I have created. You have the chance to lay your king down and quit while you can. We can both go our own way without any needless pain."

Matt nodded unconcerned. "I don't play games. In the real world, where I live, justice wins. I guess you could say, since you're in my jail, that the game's over."

"The game is not over until I am dead, or you are. We could have been friends." His lips turned into a sneer. "Not anymore. Christine, Truet, your family, who knows where or what could happen while I am in here?"

Matt stepped closer and held the keys up. "And I can lose my keys on the street when the miners learn who really killed their friends. Don't threaten me. All I have to do is turn my head and they'll come in here and string you three up from the Rose Street headgate. And I will hand them the keys if anything happens. I believe the death penalty is justice for the families, and all three of you have earned it many times over. Whether it's through the court of law or vigilantes, the ending remains is the same. Your best bet is to sit down and shut up!"

Wu-Pen raised his voice as Matt turned his back to leave, "I will bring you to your knees. Believe me. I will!"

Matt stopped, turned towards Wu-Pen to respond, but hesitated. There was no reason to kick a dead horse. He would let Wu-Pen have the last word and continued into the office and closed the steel door behind him.

18

Matt had spent the evening writing his arrest report as precisely as possible to bring multiple charges against Wu-Pen Tseng, Bing Jue and Uang Yang. He had never written a more comprehensive arrest report in his career. It was twenty-nine pages of handwritten accounts of murder, the facts to each murder and copies of the autopsy reports that he kept on file. All the evidence set before the court that condemned Izu and Wang Chee was once again going before the District Attorney as evidence for two new First Degree Murder charges against Wu-Pen. Although Wu-Pen did not kill Izu and Wang Chee himself, the legal definition of murder is - *intentionally causing the death of another*. The long list of lesser crimes such as: initiating a false report, initiating a false confession, tampering with a witness, and a few others were all designed to condemn two innocent brothers to death for crimes Wu-Pen planned and executed with the intent to kill. The report was complicated and took several hours with a pen and ink bottle to finish. He did not have an answer for some things and Wu-Pen would not answer when asked, but the facts were written down as clearly and detailed as his knowledge of the crimes could make it. Arrest reports were not an emotional journal. They were impersonal, black ink written on white paper with facts and what was known by the evidence and witnesses. Any personal opinions had to be stated as so and not as an unverifiable fact. Matt's personal feelings did not matter and were not expressed in the report.

Matt set his favorite pen back in the desk drawer and stood to stretch his arms and back. He was exhausted from the hours of writing and the concentration he committed to it. His fingers were cramping, and his hand ached from holding the pen. The report was finished and all he had to do was wait for the ink to dry on the last page. He pulled a pocket watch out of his desk drawer; it was just after eleven at night. The time had flown by like children playing in a creek bed on a hot summer's afternoon. Matt blew gently on the ink and then yawned with a rub of his eyes. He had an hour before Phillip would come to the office and he could go home and get some rest. When the ink was dry, he took the report and set it on top of Phillip's desk for him to write a copy.

He stepped outside of the office onto Main Street for some fresh air and stretched his legs. It was quiet and still, except for a couple of intoxicated men walking across Main Street on their way home from a saloon a block away. It was a warm spring night with a breeze that felt quite refreshing after being stuck in a stuffy office for several hours. The fresh cool air brought a jolt of life and the thought of hurrying to the dance hall to see his beloved Christine came to mind. It would be nice to see her before the dance hall closed at midnight. No one had come by the office and there was no one lingering around on the street waiting for him to leave. Even if someone had Wu-Pen's key to the entrance door, they couldn't get into the jail nor open the cell doors to get his three guests out. There was just over a half-hour window that he could take advantage of before Phillip came to the office. Matt intended to be there when he arrived so it would be a quick walk, a half an hour or so to hold, kiss and dance with his lady before he had to leave. It wouldn't be as long as Matt would like, but at least he could let her know she was loved. In the meantime, he would keep the office lit brightly and his private office door left open an inch or two with the lantern burning inside to keep the appearance that he was present. Anyone desiring to sneak inside would be hesitant to do so if they thought Matt was there. Feeling secure to leave for a bit, Matt locked the office door and listened to his bootheels on the boardwalk as he stepped with anticipation towards Bella's Dance Hall.

Matt entered the noisy dance hall and chatted with Gaylon Dirks, the dance hall security guard, for a moment before stepping into the ballroom. The band played a polka while the ladies danced with a partner. A proud smile grew across Matt's face when he spotted Christine dressed in a bright pink dress with a light blue flower design. Her long dark hair was pulled up in a mysteriously weaved decorative bun, and her smile shined as beautifully as ever. Matt leaned against the wall and watched the men near the bar asking for another drink before the dance hall closed for the night. Being midweek, most of the men had to work in the morning. Matt's eyes scanned over the men as they talked amongst each other about everything from the weather to the women on the ballroom floor. Some were rowdier than others, but it was nothing out of the ordinary.

When the music was over, he watched the gentleman dancing with Christine escort her to the bar and purchase a small glass of pink champagne for her. It was nothing more than pink lemonade to keep the dancers sober and hydrated, but the crowd of men didn't know that. Christine's eyes brightened when they connected with his. Her smile was an immediate flash of her bright white teeth. She politely excused herself from the gentleman that bought her a drink and made her way through the crowd towards him.

"Hello," she said, keeping a professional distance between them. Bella had noticed the ladies were becoming too affectionate during business hours with their favored gentlemen, and it was affecting dance ticket sales. "It's about time you come to see me. I was beginning to wonder if you were leaving me at the altar a month early."

His gaze rested on her affectionately. "You have no idea how good it is to see you."

"Hard day?" she asked with the sincere caring on her face that he loved about her.

"It's been a long one."

"You look exhausted."

"I am," he yawned. "I don't have long. I need to get back to the jail before Phillip gets there. But I figured we had time for one dance. If I could hold you for that long, it would be worth every second."

Christine's eyes closed slowly as disappointment brought the corners of her lips downward. "My next dance is with that gentleman over there waiting for me. I already have his dance ticket. Do you have to leave? I was hoping you were staying until after closing to spend some time with me. You can't come back?"

"I'm too tired. I'll tell you about my day tomorrow at lunch. We can go anywhere you want."

Her lips turned upwards. "That sounds nice. I have a few minutes before the band starts. Let's step outside and let me cool down." She told the gentleman waiting to dance with her that she'd be right back before she and Matt stepped out onto Rose Street. The cool breeze caressed her skin. "Oh, my. That breeze feels so good," she said, lifting her arms outward to cool her body. "So why is Phillip meeting you at the jail tonight?"

"I'll tell you all about it tomorrow at lunch. Until then, how about I kiss you?"

She giggled. "Why do you think I stepped outside?" She put her arms around him and they kissed. When she pulled her lips away from his she whispered, "I can't wait until we're married."

"Are you going to be able to pull yourself away from here to be my wife?" he asked, nodding toward the dance hall.

Her nose wrinkled skeptically with a coy smile. "I could. Or maybe I'll just keep dancing until I earn enough to build my dream house on top of that hill where we first kissed. Remember, I stomped out the basic design of my dream house in the snow? I want a porch that goes all the way around the house, so we can cuddle and watch the sunrise in the east and the sunset to the west."

He loved the excitement that lit up her face when she talked about her dream house. "I remember." He paused, thoughtfully. "I don't know if I ever told you, but after you were shot and in surgery, I went up on the hill and fell to my knees and prayed. Your tracks in the snow were cemented into my mind. I didn't care about anything else; I knew right then and there that I wanted to spend the rest of my life with you."

She kissed him softly. "That surgery ruined my stomach. I may never be able to have children again, you know," she said softly with a heartbroken touch to her voice. "And the scar is so ugly. You might want an annulment after our honeymoon."

"You have mentioned the scar across your stomach before, but I'll tell you a secret, I don't care. Even if that bullet had pierced your spine and you could never walk again, I'd still want to marry you. I love you, for you, Christine. Not your stomach. And as far as children go, that's for the Lord to decide. Whether the Lord blesses us with children or not, I'll still be thankful and blessed with you as my wife."

Her lips tightened. "I love you, Matthew." She kissed him softly. "Do you think Sunday afternoon we could go back up there to have a picnic and watch the sunset?"

"That sounds like a good plan."

The door opened, and the gentleman who was waiting for a dance stopped in his tracks when he saw Christine in Matt's arms. "Oh! Sorry, Marshal," he said respectfully.

Christine released her arms from Matt. "Oh, hi," she said with a slightly embarrassed smile to be caught. She explained to Matt, "I have to go dance."

The gentleman raised his hands apologetically. "No, it's okay. I don't want to interrupt."

"Nonsense," Matt said. "You paid for your ticket. Go enjoy your dance."

Matt walked back to the marshal's office, feeling the exhilaration of holding Christine and the idea of someday building her perfect dream house on the hill. The idea of snuggling on the porch with her to watch the sunset and talk under the stars until the sunrise became a dream to pray for. What a wonderful time it would be if they could do that just once, but a lifetime of opportunities to sit and watch the sunset together would be paradise. He made good money now that he was a U.S. Marshal and could afford to live well enough, but perhaps not enough to purchase the amount of acreage the hill contained. It would cost quite a bit to build a house like Christine wanted on the hill. The house was one thing, but the most significant issue would be digging a well deep enough to hit water. He would have to hire a crew from the Slater Silver Mine to dig a shaft deep enough to hit water from the crest of the hill. However, if it made Christine happy, he'd find a way to get it done. It might be years down the road, but the hill he could inquire about purchasing now. He had mentioned it to Lee once before, but it had not been forgotten about since then. He would talk to Lee about it tomorrow and maybe be able to surprise Christine on Sunday with a bill of sale during their picnic.

He reached the office only moments before Phillip. He could see Phillip walking towards the office a block away as he unlocked the office door. Matt immediately busied himself making a pot of coffee, which he promised would be ready when Phillip arrived. Matt didn't think about heating the water beforehand, so he poured some water from a bucket into a pot and set it on the stove to heat.

Phillip opened the office door and stepped inside with a yawn. "Sorry, boss, I didn't get much sleep. I hope you have that coffee made."

"Almost," Matt lied. "Thanks for coming in."

"Sure," he said, removing his hat and coat. "You didn't make coffee, did you?" he asked with disappointment while watching Matt preparing to make it.

"I'm working on it. I finished writing the arrest report just after eleven. I needed a break and went over to talk with Christine for a bit. I saw you walking towards the office when I returned. I made it just in time," Matt said with a tired smile.

"I saw you. I figured you were coming back from the privy and would have coffee made at least. Fortunately, I have something to do tonight. How long is the arrest report?" Phillip asked with a yawn.

"Twenty-nine pages. It won't be fun, but it needs to be copied. I'll take it to the courthouse in the morning. Phillip, I think I'll let you finish the coffee and I'll go home. It's been quiet. Be sure to lock the door when I leave and keep a shotgun handy if one of Wu-Pen's goons wants to come in. Do not enter the jail for any reason at all, period. Just stay awake, keep the door locked and you'll be fine. Do not open the door for anyone. In the meantime, you have an arrest report to copy. It will take a few hours, but you have all night."

"Did you leave the report on your desk?" Phillip asked.

"No. It's on your desk," Matt said. His brow narrowed curiously.

"It's not there," Phillip stated. "Did you put it in a drawer?"

Like an unexpected gust of wind, his body felt a wave of alarm flow through him. "I put it right here," Matt sputtered anxiously. He moved quickly to his office and grabbed the jail keys. He opened the steel door and uncommonly, cursed. The second jail cell's door where Bing Jue had been contained was wide open. Wu-Pen's cell door was partly open with a pair of wrist shackles secured on the door and the cell's door frame. A rolled-up piece of writing paper was stuffed between the chin links of the restraints. The three men were gone.

Matt pulled the paper out of the chin link and unrolled it. He felt a cold chill run down his spine.

The note read four simple words:
'Who shall be first?'

Matt spun around and pointed his finger at Phillip. He shouted, "Take a shotgun and go wake Truet, right now! Tell him to wake my brothers and tell them to get their families to the top floor of the Monarch Hotel! I don't have time to explain it to them. Just get their families there now! I'm going to get Christine, and I'll meet you there."

"Where?" Phillip asked with a confused shrug of his shoulders.

"The hotel! Tell my brothers it is non-negotiable. Their families are in danger. Phillip, if you see Wu-Pen or his men out on the street, kill them before they kill you. Go!"

19

Matt told Phillip to carry a shotgun because there was a possibility that if Wu-Pen and his thugs were prowling the streets and saw Phillip, he would become a target. Phillip carried a sidearm along with his badge, but he had never had to use it and Matt doubted Phillip would be efficient enough to hit his target if he was attacked. Phillip had a greater chance of protecting himself with a double-barrel shotgun.

Matt slipped the thong off the hammer of his revolver as he went back towards Rose Street. Chinatown was one block over, and if he saw Wu-Pen and his two guards, he'd put two shots in each of their chests, and he had just enough experience and bullets to do so. Some men carried five bullets in their revolvers to lower the risk of an accidental shooting, but Matt learned long ago that in the life he chose, that one empty chamber slowed reaction time. He could not ever risk that again. The dance hall had closed for the night, but the lights were still lit as a few lucky men that had won the affections of their chosen lady were invited to stay longer to visit and have some quality time.

Matt banged on the door to get someone's attention. Momentarily, Gaylon Dirks unlocked the door while Bella's husband, Dave stood nearby, curious to see who was banging on the door.

Matt stepped inside uninvited. "Dave, I don't mean for you to panic. But just in case, I need you to put your pistol on, and you and Gaylon keep watch tonight. If you see any Chinese at your door before morning, kill them. I need to get Christine out of here though."

"What's wrong?" Dave asked with concern.

Matt could see the attractive red-haired dancer, Rose Blanchard coming down the stairs after changing into a more comfortable dress. She offered a seductive smile. "Are you coming to see me, Matt?" she asked.

"Rose, will you tell Christine I'm here please. Tell her she's leaving for the night. I'll be in Dave and Bella's apartment." He turned towards Gaylon. "Lock that door and sit up with your shotgun. You might have company tonight, and if you do you had better be ready."

Frightened by Matt's words and tone, Rose left immediately to tell Christine.

Bella sat on her davenport, glaring at Matt while breathing heavily. The risk to her girls and her business was endangered by Matt's relationship with Christine. Back in September, her dance hall was almost burnt down and suffered a significant amount of damage when two imbeciles named Pick Lawson and Jim Hexum mistook Christine for being a missing railroad tycoon's daughter. They caught the dance hall on fire and kidnapped her in the chaos that followed. The fault wasn't Matt's, but it would never have happened if it wasn't for Matt's relationship with Christine. In December, Martin Ballenger stalked and killed Edith Williams at the bottom of the stairs. Christine was intentionally shot as well to slow Matt down, because he would have killed Martin. What Martin did wasn't Matt's fault, but Christine would not have been shot if it wasn't for their relationship. It had taken months for Christine to recover and now once again, Christine was in danger. Bella loved Christine like a daughter, and there was a time when she encouraged Christine to take a chance on love again with Matt. Bella regretted that decision now. Matt was a good-hearted man, but he invited danger at every turn and beside him was no place for a young lady to be.

Matt finished his explanation, "So I am taking Christine to the hotel where she can be protected until I end this with Wu-Pen and his guards."

"And then what?" Bella asked sharply. The indignation smoldered behind her grit teeth.

Matt didn't understand the question. "Then she can come back."

The simplistic answer was like a stick of dynamite bursting a beaver's dam. The full volume of her wrath poured out, "No! I mean, then what? What will happen to her next because of you? I blame you for everything that has happened to her in the past year. If you had never met Christine, she wouldn't have been kidnapped, our place wouldn't have been burnt and she wouldn't have been shot! Maybe Edith wouldn't have been murdered either, if you hadn't recommended Martin to be a sheriff's deputy. He was a bum, and he would have stayed a bum if it wasn't for you!"

"Bella," Dave said calmly. "I think you're over-reacting."

"No, Dave, I'm not!" she shouted at her husband with outrage burning in her eyes. She continued to shout at Matt, "When's it ever going to stop? You're going to get Christine killed one of these days when someone takes a shot at you and hits her instead. Do you know she can't have children anymore because of you? You have caused more trouble for her than any young woman ever deserves in her lifetime. And now this!" Her stare blazed with indignation and her voice was caustic, "I'm sick of it. Once is forgivable, twice is too many, and now it's becoming a lifestyle that leads to the grave. I won't let you do that to her!"

Matt was taken back by the unexpected lashing that spewed from her mouth like a poison to his soul. He knew she liked to drink, and he could smell the alcohol on her breath, but the words hurt. "I never recommended Martin..." He was flustered and took a moment to collect his thoughts. "I'll bring Christine back when it's safe to do so." He knew she was a bit intoxicated and wasn't going to argue with her. It was just best to let her have her say and walk away. He stepped towards the apartment door to leave.

"That Chinaman was here just two days ago!" Bella shouted with her deep raspy voice. "He had eyes on several of our ladies. I swear to you if anything happens to any one of our girls, I will personally hold you accountable. And if anything happens to Christine, I will let everyone know it was you that killed her. It will be your fault!" Her hands trembled with emotion.

Matt was resigned to answer, "Wu-Pen has no interest in any of your other ladies. He wants to hurt me."

Bella spoke with a victorious tone, "That's exactly my point, Matt! Get it through your head, You are the worst person that has ever entered her life. You need to end it and give her a chance to live before she winds up as dead as everyone else you go around. You are death sentence to her and nothing more," she spat out coldly.

The door opened, and Christine stepped inside, unsure of what was happening, but had heard shouting. "Matt, what is wrong?" she asked gently. "Why am I being whisked away?"

Bella wiped her eyes with a cold sneer on her mouth.

Matt took a deep breath. "It's a long story. I'll explain on the way."

"Bella, what's wrong?" Christine asked with concern.

"Talk to your husband!" she snapped. She stood and pointed at Matt with tears growing thickly in her eyes. "One of the vows a husband takes is to protect his bride. You can't do that! You won't be able to! It's just as important as being faithful, but you can't do it." She fought the anguished tears from falling. "Christine deserves better. I won't be coming to your wedding, and Dave's not walking her down the aisle either! I won't have anything to do with your wedding!" She directed her words to Christine, "There won't be any reception here for you either, if you marry him!"

"What is going on between you two?" Christine demanded to know with a raised voice.

Bella shouted, "Your life's in danger, *again* because of him! I know you love him, Christine, but that love isn't worth dying for. My advice is when this crisis is over, end it with him before the next one kills you," Bella said and then stormed into her bedroom and slammed the door behind her.

Christine was stunned.

Dave rolled his eyes with a shake of his head with frustration. "Take her on out, Matt. Bella's had too much to drink tonight."

"Matt?" Christine gasped, still curious what had happened.

"I'll explain on the way."

The walk to the Monarch Hotel had been uneventful, though filled with caution. It was apparent that someone was watching his office, just waiting for him to leave to have the chance to free Wu-Pen and his two guards. Where they had hidden was anyone's guess, but whoever it was had the patience to stay hidden and watch until an opportunity arose.

They would not know how much time they had before Matt returned, so it had to have been quick. It was illegal for Chinese people to be out in public after dark. Whoever it was had to have been adept at staying concealed and maneuvering around at night. Aware of that, Matt walked Christine down the center of the street to leave open space between them and any alleys and corners where they could be approached. It offered enough distance for Matt to draw his weapon and shoot three men if he had to. He explained the situation as best he could to Christine while at the same time keeping his senses alert for the slightest sound or anything out of place.

They entered the hotel and found Truet leaning against the oval courtesy desk. He had set his shotgun on the desk. "I wish they'd show up if they're going to," he said tiredly.

Matt spoke bluntly, "Truet, I hope I'm wrong, but Wu-Pen's note is worth taking some caution. Is everyone upstairs?"

Truet didn't think Wu-Pen's note was anything more than an idle threat. "Albert has his family upstairs. Lee refused to come. He said he was a soldier and could take care of himself. The only reason Albert is upstairs is because Mellissa made him come here. Matt, do you really think it's necessary to scare her like this?"

"I do," Matt answered strongly to settle the discussion then and there. "Where's William?" he asked. William Fasana was the hotel's live-in security guard.

"Upstairs talking with Albert. Phillip went to

wake up Nate and get him here." He yawned. He had been sleeping soundly when Phillip pounded on the door.

"I'll take Christine upstairs and then go over and talk to Lee. When Nate gets here, will you two go to the stable and rent a wagon. I'll meet you there, and then we'll go to Luther's. I want Phillip to stay here and watch the door."

"This is going to be a long night," Truet said with a yawn.

Matt nodded in agreement. "I know. But after talking to Ah See and Tillie over in Natoma, I'm not willing to go to bed and risk losing anyone I love. You and I have seen with our own eyes what that madman is capable of doing; I can't afford to take him lightly. You didn't hear Tillie's story or what Ah See had to say. I know you're irritated and think I'm overreacting, but in this case, it might just be the wisest thing to do."

20

Wu-Pen stood in the darkness of his office looking out the window towards the backside of the dance hall two blocks away. He could see the light glowing through the closed curtains of the ladies' rooms that faced Chinatown. He always hoped Christine's room faced Chinatown, but hers did not. Once in a while, a lady or two would change their dresses and forget to close the curtains. His mind wasn't on the ladies or hoping to get a glimpse of their chemise. Not even a glimpse of the bare skin of one of the prettiest ladies would ease the burden of his heavy thoughts.

Wu-Pen had come to Branson to create a paradise, and now he was at the brink of watching all his hard work go to waste. He had finished reading the report Matt had written under candlelight at his desk. The arrest report Matt had carefully and skillfully written was damning. There would be no way to manipulate his way past the law now that

Ah See had squealed like a kicked pig. When he found Ah See, Wu-Pen decided to bake him over a fire like the pig he was. Wu-Pen's teeth ached from constantly grinding since Matt had told him he was being charged with several murders. He had not doubted his woman, Ling, would send their locksmith Heop Lee to the marshal's office with the jail keys to ask if Wu-Pen wanted to be let out of jail or not. Initially, he planned to stay there until Matt released him, but then he was informed that he was being charged with murder.

Wu-Pen was curious how Matt could convince the cowardice pig to talk when Ah See knew the consequences of betrayal. Ling sent one message with Heop, and that was that Ah See had come to Chinatown and took Meili under the marshal's protection.

Heop Lee waited for hours in the darkness and entered when Matt left the office. They needed to make their escape quick as they had no idea how soon Matt would return. Wu-Pen knew there would be a moment when Heop Lee would show up, but an immediate distraction had to be implemented to give him the time to try to plan a strategy to save his kingdom, if not just escape with his life. Ah See was the only witness that could send Wu-Pen to the gallows and if he disappeared, the Six Company's lawyers could get the charges dismissed or the trial moved to Portland where the jury could be easier to persuade. Every man had a price, and the district attorney and judge were mere human beings too. If they were incorruptible, a midnight visit to their homes often worked to help keep men in the upper echelons of the triad such as Wu-Pen, free from their crimes. He could have told Bing Jue to stay behind and kill the marshal when he returned, but the temptation to laugh in the marshal's face was too great. If Wu-Pen could locate Ah See and take him and Meili underground into the tunnels where they would never be seen again, he could continue living free and continue building the paradise he envisioned.

Wu-Pen knew he would be set free by Heop, because he had a key to every lock in the marshal's office and Matt's house as well. Knowing that, he began thinking of a plan on how to root the pig out from a flock of sheep. Ah See was more than likely at Matt's house, but Wu-Pen needed to scatter the sheep so they could go in and retrieve the pig. The note Wu-Pen left rolled up in the chain link of his shackles was an attempt to panic the marshal into thinking his family members were now targets and ideally, Matt would run around to save his loved ones while leaving his home exposed to enter and bring Ah See and Meili back to him.

It had been a good plan, but the word came back quickly that Matt's home was empty and there was no sign of Ah See and Meili. Furious, Wu-Pen sent his spies to watch Matt's two brother's homes, and another spy to locate Matt and follow him, another to follow Truet. News from the spies came slowly, but Albert Bannister's family had been ushered into the Monarch Hotel. Matt was seen escorting Christine Knapp there as well. Matt then went to

Lee's before he rented a wagon and brought his uncle Luther, cousin, Billy Jo and her two boys to the hotel. It was clear that Matt was protecting his loved ones at the hotel where it would be much harder for Wu-Pen to get to them. The last thing Matt did was go back to Lee Bannister's house and took his two young nieces to the hotel. Lee and his beautiful wife remained at home. Not one of the six spies he had sent out into the night had a single glimpse of Ah See.

Wu-Pen turned from the window to look at Uang Yang unfavorably in the flickering candlelight. He spoke harshly in their native language, "You failed to do a simple thing! I should have your head, and I will if you fail me again. All we have accomplished is at risk and you are to blame. I depended on you to kill Ah See. If you had done that simple thing, we would sleep peacefully tonight instead of sending out spies to find the man you failed to kill! Uang, I should cut your queue off and send you home, but if I wanted you dead, I'd take pleasure in doing it, myself! Fail me again, and I will. Understood?"

"Yes," Uang said shamefully, followed by a respectful bow.

"I am giving you a chance to win back my favor. Matt has taken his woman and all of his family to the hotel for safe keeping." Wu-Pen smiled for the first time, pleased by how successful his strategy of writing the note had been. "The man is too predictable. Matt did take his nieces to the hotel, but his brother, Lee and his wife remain at home. Ah See and Meili must be hiding in Lee's big house. It is now three in the morning. Go there and bring Ah See and Meili back to me. Do not to harm Lee or his wife. He is a benefit to me as a friend. Through him, we can buy American land. I repeat, do not harm Lee or his wife or I will have your queue hanging on my wall. If the marshal tries to stop you, kill him only if you have to, otherwise bring him to me. He had his chance to be my friend. Can you achieve this, Uang?"

"Yes," he answered.

"Do you know where Lee lives? Heop Lee will go with you and unlock the door," Wu-Pen said.

"Ah See will be here within the hour. My honor upon it," Uang slurred his words from missing six teeth. His mouth throbbed, but there was no tolerance for showing pain.

"Honor?" Wu-Pen questioned. "You'll win back your honor when you kill the man that defeated you. Until then, you have no honor. Go, and win back my favor, at least."

Uang and Heop wore black clothing to blend into the darkness and wore black hoods that pulled over their heads and covered most of their face. They maneuvered carefully around the Branson city limits to the southeast corner of town where Branson's wealthiest built large homes on four main streets on a hill. Lee Bannister's home was on Liberty Street. It was a large Victorian house on a corner with a wrought iron fenced yard and a carriage house with live-in caretakers. The house was dark and quiet. The two men hopped the fence and quietly made their way to the large porch. Heop used his skills to pick the lock and opened the door. A chain lock stopped the door from opening and left an inch of room between the door and the door jamb. Heop frowned. He tried to use his fingers to manipulate the chain lock, but there wasn't enough room to slide the lock out without closing the door. He whispered, "The chain is too short. I am unable to unlock it. I did not bring cutters."

"Move," Uang said, losing his patience. Heop stepped aside, and Uang kicked the door forcefully, breaking the chain. The door flew open and hit the doorstop mounted on the floor with a loud bang. Uang stepped inside, determined to find Ah See.

"I'm leaving," Heop said. He was afraid of being caught in public or, worse, being shot for trespassing. Certainly, the loud noise woke up the homeowners and perhaps a neighbor or two. His purpose was to open locks and make keys. When it came to violence, he wanted no part of it.

"No, you're not! Help me look for Ah See," Uang spoke viscously. He was in no mood for cowards, and he would not fail Wu-Pen again.

Heop was frightened. "The door is open. There is nothing more I can do."

"You have eyes. Look for him! If not, you will not have eyes to see anymore." Uang's stone cold expression could be seen in the faint light of a low burning kerosene lantern placed securely in a holder on the wall. The lantern lit the hallway leading to a large sitting room with a staircase at the end of it. To the left was another staircase going up to the second floor. Under the staircase was a doorway leading to a playroom with a dollhouse and a collection of young girls' toys and books. To the right was the parlor with seating and a bar. The next door to the right was Lee's home office with a large desk, file cabinets and built-in bookshelves filled with a library of books. Behind the sitting room were the dining room and kitchen. In the kitchen, a stairway lowered into the cellar. Uang knew the people upstairs had woken, and he moved quickly through the house room by room, looking for Ah See. He stepped quietly into the large sitting room where Heop stood in the faint light like a small rodent that had been flicked on the head and was too stunned to move.

Uang spoke low, "Wait here, I'm going downstairs. I'm sure he's hiding down there like a rat. Watch the stairs."

Heop watched Uang move quickly across the room and disappear behind a corner into the kitchen. He could manage the stairs, but there was no way he was ascending them. He could hear the homeowner's footsteps walking around and probably waiting for them in the dark with a gun. He was not a fighter, and he was too old to get into one. Younger men, like Uang could do the fighting; he would wait and let Uang lead the searching upstairs if Ah See was not in the cellar.

Regina had trouble sleeping with a threat hanging over their home. Lee was an old calvary man still in his prime and would not be frightened out of his home. Matt seemed quite sincere with concern for their well-being, but Lee was in the middle of a business deal with Wu-Pen and highly doubted there was any threat towards him and his family. Matt had come back later and asked to take the girls to the hotel as a precaution. The things he said about Wu-Pen turned Regina's stomach and frightened her. Lee remained unconcerned and initially refused, but Regina was frightened and overrode Lee. It was better knowing the girls would be safe with the rest of the family if anything were to happen. Lee was angry about it, but she insisted that Matt take the girls with him. The girls didn't mind; it just sounded like fun to them.

Regina had slept uneasily and was almost back to sleep when the door burst open. Alarmed and terrified, she woke Lee from a sound sleep. He got out of bed, turned the oil lantern up and pulled on his pants. He grabbed his revolver out of the drawer beside his bed and checked the cylinder to verify it was loaded. She could tell Lee was concerned and yet, perhaps in disbelief, that his new friend was attacking his home.

"Lee, just let them take what they want," Regina suggested, afraid that he would go downstairs and leave her alone.

Lee moved over to a gun cabinet, pulled a shotgun out, shoved in two shells, and closed the barrel. He looked at his frightened wife. "They're not here to take anything except our lives. That isn't going to happen without a fight. You hold the shotgun. Pull the hammers back until they click and pull one trigger for one barrel and then the other if you need to. You can't hardly miss if they come in here, so you'll be fine."

Lee kissed her and left the room carrying his revolver. He stepped softly and heard Chinese being whispered from the sitting room at the bottom of the stairs. He knew at least two of them were in his home and hoped they would come up the stairs, but they did not seem intent on doing so. He could hear one of them leave the sitting room and worried the man was intent on coming up the other staircase behind him. He turned and ran on his toes to the top of the other staircase. He listened intently and could hear nothing. Slowly, he descended the stairs over the girl's playroom and saw his front door wide open. He turned and crept down the hallway keeping his shoulder close to the wall to cast less of a shadow in the dim light. He peeked around the family room corner and saw a man dressed in black standing near the bottom of the staircase, thinking about going up towards the bedrooms. The very idea of a man breaking into the security of his home at night could only mean an intent to harm his family. It enraged Lee.

He aimed the revolver and stepped out from the corner. "Psst!" he whispered. The man dressed in black by the stairs turned towards him, revealing a broader target. Lee pulled the trigger, and the hammer fell with a loud discharge of the bullet firing. The aim was dead on with the bullet striking the man in the heart killing him instantly as he fell to his back, leaving his feet crossed.

The question of where the other man could be in the house was answered when Lee heard the sound of a canning jar break through the floorboards in the cellar. Lee turned towards the accessway to the dining room and kitchen. He could hear Regina begin to call out his name fearfully. Lee could not answer her without revealing where he was to the other trespasser. He had become the hunter instead of the hunted, and the smell of black powder from a freshly fired gun pleased his senses. His heart beat faster and his senses were quick to notice everything, including the pitter-patter of his wife hurrying across the hallway towards the stairs above him.

"Lee? Lee?" Regina called as she took a few steps down the stairs. She turned an oil lamp up along the stairwell that lit up the room. She gasped immediately upon seeing the dead body of a man dressed in black at the bottom of the stairs.

Lee shot a stern glare at her standing midway down the stairs. "Get back upstairs and lock the door!" he shouted impatiently.

A black blur ran out of the dining room door while his attention was on Regina. The man in black caught Lee's attention, but before he could fire another shot, the man dove to the floor rolled through the dive and brought both of his feet upwards into Lee's abdomen. Lee's wind was knocked out of him immediately while his feet left the ground with the upward thrust of the double kick. Lee fell to the floor landing face down. He had dropped the revolver when he was kicked and at the moment struggled to get a breath of air.

Regina screamed and ran upstairs in a panic to her bedroom and locked the door before running to a corner with the shotgun in her hands. Tears streamed down her cheeks, terrified for her husband.

Lee put his palms against the floor and forced himself to stand. The blow to his abdomen was perfectly placed and took the will to fight out of him. He struggled to get a breath and got to his hands and knees. He would have liked to have laid there, but a stranger was in his house, and he could not stay down. He would fight to the death before he surrendered and gave up in his own home. Soldiers fight and Lee had always enjoyed a good fight.

Uang picked up the revolver and threw it out a window into the yard. The breaking glass was loud and echoed through the night like a woman's scream, but there was no need for silence now that Lee had fired a gun to kill Heop. Wu-Pen had given orders not to harm Lee or his wife, but Uang struggled against the temptation to destroy the American right then and there. It would be easy to do. Uang brought a downward heel kick into Lee's kidney while he was on his hands and knees. He watched Lee arch his back and grimace in pain. Uang smirked with pleasure; he loved to see the enemy in pain. The kick would double the agony of being winded and unable to breathe for a few minutes, but that was not quite long enough. Uang drove his knee into Lee's rib cage, and when Lee rolled to his back, Uang stomped on his face bouncing the back of Lee's head against the hardwood floor.

Time was short, and Ah See was yet to be found. Lee was writhing painfully on the floor. If not for Wu-Pen's words, Uang would hurt the man to keep him there, but he was hesitant to hurt Lee and lose more of Wu-Pen's favor. Uang moved around Heop's body and got three steps up the stairs when he heard Lee say something that he did not understand in language but did understand the hand motions of a man refusing to give up.

Lee forced himself unsteadily up to his feet. "Come on!" He waved towards himself with his hands inviting Uang to finish the fight. "You're going to have to kill me before you can go upstairs."

Uang could dash upstairs, locate Ah See and leave, but he knew Lee would follow him and become a nuisance very much like a fly that won't leave a man alone. He may even have another gun. It was better to knock him unconscious now. Uang jumped over Heop's body quite aware that time was wasting, and the gunshot could bring concerned neighbors with their weapons. If Uang were lucky, Matt would show up alone and he could end all Wu-Pen's troubles in one night. It was late, but he still had a moment to toy with a man wanting to fight him.

Lee was worn down but held his open hands up in a fighting position while he circled away from the stairs to lead Uang away from them. Uang followed casually with his hands at his sides like it was a casual stroll across town. Uang smirked under the hood that covered his face. It wasn't uncommon for a man of the arts to keep his hands unclenched, but it was most unusual for the Americans he had either fought or watched fight. Most held their hands clenched in a tight fist and reduced their efficiency and speed, making them easy to defeat. Even the massive man that had beaten Uang the day before clenched his fists, but he had gotten so close it was hard to defend an unseen uppercut that came faster and harder than Uang expected. It wouldn't be the same when they fought again. A man with opened hands could grab, block, strike, and move freely, and knowing so, Uang stayed just far enough away to stay out of Lee's arm length but well within Uang's kicking distance.

Lee hopped forward and threw a hard overhand right towards Uang's face. Uang stepped back and pulled his head back as the hand transforming into a solid fist passed by without touching him. When Lee composed himself and raised his hands again, Uang fired a fast straight right jab that knocked Lee's head back with a solid blow in the nose. As Uang recoiled his arm, he stepped forward quickly and drove his right elbow into the side of Lee's head with force.

The two blows came faster than Lee had ever experienced. In his youth, he enjoyed fighting, but he had never witnessed such speed, footwork, or precise aim even in the room's dim light. The jab to the nose hurt and watered his eyes. He could feel his nose begin to bleed, and the elbow blow to his head had stunned him. Quickly understanding that he was overmatched by skill, Lee scanned his masked opponent from head to toe with more caution and the one thing he noticed above all else was the smaller man stood as if he didn't have a care in the world. It pissed Lee off not to be taken as more of a threat. With renewed determination, Lee decided to take the smaller man to the ground and use his body weight to hold him down and let his rage and brute strength bash the man's head until he was unconscious or dead. Lee lowered his head and tucked in his chin and charged forward to tackle the stranger down.

Uang was not surprised by the charge and had prepared for it by stepping back to leave enough room to plant his left foot and kick his right leg high enough to connect with Lee's forehead. Lee's head snapped back while his body weight came forward, dropping him to his back on the floor like a heavy bag of grain. Lee was dazed and laid on the floor to let his equilibrium settle for a moment.

A brief laugh broke loose from Uang's lips before he spoke in Chinese, "Stay down before you get hurt." He turned away from Lee to find Ah See.

Lee shook the cobwebs from his head. He never saw the foot coming, but he felt the aftereffects. He watched Uang step over Heop's body to go upstairs. Afraid for Regina, Lee planted a foot under him and stood up. "Hey!" he shouted. "Don't you go near my wife. I'm not dead yet." He waved Uang back towards him again.

Uang was growing frustrated. He had tried not to hurt Wu-Pen's friend, but he was making it hard not to. A dislocated shoulder, a separated elbow, a fractured wrist, an injured knee or ankle, the options were many to leave him hurt, but he was afraid that Wu-Pen would be angry at him if he hurt Lee. He could not afford to anger Wu-Pen any more than he had. Uang went down the stairs and stepped over Heop's body for the last time. This time he would leave the man unconscious.

Lee turned and ran into his office, where he kept his cavalry saber mounted on the wall. He grabbed the black leather scabbard off the wall, pulled the forty-inch blade out of the scabbard, and turned to face Uang as he entered the office. "Come on!" Lee challenged. "Kick me now!" The comfort of the saber in his hand felt like an old friend from his youth in the 7th Cavalry Company E, which made a name for itself in the Battle of Henry Creek during the Snake War. Not many of the men in Company E carried sabers, but Lee had taken quite a liking to it and used it on a few occasions in close-quarter combat.

Uang moved back slowly while keeping eye contact with the wild-eyed man wielding a sword. Wu-Pen had told him not to hurt Lee or his wife, but that was before Lee killed Heop. Now that Lee was holding a weapon, Uang could honestly claim that Lee's death was self-defense. Uang slowly backed out of the office and down the hallway into the sitting room, where he had much more room to maneuver. Just because a man holds a sword does not mean he knows how to use it. One wild swing by Lee and Uang could move in close enough to make the weapon useless. Lee's death would be short and sweet. Knowing Lee nor his wife would survive to tell the story, Uang pulled the hood off his head, exposing his face and tossed it over by Heop's body to pick up later. He spoke in Chinese, "I didn't want to kill you, but now I will,"

Lee stepped forward with the saber in his right hand held up above his right shoulder, ready to slash it in front of him. It only took a moment to recognize him as Wu-Pen's security guard, and although it surprised him, it only made him more determined to kill the man. Uang was ready to spring forward, and Lee knew it. The Chinese man was fast and agile, and if he got a hold of the saber like he had the gun, Lee could read it in the man's expression that he would not hesitate to kill him. Adrenaline ran high as Lee knew he had one shot of getting it right before he was kicked or hit. He silently said a prayer and wished Regina would come down the stairs and shoot the man with the shotgun, but she was nowhere to be seen. On the silent count of three, he grabbed the sword's handle with both hands and swung the saber as hard as he could in a wide arc at the man's chest level. He missed, and he knew Uang was stepping forward. The swing's momentum turned Lee's body, and he intentionally spun around and dropped to his knees as he brought the sword around again.

Uang had reacted quickly at the first swing and stepped right into the blade as it lowered and came around again. It was too late to avoid it, and although he tried to leap over the blade, it sank deep into the flesh of his right leg just above the knee, slicing through the muscle down into the bone. Uang cried out and fell to his back on the floor, holding the gash across his leg. He watched Lee stand above him with no mercy in his eyes and the cold sneer of victory appear on Lee's lips. He watched Lee raise the sword with both hands . Uang knew his time on earth was through.

Lee raised the sword vertically above Uang's chest with both hands on the hilt and plunged the sword through Uang's heart with enough force to drive the blade's tip into the floor. Lee released the sword and took a few deep breaths to relax. He stepped over the dead body at the bottom of the stairs, and called loudly, "Regina, it's safe." He took another deep breath and repeated, "You can come down now."

21

It had been years since William Fasana had the privilege of seeing Lee wear his gun belt like he used to when they were young. Lee's nose was bloody, but the no nonsense fighting man he had once known was back. Lee brought Regina to the hotel to keep her safe, and left the shotgun with Albert to watch over everyone in a hotel suite with two bedrooms and a large sitting room. Lee and William woke Matt from his one hour of sleep to go with them to remove the bodies from Lee's house. They went to the livery stable and rented the same wagon Matt used earlier to bring Luther and his family to town.

Matt drove the wagon towards the house while Lee narrated what had happened and how surprised he was since they had a large business deal in the works. The negotiations would secure four hundred acres to Wu-Pen under the name John Bearden, a San Francisco lawyer who had agreed to purchase the land and rent it to the Chinese community outside of Branson. It wasn't entirely as legal as it seemed. John Bearden was one of the Six Companies lawyers that often lent his name and signature to purchase land and other things for the Chinese at a price. The transaction appeared legal and put a good amount of money in Lee's bank account. As far as Lee was concerned, it was none of his business who John Bearden was or what he did with the land. The deal was almost done as they waited for a counteroffer to arrive from San Francisco . Lee heatedly told William and Matt about what he felt was a betrayal as they rode in the wagon to Lee's house during the last hour of darkness before the sunrise.

"If Wu-Pen was smart, he would have waited until the contract was finalized before sending his goon to kill me. Now I'm going to burn the contract and send a note to Wu-Pen stating the land will be his as soon as he can sign the ashes."

Matt was tired and irritable. "It's against the law for him to own land, Lee. You can't be swindling deals illegally. How can I say on one hand that I want to end the city's corruption, and my brother is making illegal business deals to line his pocket? I finally got the sheriff toeing a line of semi-integrity, and if he hears that I'm fine with you making corrupt deals, where does my integrity stand? Do you understand what I'm saying? The corruption needs to stop."

Lee grimaced. "I had two men break into my house and I killed them. Don't you think I have more on my mind than being lectured?"

"I told you a long time ago not to trust Wu-Pen. I warned you tonight that he might send people to your house, and you didn't believe me then either. I'm not a child, Lee. Start listening! One of these days, you're going to get caught breaking the law and I will arrest you. I won't ruin my reputation because of your slithering business deals."

"Shut up," Lee said with a roll of his head. "It wasn't a slithering deal. It was all on the up and up. And you wouldn't know the difference if I hadn't told you. I cover my backtrail. It was perfectly legal. Besides, he was paying me at least three times what the land is worth."

William Fasana sat on the narrow side rail behind the bench seat the two brothers shared. He was thirty-nine and a lifelong bachelor, who made a living gambling. He wasn't as tall or broad shouldered as his cousins, but rather lean and feisty. His long and wavy blond hair was in a ponytail and he maintained a well-groomed goatee around his mouth. William's face was weathered and looked as dangerous as he was known to be. Unlike his cousins who had brown eyes, William's were sky blue. "That sounds like a good deal. I would have dropped some silver ore, spread it around, and charged ten times the worth pointing out that there appeared to be plenty of silver hidden in the ground. It would help if you started doing that, Lee. The worst that could happen is the buyers could try mining and find nothing except dirt and rocks. If they come to you with questions, you could just say, 'Huh! It must have fallen off the ore wagons when they passed through here a few years back when the road washed out.'"

Lee peered at Matt with a slight narrowing at the corner of his eyes. "I'm far too honest for that. William, talk to me in private about your ideas from here on out. We don't want Matt to arrest us for talking business."

Matt pulled the wagon beside Lee's wrought iron gate to his yard and set the brake. "I'm serious, Lee. I warned you about Wu-Pen, I warned you tonight, and I'm warning you now, keep your business on the up and up. No more slithering deals."

"It wasn't a slithering deal. It was brilliant."

William grinned while he jiggled the saber's hilt as it stood upright out of Uang's chest. "Nice," he said approvingly. "Matt, you should have seen your brother back when we were young, with this thing in his hand. He was a sword-wielding knight in shining armor, especially during the Henry Creek fight, right?" he asked Lee. "Your brother saved my life and Adam's too. Hell, half of the men in the company were saved by Lee's sword and revolver, I kid you not. If we had to fight for another ten minutes, I swear we would have been out of ammunition and all of us would have been killed. This sword right here," he patted the brass handle, "saved us. It's good to see you still use it, Lee."

"Yeah," Lee said without enthusiasm, "I didn't have much choice. Help me get these bodies into the wagon. I'm going with you to drop them off," he said to Matt. "I have a few words for Wu-Pen."

"That's Uang Yang," Matt commented, looking at the toothless mouth and beaten face.

William chuckled to himself. "Uang Yang, ying ding, dong long, long dong, soap dope. Do you think Chinese name their kids by rolling a couple of dice and then start rhyming until they get to that number? What's the other one's name? Castle Fassel? Jimmy Whimmy?"

"I don't know, but I need a drink. You?" Lee asked.

"Always," William answered.

Matt pulled the hood off Heop's head. He had hoped it was Bing Jue and was disappointed to see an old man. "I don't know his name, but I recognize him as one of the men that worked in my office."

"He's probably the one that made copies of your keys. They unlocked my door but had to break the chain lock," Lee offered.

"Well," William added, "he's dead now. Surprisingly, I'm not emotionally upset and crying about it. Are you, Lee?"

"No."

William motioned towards Matt, who was kneeling by the dead man. "He is. Are you crying, Matt?"

"No, I'm not crying. Why would you ask that?" he asked William. The stupidity of the question aggravated him.

"Because you have been moodier than a woman all night long. I used to ask my mom, 'Hey Mom, what's for supper?' and she'd snap like a snapping turtle just before the smack for the asking. Talking to you tonight is like being around my mom, and boy, howdy, I'm just waiting for the smack. I dare not mention that I'm hungry." He furrowed his brow and added, "I think I'll name my first-born son Smack Snap or Snap Smack; I'll have to write them out and see which one looks more professional. Either way, he'll be named in my mom's honor. It rhymes. Yeah?"

Matt stared at William dumbfounded for a moment. Sometimes it was best to leave the side trails alone and stick to the main point of William's dialogue. "If I've been moody, I apologize. I have a lot on my mind, I suppose."

"When you and Christine have a son, no, a daughter, you can name her, Kind Mind. Your son will be named William Kill'em. Which I think you'll be saying later on today when we go Wu-Pen hunting." William offered.

"William, knock it off. Let's get these bodies picked up. I'd like to get a few hours of sleep if I can." Matt yawned.

They loaded the two bodies into the wagon, and Matt drove into Chinatown and parked the wagon below Wu-Pen's office windows. William stood in the back of the wagon, cupped his hands over his mouth and hollered, "Hey, you up there, Ding-a-Ling and Ling Ding Dong, wake up! See what happens when you go against my family? Now you involved me! I'm not near as nice as my cousins, so prepare to join your pals, Bullet Cool-it and Sword-in-the-Goard. That's what we call your friends now. Here you go." He picked Heop's arms up as Matt grabbed his ankles and tossed him out of the wagon to the road. They did the same with Uang's body.

Lee cupped his hands over his mouth and shouted, "Wu-Pen, our deal is over! I'll keep the down payment to fix my blood-stained floors. If you come around my family again, I'll put a bullet in your head!"

William stared up at Wu-Pen's office window. He grinned when he saw the curtain move slightly. "Hey, Matt," he called out loudly. "What do you call two dead Chinese home invaders dressed in black?"

It wasn't a joke, and he was in no mood for one.

William didn't wait for him to answer. "Well, Matt, you're supposed to say, 'I don't know William, what do you call them?'" He paused for effect with a large grin.

Lee answered with his attention on the office windows, "What do you call them, William?"

"Worm Chinese food!" He laughed heartedly.

A slow growing smile turned into a quiet laugh. "I knew you were going there," Lee said through a tooth filled grin.

Matt ignored them and shouted, "Uang failed again. I can rewrite my report, and you're still going to hang. Nothing's changed. Turn yourself in this morning, and you'll end up saving yourself a lot of trouble. And maybe even the lives of some of your friends. Let's go, boys."

"You didn't think that was funny, Matt?" William asked, still humored by his joke.

"No," Matt answered abrasively.

William rolled his head with disappointment. "Well, you would if you weren't so dang moody! I swear, are you having menstrual cramps? Do you need some laudanum?"

Matt stopped the wagon and set the brake. He turned around on the bench seat to make eye contact with his cousin. Matt was in a foul mood. "No, William! Wu-Pen is not a joke. There is nothing funny about how the Chinese name their children or what they eat. It's who they are. They might find the name William hilarious because in Chinese, your name might mean defecating. We don't speak their language or have any idea what the names mean. I assure you it is far beyond rhyming." Matt shook his head in frustration. "The Chinese are no different than us. They have different customs, but that is all. I found no humor in your joke. But if that joke spreads around Chinatown, you just ruined a piece of the trust I have with some of the people there. You just hit the wedge on its head, leading to more strife between the Chinese and us. Enough! We were never taught to be bigots in our family, don't start now with the Chinese."

"Wow," William said slowly. "For a moment, I thought Aunt Mary was here reaming my ass. You made your point, but you need to take a few swigs of laudanum and settle those cramps down. You are very moody tonight."

Lee quickly nodded in agreement. "Yeah, he is. Between my so-called slithering deals and your bad jokes, I don't know which of us took the greater lashing. Matt, please don't go running to Aunt Mary to tattle tale on us awful, naughty boys. I don't know if either one of us could endure another verbal scolding without breaking down and crying." The sarcasm in his tone could not be missed.

Matt's heart was troubled. It wasn't Wu-Pen's escape or the attack on his brother or the dead bodies he had thrown to the street that occupied his mind. It wasn't Lee's shady deals or even William's jokes and babbling mouth that ran like a bubbling brook that weighed his spirits down like a millstone tied around his neck. Bella's words were like the sword driven through Uang's chest. They pierced his heart and stayed there. The words were true. None of those things Bella mentioned would have happened to Christine if he had never met her. It haunted him like a dense fog and he could not pull himself out of the condemning thoughts of it.

"I don't think Aunt Mary has menstrual cramps anymore," William added thoughtfully. "Her scolding wouldn't be as *painful*," he emphasized, "because she doesn't experience the agony of the cramps like Matt is presently." He nudged Lee on the back of his shoulder. "Hey, if you want to name your next daughter after your brother, can I suggest, Crampy Mattie? It's fitting."

Matt smiled for the first time. "Will you two knock it off."

Wu-Pen grit his teeth in fury as he watched and listened to the three men standing over the bodies of his dead friends.

"What did he say?" Bing Jue asked again. He was curious why the Americans were laughing. It was stunning to think Uang could fail at anything, yet he was dead, and they were laughing.

Wu-Pen watched the wagon leave with a stone-cold expression on his face.

"What did they say?" Bing asked again.

"Wu-Pen, what did the wicked Americans say?" Ling Tseng asked as she held his arm.

Wu-Pen spoke with a soft and troubled voice, "Bing, have the bodies taken in and prepared for burial. I will write to notify their families and arrange to have their bodies shipped back home. They have earned that honor. Please leave me. I must think."

"May I ask what they said?" Bing asked again. He was angry and wanted the Americans' blood on his hands.

In the same melancholy tone, Wu-Pen responded, "You would leave me unprotected to go kill them if I told you. I will tell you later. Please leave me. I must be alone and think." When Bing and Ling had left his office, Wu-Pen sat at his desk and opened a drawer to pull out a map of the city he had bought from Lee. He laid it on his desktop and rested his chin on his folded hands as he studied at the town's layout. Pencil marks traced the underground tunnel work through Chinatown and hash marks where he had planned for the tunnels to go. His dream was to have a system of tunnels that would stretch across town in various directions where his people could do his will without ever worrying about being seen, whether it was day or night. Exits out of the tunnels had to be precisely planned to line up under buildings or houses where the foundations were high enough to create an opening. They were a long time off from worrying about that, though. The tunnels traveled no further than Chinatown presently. It wasn't often that he felt defeated, but at the moment, Wu-Pen Tseng was moving his King in defense.

A man with nothing to lose made desperate attempts, and occasionally they succeeded, but a man with much to lose had to act wisely. Defeat brought lowered heads which was already a lost fight. There had to be a way to defeat the marshal and save what Wu-Pen had created. He wasn't good at losing, and defeat was not acceptable. Emotions are a funny thing, one could feel defeated, but it didn't mean they were. One could feel happy, but it would only last until they stubbed their toe. Emotions fluctuated like the swells in the open Pacific. There had to be a way to hit hard where it was least expected and leave no trace that it was him. Staying focused was the difference between achieving or missing a goal. Matt's goal was to hang Wu-Pen while it was Wu-Pen's goal to remain free and continue to live as he did. Someone had to win, and someone was going to lose. Matt played by the rules while Wu-Pen had no rules to follow other than do what he must to win.

He heard the men outside lifting the bodies and peeked out the broken window Uang jumped out of to watch his valuable old friends being carried away. It was sad to lose Heop Lee and Uang Yang. Uang may have lost his final two battles, but he was a spectacular asset for four years. Uang liked to toy with lesser fighters, and that was probably his only weakness, pride. Wu-Pen guessed it played a part in both of his failures. On the other hand, Bing Jue had no mercy and did as he was told without question.

Wu-Pen noticed the group of men he had hired to level the streets of Branson with the excess soil from the tunnels. The men were hauling their wagon of dirt and hand carts filled with hand tools towards Main Street. His eyes widened with a hint of hope. He went to his map and studied it carefully. A devious smile appeared on his lips. The fight wasn't over yet. He opened a window and shouted, "Bing Jue! Come here, hurry!"

Chess is a brilliant game, but even an expert can be surprised by a lesser player. Sometimes a single pawn can change the game if it is positioned right whether by chance, luck or providence didn't matter. An overlooked pawn was going to save his kingdom today.

22

Matt was exhausted as he sat across the table from Christine as they had breakfast. Matt had not slept and was quieter than usual as he sipped on his coffee.

"I can't stay here today," Christine said equally as tired as Matt was. "I have to go back to the dance hall and get some sleep before working tonight. I stayed up too late talking with Billy Jo and Regina. Your nieces slept with Billy Jo and me and they are very sweet girls, but they are also bed hogs." A small smile appeared on her lips as she thought of the uncomfortable night. She was glad to put it behind her and looked forward to getting some sleep.

Matt's voice seemed dull and lifeless, "You can't leave the hotel. Not until I have Wu-Pen back in jail. Once he is, you can."

She covered her mouth to yawn. "You don't understand. I got no sleep last night. I won't get any today either if I stay here. I don't think your nieces will let me."

"I'll get you a room of your own where you can. Until Wu-Pen is back in jail, no one can leave, for their safety," Matt explained. They had no time to talk since he brought her to the hotel, without being interrupted by one of the other family members, especially the children who took a particular liking to Christine.

She set her fork down irritably. "Don't tell me Bella is right? Is this the life that we will be living? Being forced to hide every time someone has an issue with you?"

Matt frowned. He didn't know what to say. Bella's words had bothered him like the ringing in one's ears after having a firearm discharged at close range. "I hope not. I've never been married before, I don't know," he answered softly. It was true. If it weren't for him, she never would have been kidnapped or shot. She would not have the ugly scar on her belly or bad ovaries and still be able to have children. Guilt swept in like a flash flood after a hard rain and washed a part of him away.

"Matt, I won't live my life hiding," Christine said.

"I know," he said softly. "I can't control what men like Wu-Pen do. I can only do what I must to keep you safe." His eyes burned with a touch of moisture. "What Bella said...was true." He swallowed uncomfortably. "Most of the time, a man can arrest these criminals, and nothing comes from it. But occasionally, I would be lying to you if I said there would never be anything to worry about. The Dobson Gang traveled all the way from Texas to kill Uncle Charlie. Wu-Pen made specific threats towards you and my family." He paused before continuing, "It's all I can do to try to protect you all the best I can until I either have him back in jail or kill him. I don't know what the future holds, though, Christine. Your job is to dance. You know what to expect every night because it's routine. My job isn't like that. I never know what will happen on any given day or where it will take me or for how long I'll be gone. I could be gone for a few days to weeks. I wish I could say I will give it up and manage a store to be more dependable, but the fact is, I can't. I love what I do. It's who I am." His eyes, glossy and deeply morose, held on her hinting that he hesitated to continue.

"What are you getting at, Matt?" she asked with concern.

He lowered his head for a moment. His head lifted and he took a deep breath before answering, "I don't want to get you killed. If you marry me – I will." His lips tightened together emotionally.

Her brow furrowed with the sting of the words. Her mouth opened, but no words came out. "We…" she stopped to collect her thoughts. "We talked about this. I thought we were leaving our lives in the Lord's hands and just going to enjoy our time together. All I said was I don't like hiding. I didn't say I didn't want to marry you."

He blinked the moisture away and frowned. "I know this isn't the time or place, but…"

Mellissa Bannister entered the restaurant with her sons and stopped to their table. The joy of life lit her face as brightly as ever. She asked, "Do you mind if the boys and I join you? We can pull up another chair for Joshua."

Matt glanced up at her. "It's not a good time."

"Oh!" she was taken back by his sullen appearance. "Okay. Well, I hope everything is okay. I'll talk to you later," she said to Christine.

"Of course," Christine replied and then put her attention back on Matt. "It's not a good time for what, Matt?" Her unsettled anxiousness showed on her beautiful face.

His lips squeezed together. "I don't know if we should get married, Christine."

"Why?" Her voice had taken a sharper tone. Her breathing grew shallow and quick.

"Because Bella is right. I'll only get you killed, and I can't live with that."

Her head rolled back with aggravation. "Wasn't it just the other day that you said you'd love me and want to marry me even if I had been crippled?"

He nodded. "I would," he replied softly. His voice quivered as he continued, "But I'd never forgive myself."

She tossed her fork down onto her plate, causing a loud clang. "I'm going home! I don't understand where this is coming from. I don't even know what to say. If you don't want to get married, then tell me!"

"Whoa…" came William's voice from four tables away, where he sat with Lee and Regina's family.

Matt's face was reddened by the attention her actions had caused. The chattering at other tables had stopped to watch them. "I would like to, but I am not good for you."

Her eyes welled in tears while her bottom lip began to tremble. Her breath quickened. "Goodbye, Matthew!" she stood to leave.

Matt stood and reached for her hand. "Christine…"

She yanked her hand back and shouted, "Leave me alone! Just leave me alone! Period. Don't follow me. I'll be fine! One of us can't be afraid to live life!" She stormed out of the restaurant.

Matt could feel the floor move under his feet as his heart plummeted to the depths of his soul. He never imagined that his relationship with Christine would be troubled and potentially end. He never intended to end his engagement, but it appeared he might have. Hollowness is perhaps the worst emotion a man can feel as he watched Christine walk past the restaurant's windows with tears streaming down her face.

"What did you say to her?" Albert asked from a few tables away.

Matt could not respond.

William answered loudly, "He's having menstrual cramps. He's been moody all night long, just like my mom. She left us too, you know. She walked out a lot like that, very reminiscent. Mellissa, do you have any laudanum Matt can take for his cramping?"

Mellissa's eyes bore into William disapprovingly. "Hush, William."

Matt turned and pointed a finger at his cousin warningly. His reddened eyes revealed there was no empty threat in him. "One more word, William, and the doctor will be wiring your mouth shut!"

Matt left the restaurant without another word. He would follow Christine to make sure she reached the dance hall safely, at least. He loved her too much to see her get hurt on account of who he was and a badge he could never lay down. It was all he knew, and even if it condemned him to a life of loneliness, the badge of the law would still be who and what he was.

Christine banged on the locked dance hall door. She was enraged and had a few choice words for Bella burning on her tongue. She banged on the door again. It was still early, and from the nature of the business, no one woke up too early after being up late. It took a few minutes, but the young blonde-haired lady named Angela came downstairs with a blanket wrapped around her and peeked out of the curtain to see Christine. She opened the door with concern. "Christine, what is wrong?"

"Where's Bella? In her room?" Christine asked as she charged inside.

"I suppose," Angela said. She glanced outside in the morning sunshine and spotted Matt watching them. "Why is Matt way over there and not with you?"

Christine glanced outside spotting Matt and then stepped into the ballroom while Angela locked the door. "That's a good question that I'm about to find out." She knocked loudly on Dave and Bella's apartment door. After a few moments, Dave opened the door.

Christine's tone wasn't friendly, "I need to talk

212

to Bella."

Momentarily, Bella came out of her room wearing a rope. "What is it, Christine?" She didn't feel too good being woken up so early. "Angela, be a doll and make some coffee, please."

"What did you say to Matt?" Christine demanded to know.

"What?" she asked while taking a seat on her davenport. She closed her eyes and rubbed her temples to relieve the slight aching. She took notice of Christine and asked, "What can I do for you, Christine?"

"Last night before I came downstairs, what did you say to Matt?" She was angry, but her voice was restrained.

Bella wrinkled her brow, trying to remember. "You heard me. Why?"

"What did you say?" she pleaded emotionally. "He doesn't want to marry me, now, Bella. What in the hell did you say to him?" Tears quickly flooded her eyes and drained down her cheeks. Her stomach muscles convulsed as she fought to remain in control of her weakening willpower from bursting into sobs.

Bella felt a cold chill run down her spine with Christine's words. "Oh, dear. Come in and sit down."

"I don't want to sit down! Please, just tell me what you said."

Bella seemed lost for words to see Christine on the brink of tears. "Christine, I was drunk."

"I don't care!" she shouted. "Just tell me what you said to him."

Dave asked, "Didn't Matt tell you when you two left?"

"All he said was Bella was afraid I'd get hurt and live my life hiding if we got married. He was concerned about other things at the time. He didn't go into great detail, and we haven't had had a chance to talk since then. I wasn't expecting him to say we shouldn't get married!" She stomped her foot, and asked emotionally, "What did you say?" Her voice cracked as a sob broke loose. She covered her mouth to help hold herself together.

Dave answered, "She told him it was his fault that you were taken by those men and them burning our business. It was his fault that you were shot, and Edith being killed too. She told him you would have been better off if you never met him. And that he was going to get you killed eventually."

Bella began weeping as she listened to her husband. "I'm so sorry."

A tear rolled down Christine's soft cheek, as she stood slack jawed and shook her head slightly. "Why? Why would you do that? I love him. I want to spend my life with him, and you destroyed him. You destroyed us."

"I was drunk," Bella gasped. "I know those were not his fault."

"Apparently, you don't know that, or you wouldn't have said it!" Christine snapped sharply .

"I didn't mean it. But while we are on the subject, doesn't it scare you to know you could be killed because someone wants to hurt him, even by accident?" Bella asked. She remembered perfectly well

214

what she had said the night before. She was drunk and perhaps did say more than she needed, but the general idea was honest concern with a touch of resentment for all that had happened to her since meeting him.

"No," Christine answered with a groan. "Do you not understand that I love him? If I die, I die. But I won't be scared out of a life with the man I love because I'm afraid of what might happen. We are all going to die. I just pray the Lord will protect us both so we can grow old together before we do. What if Matt marries another woman because I'm too scared to marry him, and then in fifty years I run into them, and find out she was never once in danger? Not one time and they had a wonderful life. Do you think I might say it could have been me? I want to take that risk and love every minute of it whether we have a year together, thirty or fifty years. I will never regret marrying the man I'm in love with. I know what he does for a living, but he's a good man, Bella. He's such a good man that he is afraid to marry me now just in case I am hurt again. Do you not think he carries enough guilt knowing that? He's been different all night, and now, I know why." She sniffled and wiped the tears from her face. "May God forgive you if you ruined my engagement, because I will not. Not for a very long time, if ever!" She turned away to leave.

"Christine," Bella called after her. "I'm sorry."

"Just leave me alone!" Christine went to her room and collapsed on her bed. Hugging her pillow, she wept.

23

Phillip Forrester and Nate Robertson were sitting at the table near the woodstove, talking quietly. Rumors were spreading fast about the home invasion at Lee Bannister's house, and the gossip was Lee killed two men. Phillip tried to ask Matt about it but was told to leave him alone, with a harsh, red-eyed glare. It didn't take much more than that to know Matt was in a nasty mood. They hadn't bothered him since. A lingering knowledge of them going back into Chinatown hung in the air, but Matt's silence left an unsettling ambiance hovering over the office.

Truet Davis had stayed the night at Luther's to protect Ah See and Meili. Matt had intended to take them to the hotel, but Ah See feared Wu-Pen would have Matt followed to locate him and Meili and assassinate them on the way. Ah See had the idea to stay at Luther's while Matt took his relatives to the hotel. If he were followed, the spies would not think Ah See would be left alone. It was the safest gamble, and Ah See wanted to take that risk with a promise of using no lights or exiting the house for any reason. Matt agreed to it but also had Truet ride out of town towards Willow Falls for five miles before cutting back across the open country to Luther's. If Truet were followed, they would think he was leaving town to the west and far from Luther's homestead to the north of town. The night at Luther's had been uneventful. Truet entered the town from the west as a precaution. The extra riding caused him to arrive later than usual. He entered the office and laid his shotgun on his desk while looking suspiciously at his younger deputies.

"You boys look spooked. Is the coffee bad?" he asked with a smile, nearing the woodstove to pour a cup of coffee.

"No. Matt's in a *bad* mood," Nate emphasized quietly.

Phillip agreed.

"Oh yeah? Did anything happen last night?" Truet asked.

"Matt hasn't said a word. But the rumor is Lee's house was attacked, and Lee killed a couple of Chinese men," Phillip explained. "I asked Matt about it, but he just told me to close his door and leave him alone."

Truet sipped the coffee. "Well, leave him alone." He walked to Matt's private office, knocked once and opened the door, closing it behind him as he entered. He furrowed his brow when Matt watched at him with a scowl. Truet sat down in the chair across the desk. "Want to talk about it?"

Matt drew a deep breath. "No. Any troubles overnight?"

"No problem at all. Rumor says Lee was attacked. Is the family, okay?"

Matt covered his mouth as he yawned. "Lee and Regina are fine. I took the girls to the hotel before that happened, which I am glad of because they didn't need to see that bloody mess. Lee shot one and used his sword to kill Uang, Wu-Pen's guard."

"Really?" Truet asked surprised. "I'll be honest. I didn't think anything would happen last night. I certainly didn't think he'd go after anyone in your family. Ah See, you and me, maybe yes, but not them. Well, praise the Lord that they are all safe."

"Yeah," Matt said, heavily burdened. He could not get the heartbreaking vision of Christine's anguished expression while leaving the restaurant out of his mind. He had not intended for the conversation to occur, but he was honest, and it rolled down a steep hill like a boulder crashing down a cliffside from there. The weight of guilt can be as cumbersome as one man dragging an iron rail to lay new tracks for the Pacific Railroad. The weight can bend a man over and break him down with every step he takes. Bella's words the night before cut into his soul like Lee's sword penetrated Uang's chest. He could argue, but the fact was her words were true. He loved Christine more than himself, and it siphoned the life right out of him the more he thought about it. His heart was empty of joy and sorrow-filled, but it assured Christine would live a long and good life if he wasn't a part of his life. Sometimes love does more extraordinary things when it is not allowed to blossom. He loved her enough to let her go.

"So, what's on your mind?" Truet asked.

Matt didn't feel like talking about it. "We're going in to arrest or kill Wu-Pen today. I don't care which. Uang is dead, so that leaves Bing and whatever other guards he may have. We're not using the sheriff or his deputies this time. Wu-Pen will be expecting us, so we're going in hard and searching every building, whether we are welcome or not, until we find him. If someone gets in your way, get them out of your way by any means necessary. If Bing wants to fight, do not hesitate to shoot him. I'm going to personally drag Wu-Pen by his hair back to jail or put a bullet in his head, one of the two."

Truet could see the fury in Matt's eyes and knew there was much more on his mind than what he was saying. "That's fine. You sound irritated."

"I've been up all night and I want to get this done." He tried to explain quickly, but the sadness could not be hidden. The heaviness of the iron rail could be hidden for a moment or two, but the strain of carrying such a burden eventually reveals itself. Matt's jaw clenched as his lips pushed together tightly. "I called off the engagement with Christine."

"What?" Truet was stunned. "Why?"

Matt folded his hands on the desktop. His fingers interlaced, lifted and fell continuously. His eyes downward, glazed and reddened with exhaustion, heartbreak and misery. "I don't want to talk about it right now. Let's just say I think she is better off without me. Get these boys ready to bring in Wu-Pen and Bing." He stood.

"Matt, I'm confused. Can you explain why you called off your engagement?"

"Not right now. Get the boys ready to go."

"Wait a minute," Truet said. "Matt, I'm getting concerned about you and I'll tell you why. You haven't been to church since Reverend Ash was killed and your Bible has been setting on the kitchen counter since we came back from his funeral. I don't know how that has affected you, but I do know it did. Remember that talk you gave about being part his legacy? You're not living it. Maybe you haven't noticed, but you're getting angrier. You're my best friend and I'm not criticizing you, but buddy, you're losing that spirit of hope that we all love about you. I don't know what happened between you and Christine, but you need to ask yourself where you are in your Christian walk before you make that decision. You have to read your Bible again and get back to who you are. Have you noticed how quick you get irritated now, even with me? You never used to. Remember, some of the most unhappy people are Christians who have fallen away from the Lord. You need to spend some time with the Jesus, my friend. Wipe the dust off that Bible and read it."

Matt lowered his head and exhaled. "I suppose you're probably right. But at the moment, I drank too much coffee and need to visit the privy. I'll be right back."

Truet chuckled. "You do that, but then we're talking about Christine. Wu-Pen can wait a few minutes. I need you thinking about the task at hand and not Christine when we go in there."

Matt went around the block to the nearest public privy on Main Street. There were two public privies spread out by five blocks located behind the buildings on Main Street. Matt turned left on Ninth Street and saw the Chinese crew leveling the street between Main and Ash Streets in front of the community privy. The Chinese all wore various clothing colors, but all wore a wide-brimmed hat to keep the sun off their heads. A few scraped the ruts down, others hauled dirt out of a wagon and filled the ruts, while others packed the earth with heavy iron plates with a handle called a stamper that packed the soil down. A wagon full of dirt being pulled by a mule was parked in front of the privy. Two smaller handcarts about four feet long and three feet wide were used to shovel dirt into and transport to where they were working. The group were hardworking men who had done a great job all along Main Street, and now they could be found fixing the side streets one block at a time.

Matt gave a quick nod to one of the men that had made eye contact with him and walked into the privy. The public privy was built with a separation wall between a long wooden bench seat with multiple holes cut into it on one side and a six-inch-wide metal trough built in the floor on the other. A man named Herbert Locke stood at one corner of the drain relieving himself. Herbert ran a general store with a clock repair shop not too far from the Marshal's Office. He glanced over and said, "I hear you had a busy night, Marshal."

"Yep," Matt said, not wanting to elaborate.

"I had a rough night of sleep myself. My neighbor's dog kept barking all night. I don't know what it barks at; it barks all the time. Do you suppose you could go over to Walt Hunsaker's place and shoot his dog for me? I'd trade you a mantel clock for it."

The corner of Matt's lips raised just a touch. "No, I don't think I can."

"Can I?" Herbert asked.

"You could, but you would probably be sued, and it wouldn't help your friendship with him. Have you tried talking to him?"

"I have tried talking to him. He loves the old flea-bitten mutt. The mutt is already ruining our neighborly friendship. I hate that dog. Is it against the law to take some twine and tie its mouth shut at night?"

Matt couldn't help but to laugh lightly at the idea. "The dog's not your property, so I wouldn't. I suggest you complain to Sheriff Tim Wright and see what he says. It's in his jurisdiction, not mine. Sorry, I couldn't help you more," he said as Herbert buttoned his pants to leave.

"You still can. I won't say anything if you shoot the dog from a distance. I know you're a good rifle shot. No one will know. I'll toss in a wall-mounted cuckoo clock made in Germany," Herbert upped his offer.

Matt grinned for the first time. "I'm afraid not,

Herb. I won't shoot a man's dog unless I have to. Talk to Tim."

"It's worth asking anyway. Nice talking to you, Matt," he said as he left the privy.

Matt was buttoning his pants when he heard a strange voice with a Chinese accent say, "Mar-shal." He turned around and saw Bing Jue dressed in laborer's clothing and a wide-brimmed hat. Alarmed, Matt tried to reach for his gun, but a swift blow to the side of his neck was the last thing he'd see before falling to the floor unconscious.

"Quick," Bing Jue spoke in Chinese to three other men behind him. "Pull the cart to the door and have that blanket ready." He knelt and pulled a rag and small bottle of ether out of a pocket and covered Matt's nose and mouth with the rag to keep him unconscious. The blow to the carotid artery was only effective for a moment or two. The ether would keep Matt unconscious for a while.

One of the others wheeled a handcart to the door. They set Matt's body into the cart and covered it with a dirt brown blanket when it was clear. Three of the men began shoveling dirt on top of Matt to hide him underneath. When he was no longer visible, Bing walked beside the cart as it was pushed into Chinatown. The others moved the wagon from the privy up the street and kept working as if nothing had happened.

24

An hour later, Truet knocked on the door of Bella's Dance Hall. He had been there before but never enough to know any of the employees very well. He had never bought a dance ticket or had any interest in going there since he had met Annie Lenning. Truet was a man that gave his loyalty to what he committed to, whether it was a faithful relationship, a friendship or a project like the cabinets he was making for a friend, on his time off work . He had been loyal to his wife Jenny Mae until her death. Now he was committed to Annie Lenning and their growing courtship. The dance hall was an addictive staple for some men in the community, but it held no interest to him. A quiet night at home reading a good book or working in the local carpenter's woodshop on a project was more fulfilling. Working with wood was a love that he had, and now that he could work on projects that he wanted to build, it was far more relaxing and enjoyable than when he labored as a carpenter building projects that he didn't necessarily enjoy. He knocked louder until Bella's husband, Dave, answered the door.

"Good morning. Is Matt around here?" Truet asked.

"No," Dave answered sharply. An argument had followed between him and Bella after Christine had left them. Dave was still irritated. Like Bella, he also cared for all the young ladies in their care, and the fallout from Bella's drinking could ruin the familial ties with one of their most cherished ladies. Christine refused to talk to either one of them.

"Could I speak with Christine for a moment?"

"I'll let her know you're here, but I don't know if she'll want to talk to you. Come on in." He closed and locked the door. "Wait here. I'll be back and let you know." He went upstairs, and before too long, he came down and told him she needed to get dressed but would be coming down.

Christine descended the stairs wearing a plain colored gray cotton dress for everyday chores. Her hair was down and covered part of her face. She pulled her hair back behind her shoulders and sat on the lower steps. She was exhausted, and her eyes were reddened from crying. "Most of the girls are sleeping, and I don't want to walk into the ballroom or see Bella." She rested her chin on her hands with her elbows on her knees. "I hope you don't mind."

"Not at all. Have you seen Matt this morning? He said he'd be right back from the privy and I haven't seen him since. That was more than an hour ago. I figured he came here to see you after what he told me."

"What did he tell you?" she asked.

"That he ended the engagement."

Her eyes closed and she began to weep. "Matt didn't tell me that," she whimpered.

Truet's heart sank, watching her hear the words spoken to her for the first time. "Can I ask what happened? I don't understand?"

She wiped tears from her cheeks while her lip trembled. "I don't know. Bella was drinking..." She explained what Bella had said to him the night before. "And this morning, he was just different." She wiped the tears from her cheeks again to no avail as new tears slithered out of her eyes like a small spring during the winter thaw.

"I'm sorry, Christine. I was stunned when he told me. I know he loves you very much. I don't understand exactly. I don't know anything more than that. Like, I said, I haven't seen him since."

Christine sniffled and wiped her face of the tears. "Bella had no business saying those things to him. I know who Matt is and what he does. I know there are evil people in the world. For Pete's sake, my husband Richard was stabbed to death in Denver just for bumping into a man. I know the risks." She looked at Truet as another tear slipped out of her water-filled eyes. "But to spend my life with the man I love is worth the risk. It's not anyone else's business except Matt's and mine. I can't imagine being blamed for injuring another person or, worse, the murder of Edith. I know Matt, and I doubt he can even look himself in the mirror right now. You know he still regrets holding a shotgun the day Reverend Ash was killed. He said he could have killed Jude Maddox if he had his Winchester or revolver in his hand." She paused before saying just above a whisper, "I think my engagement is over, Truet." She covered her face with her hands and wept.

"I'm sorry," Truet said with sincere empathy. "I believe he is angry at himself, maybe even the Lord for not being able to save Reverend Ash. As you know he hasn't been to church, but he hasn't touched his Bible since then either. I mentioned it him this morning, and I haven't seen him since. I don't know if he's missing or off praying somewhere."

She wiped her face of the tears. "He probably went somewhere to pray then. One thing I had to learn about Matt is he likes to be alone when there is something on his mind. But back to what Bella said to him, blame costs, and when you are blamed for someone else's choices, there's no way to win. The Lord has always been with me and protected me. There was always someone there to help me. I think that's a series of miracles and never once have I blamed Matt for any of it. I blame the men responsible for their actions and no one else. Matt was trying to protect me last night. What more can he do?" She asked with a hopeless shrug of her shoulders.

Truet leaned against the wall across from the stairs. "I know he would give his life before he put you in danger. Don't give up on him yet, Christine."

"I'm not the one ending it. I'm praying he won't give up on me. Anyway, I must get some sleep. I hardly slept at all last night. When you find Matt, will you tell him to please come see me? I feel like my world is crashing down and there is nothing I can do except watch everything I dreamed of fall to pieces. I suppose that means I'm broken."

He was saddened to watch the usually cheerful and spirit-filled lady who could brighten up a room become so sullen and downcast. Her heart was broken, and it weighed heavily on his heart to know his friend was losing what Annie referred to as the greatest blessing in his life. "For what it's worth, I hope Matt spoke not from his heart but from the exhaustion after a long and stressful night."

"Me too," she said unenthusiastically. She grabbed the rail and stood. "Thank you."

"You're welcome. Again, I have no words to express how surprised I was to hear him say that because he loves you very much. I'll tell him you want to talk to him when I see him. It won't be until much later today, probably. We have an arrest to make."

"Truet, when you find him, tell him I love him."

He gave a sad half-smile. "I will do that."

The cowbell above the marshal's office door rang as it opened. Phillip Forrester anxiously watched Truet enter alone. "Any luck finding Matt?"

"No. Matt's not at the house, the hotel or talking with Christine. I don't know where he is. I was hoping he was back here by now."

"No. I'm getting kind of worried. How upset was he this morning?" Phillip asked.

Truet rubbed the stubble of whiskers on his face.

"Hard to say with him sometimes. Matt can hide his feelings fairly well. I can tell you a man who ends his engagement is usually pretty upset. It wouldn't be like him to just leave when we have a job to do, though. He wanted to get Wu-Pen and told me to get you two ready to go."

"So…what are we supposed to do?" Nate Robertson asked curiously.

Truet shrugged his shoulders not having a plan. "Let's lock the door and spread out. I'll check the livery stable and the east side of town. Nate, you head over to Rose Street and work your way over from there. Phillip, you check the stores and privies on Main Street. Check your pocket watches and we will meet back here in one hour. That doesn't give us much time, so no small talk. If someone hasn't seen Matt, move on. I'll see you two back here in one hour."

An hour later, the only bit of information discovered was by Phillip when he went into Herbert Locke's general store. Herbert had spoken to Matt in the privy. Truet wasted no time walking the short distance to the store to talk to Herbert.

"Phillip stated that you had spoken to Matt this morning in the privy. He hasn't been seen since. He was supposed to come right back to the office. Did he mention going anywhere?" Truet asked Herbert.

"No. He said very little. Is he missing?" Herbert questioned.

"I wouldn't say that, but he never came back to the office, and we had plans. You're the last person to see him that we know of. Did he leave at the same time you did? Did you see which way he went?"

"I left before he did, but he would have left maybe a minute or two after me."

"Did you see anyone else on the street that might've seen which way he went?"

"Just the Chinese working on the road," Herbert said.

A cold chill ran down Truet's spine. "Were they working near the privy?"

"Yeah. I had to walk around their wagon of dirt to get into the privy. I wanted to tell them to move it, but they wouldn't understand me anyway."

Truet was quickly growing worried. "Were there any of them standing near the wagon when you left? You know, like they were going to go inside the privy?" he asked.

"There was a couple of them getting ready to load one of their hand carts like they do, yeah. It was nothing out of the ordinary."

"Thank you," Truet said and went back to the marshal's office. He stepped inside and rested his hands on the rail of the three-foot partition fence with his head downcast in thought.

"Truet, what's wrong?" Nate asked with concern.

Truet's face was as easy to read as the weather on a hot summer's day. Panic wanted to take over his normally calm demeanor, but he fought it down. There may have been a reasonable explanation why Matt hadn't come back to the office, but after learning that the Chinese were working where Matt was last seen could not be ignored.

"Truet?" Nate pressed.

Truet's mind swirled around in circles, unable to comprehend the thought of Matt being taken by the Chinese. He refused to believe it. His voice was subdued, "Sometimes, Matt will go sit by the falls on Premro Island to be alone. Nate, I need you to hurry over there, run back here, and let me know if he is there. I need you to hurry."

"What's going on?" Nate asked.

"Go!" Truet shouted unexpectedly. Nate knew better than to keep asking questions. He hurried out the door.

Phillip Forrester sat at his desk, observing Truet. It was easy to see he was tense and deep in thought. "Truet, what is going on?"

"Let's just say I hope I'm wrong and Matt's sitting by the river because I don't know where else to look. In the meantime, I need you to run to the livery stable and bring my horse here. Bring Matt's too. Make it fast, Phillip. If Matt is not at the falls, I will bring Ah See and his sister here. And that's all I'm going to say for now. Get going."

Matt had said many times, if you don't want your plans ruined, it was better not to mention them. Sometimes it was best to play blind, deaf and dumb until you were ready to strike. Deep down, Truet knew Matt wasn't at the river. He would have to bring Ah See and his sister to town to translate when he arrested the Chinese men working on the street. Nate and Phillip would soon discover that Truet Davis could be a dangerous man.

231

25

Joe Thorn borrowed a bottle of Ipecac Syrup from a neighbor and poured some in his coffee flask to put in his lunch pail, which was nothing more than a tin pail with a handle and a lid. Since Billy Jo had been gone, his lunches had been meager coffee, boiled eggs, dried raisins that had been left in the cabinet and slices of cooked bacon he made the night before for his supper. It wasn't just Billy Jo's cooking that he missed. He missed her. He missed playing with his boys when he came home from work and the woman he wanted to marry. He drank his flask of coffee at lunch and didn't have to fake feeling ill and vomiting extensively in the mine. Sick and too weak to continue to work, he went home for the day. He washed up and walked into town. He went to Billy Jo's house and knocked on the door, but a spider's web at the top of the door connected to the door jamb told him the door had not been opened in a while. Her father's house, nearly two miles out of town was the only other place where she and boys could be. It would be a much further walk than he planned, but he loved her enough to take that extra step to win her back.

It had been quite a shock to be told that Billy Jo had taken an interest in another man, but to discover she kissed him was more than he could tolerate. Wes Wasson had no business coming into his home and mentioning Viola Goddard and accusing him of raping Billy Jo's friend at his own dinner table. The incident with Viola was a long time ago, and Joe had not spent much time thinking about her or the little girl she claimed was his. At the time, he vehemently denied it and ran Viola off as cruelly as a heartless man could to protect his relationship with Billy Jo and his son. He had seen Viola around town over the years quite a bit, but he had never spoken to her beyond ordering drinks at Ugly John's Saloon. It took a little time for Joe to think about it, but it became apparent that Wes intended to use Viola like a lumberman's wedge to create the fall between Billy Jo and himself. Wedges were designed to separate and create distance, and Wes's plan had worked well. The distance between Billy Jo and himself had never seemed further since she learned about Viola. Joe was now a living soul of regret and hoped he had not ruined the relationships he had forged with his family over the past two months. Wes would pay for the trouble he caused one of these nights when they ran into each other again, but until then, he wanted to win his fiancée back. It wouldn't be easy now that Billy

Jo knew the truth about Viola, and that Joe had a daughter that he had always denied. He knew the little girl named Bonnie was his daughter, but he was afraid of Billy Jo finding out the truth of how that little girl came about. The word *sorry* wasn't enough to right all the wrongs he had committed.

Luther's house appeared empty as he approached. He knocked on the door, but there was no answer other than Luther's dog barking at the door. He knocked again with the same result. He walked behind the house to the barn and Luther's wagon was parked beside the barn and the mules were in the pasture. He glanced towards the house, curious where they could be and caught sight of the back door window's curtain closing and an inch or two, where someone had peeked out. He went to the back door and knocked loudly. There was still no sound except for the dog barking.

He knew Billy Jo was angry and didn't want to talk to him. But he had come all that way to speak to her. He spoke loudly through the door so that she would hear him clearly, "Billy Jo, shut the dog up, for crying out loud! Look, I'm sorry. I want you to come home. I..." he hesitated growing annoyed with the dog. He chose his words carefully. "I was angry. I wish I had reacted differently. I really do. Can we talk?" There was only the dog's annoying barking in response. "Billy Jo, I just want a chance to talk. If you don't want to come home, I'll understand and leave. But please, give me a moment." He waited with no response. "I didn't come here to fight. Well, Sweetheart, I tried. I guess if you don't want to talk to me, then I will go. I know I messed up, Billy Jo. I'm sorry I said what I did to you. I won't ask you to forgive me, because maybe you won't, but I am sorry. I love you and the boys." He left the back door feeling a heavy heartedness he had not felt since he was trapped in the mine and desperately wanting a chance to survive and be a better man for his family. He proved he could be a better man and a father until Wes came over. That incident would have riled the mildest of men. He walked around the house to leave and glanced back, hoping to see Billy Jo open the door, but it remained closed. For a brief second, he caught a glimpse of a Chinese face with black hair peeking out the window. The face disappeared and the curtains swayed.

"What the? Was that a Chinaman?" he asked curiously. The rumor of two Chinese men breaking into Lee Bannister's home had reached the mine that morning. Blindsided by the fear that the Chinese had broken into Luther's home as well and concerned for his fiancée and two sons, Joe stormed onto the porch and banged on the door. "Open the door!" he demanded loudly. When there was no reply except for the dog, he picked up a chunk of black obsidian that was set on the porch with a few others that Luther had collected to try his hand at making arrowheads as his forefathers had. Joe held the obsidian and broke the glass out of the door's window. He heard a frightened scream of a girl come from inside. He tossed the volcanic rock aside and reached in to unlock the door. He entered just as a small Chinese man came into the room. Joe thought he heard his name being called from outside but seeing the stranger where his family was supposed to be, was far more alarming.

Ah See was more surprised than scared to have a man break into Luther's home. The man was rage filled and approached Ah See with violence etched on his face. Ah See raised his hands to show his peaceful intent. "No, no, no trouble," is all he got out of his mouth before a hard right fist connected his jaw, and he quickly dropped to the floor. Dazed by the blow, he tried to focus on a spinning room. Ah See could feel himself being picked up and slammed against the wall like a child's doll. He could hear Meili scream over the noise of the dog's consistent barking. Dazed, like in a dream world where everything moved in slow motion without any explanation why he was being attacked by a stranger, he tried to make sense of it and speak, but a hard right fist was driven deep into his abdomen. The hard blow forced the air out of him and left a void of space that doubled him over and dropped him to his knees, unable to suck in enough oxygen to utter a word.

Joe hollered anxiously, "Billy Jo?" He listened for any reply but couldn't hear anything over the dog barking which stood in front of a young Chinese girl protectively. Meili stood with her body partly turned towards the corner with a terrified expression. She sobbed and kept her hands close to her face protectively as she buried her neck into her shoulders.

Joe swiftly kicked Ah See in the side of the head

with his heavy boots. "Where is she? Where is my family?" he shouted wrathfully.

Luther's Red Tick Hound named Red lurched forward and nipped Joe's leg and yanked on his jeans. Joe tried to kick the dog, but it jumped back and lowered its front legs, barking and growling viciously. Joe grabbed the fire poker from near the woodstove and approached the dog intending to kill it. Meili recognized his intention and left the protection of the corner and quickly kneeled beside Red and wrapped her arms around the angry dog. Joe raised the fire poker to hit them both.

A gun shot scared him as he heard the bullet whisp past his face and hit the wall not a foot away from him. The voice of Truet Davis was fierce, "Put it down now! I won't miss again, Joe." Truet stood in the front door and had just enough time to pull his weapon and shoot to stop Joe from striking Meili. He thanked the Lord he had arrived when he did or Meili and Ah See might have been killed.

Joe lowered the fire poker. "Truet?" He was confused.

"Drop it!" Truet demanded over the dog's annoying barking.

Joe dropped the fire poker and explained, "These Chinese broke into Luther's home. I don't know what they did with Billy Jo and my boys."

Truet lowered his gun. "Your family is fine," Truet explained as he passed by Joe to kneel beside Ah See. "Your family is at the Monarch Hotel in room fourteen. Relax. They are fine." He spoke to Ah See, "Are you okay?"

"I'll be fine," Ah See said with a painful grimace while holding his ear where Joe kicked him.

"Who is he?" Joe asked, confused. "And why are they here?"

Truet spoke irritably, "If you had hurt this man or that girl, I would have shot you! You're lucky I got here when I did. You have no idea how lucky you are." He exhaled to calm his nerves. "He was watching the house for Luther," Truet explained with a lie. "You attacked an innocent man for doing what he was asked to do. You'll find your family at the hotel, Joe."

Joe scoffed defensively. "He didn't answer the door. How was I supposed to know? I thought he was robbing the house like they did Lee's last night," Joe explained. "He should have answered the door and yapped in Chinese or something instead of hiding in here like rats in an oat bag."

"He speaks English. He was told not to answer the door because I doubt people like you would have believed him anyway. Go see your family, Joe."

26

Truet took Ah See and Meili to the Monarch Hotel and spoke with William Fasana and the hotel's manager, Roger King, about a room to put Meili and Ah See in until the threat was over. They put Meili in a room with instructions to stay there.

William Fasana joined Truet and Nate as they took Ah See to arrest every Chinese man who worked on the road leveling crew. The Chinese men worked on Ninth Street between Main and Ash Streets leveling, filling in and stamping the dirt laid down. Truet had asked William to block the Main Street end while he and Nate went to the Ash Street end with the idea of herding all the men into the middle without allowing any of them to escape.

Ah See stood the middle of Ninth Street and spoke in their common language to call all the men working on the road to him and explained that both ends of the street were secured by lawmen and they would shoot anyone who tried to run. He explained they would not be hurt, but they would be taken to the marshal's office to answer some questions.

Truet watched the men ask Ah See questions while eyeing the lawmen anxiously. The men were apprehensive, and it showed in their expressions after seeing William holding both of his revolvers in his hands with a stone-cold blank expression on his weathered face like he was waiting for a target to shoot. Nate was uneasy while holding a shotgun in his hands. Truet had his revolver holstered and motioned with his hands for the men to start moseying towards the jail.

With an angry scowl on his face, one of the Chinese men held a shovel in his hands. He spun around and threw the shovel at Truet before running towards Chinatown. Truet dodged the shovel and watched Nate lift the shotgun to his shoulder and pull the trigger. Nothing happened.

"Crap!" Nate yelled and lowered the shotgun to pull back one of the two hammers.

Truet pulled his revolver, set the bead of his Colt on the man's upper back and pulled the trigger before the man could turn the corner. The percussion startled the people on Main Street nearby as it echoed throughout the quiet and busy town. The man's body fell out of control to the freshly smoothed dirt and moved only a moment before going still.

Truet glared at Nate angrily and shouted, "You have to pull the hammers back! Don't let that happen again, Nate. Someone's life could depend on you next time. Be ready!" He turned to Ah See.

"You told them not to run?"

"Yes," he nodded repeatedly. He was as stunned as the others to see one of his countrymen shot dead in front of him.

Truet scanned the faces of each one of the Chinese men who were quite frightened now. "Tell them I'm not playing. If you want to run, you will be shot! Tell them that."

William had a strange approving grin. "The wagon blocked my shot, or I would have driven him into the ground myself. Nice shot. I'll keep two of these men here, make sure that one's dead, and have them throw the body into the wagon. Cover him up with some dirt and bring the two men to the office. Ah See, translate that. Let them know I'll shoot them the moment they try to run. Guaranteed."

Truet had all the men sit on the floor along the back wall of the office. He had asked questions about Matt's disappearance, but the men seemed hesitant to answer. Truet was becoming angrier the longer it took to get any answers. He spoke in a low volume, but the wrath he was feeling was not hidden in his tone. "Ah See, tell these men I want some damn answers because I do not believe them. Matt is, I don't know where, but if he is killed, these men are going to be just as guilty as Wu-Pen if they don't start talking!" he shouted and threw a tin coffee cup at the wall above them. It hit with force and ricocheted onto the floor.

"They are too afraid of Wu-Pen to say anything," Ah See explained to Truet.

"Tell them Wu-Pen is going to be hung if I don't kill him first! They have nothing to be afraid of. I'll keep them safe for crying out loud. Just tell me what I need to know! Where is Matt? Was he taken by Wu-Pen this morning? Tell them, if Matt is dead, I will hang every one of them one by one myself!"

Ah See translated, and one man spoke to him.

"What did he say?" Truet asked.

"He said they don't know anything."

"Do you believe him?" Truet asked.

Ah See shook his head. "I do not. They are afraid of Wu-Pen, not you."

William leaned against the wall beside Matt's private office, observing the men as he listened. He was growing more impatient, worried and frustrated by the minute. "Let's shoot one of them and maybe they'll start talking."

"I already did," Truet answered with frustration in his voice.

"Then let's throw them in jail and go to Chinatown and find Matt ourselves! We're wasting time here," William said heatedly.

Ah See turned his attention back to the men sitting on the floor. He spoke in Chinese, "Wu-Pen cannot stay here. He took the marshal and that will not be overlooked. His rule over us is over. He cannot stay here and not be hung for that crime. If you want to stay here, you must speak the truth and tell them what they want to know. You all know the marshal is in danger if not dead already. If you can save him, do so now and save yourself from a needless death like Izu and Wang. They did not commit those crimes. Wu-Pen did and then blamed them. I, like you, was too scared to speak the truth. Now I live with the guilt that I could have saved my friends, but shamefully, I did not. Matt is a friend to us. Wu-Pen is not. It could be any one of you next time Wu-Pen needs a man to die for him. Remember, Po, the life we had before Wu-Pen came here? It could be good like that again."

Po Chan was one of the road crew laborers sitting on the floor. He replied nervously, "Bing Jue and two of his students worked with us this morning. None of us helped them, but yes, they took the marshal to Wu-Pen."

Ah See thanked Po and turned to Truet. "Yes, Bing Jue and his students took Matt this morning. None of these men helped."

"Where is he now?" Truet asked.

"They do not know. The tunnels more than likely."

"What tunnels?"

"The tunnels underground leading to all the buildings in Chinatown. It is safer to go from place to place at night."

"How do we get in there?"

"Under rugs, you will see a way into the tunnels."

"That's where we will look. Tell them..." He paused. He thought about letting the men leave but changed his mind to ensure none of them went scurrying to Wu-Pen. "Let them know they'll be kept here until we have Matt and Wu-Pen. Phillip, open the jail cells and put them in there."

Jinhai Zhang watched Lucille Barton's expression brighten like the sun breaking through a cloudy sky. He had handed her a white vase she wanted yellow roses painted on. Her smile alone revealed she loved his work and was pleased to have him working with her. The way she touched his hand and said, "Thank you," always brought a smile to his aging face. Some people can become a ray of sunlight in the life of another and Lucille had certainly become his. What had started with mistrust and hesitancy had become a friendship that lacked communication of the same language. However, the language of expression, respect and appreciation spoke louder than words often did. Little by little, he caught a few words of English and likewise, she learned a few words in Chinese, enough to get through the day. He pulled a table cart over to his painting station with six mugs on it. Lucille had come up with a way to communicate what she wanted by either drawing a picture and dabbing colors on the side or leaving the page blank, which meant he was free to do whatever his artistic talents led him to create.

There was a knock on the locked door; Jinhai glanced up and frowned. A Chinese man named Hop Sun was at the window jabbing his finger towards Jinhai urgently. He went to the door.

Hop Sun spoke in Chinese, "Jinhai, this is for you from Wu-Pen." He handed a small scroll to Jinhai. Hop Sun appeared unsettled. "I don't know why, but the lawman killed Gen Chen and took the whole road crew to the jail. Ah See is with the lawman. I saw them all sitting on the floor. Ah See is talking for them about something. Read that message immediately. That's the only message I received to tell you. I must go before the lawmen grab me too."

Jinhai closed the door. He untied the small ribbon that held the scroll closed. He opened it and read the writing. His mouth fell open while the color left his face. He could not pull his eyes off the words written by Wu-Pen.

"Jin," Lucille asked, "is everything okay?"

The words meant little, but the sincere concern of her face translated the meaning. He offered a fake smile that probably couldn't fool anyone that had seen him smile before. His heart quickened, and he felt faint from the blood rushing through him. His throat tightened as he raised a single finger to indicate that he would be back. He left the pottery shop and walked with trembling hands and greatly troubled, towards to the marshal's office.

He walked slowly past the bay windows and glanced inside just in time to witness Truet throw a cup at the wall and shout. He hid around the corner for a little while before the door opened and the American lawmen and Ah See came out of the building. Frightened, Jinhai stepped onto the boardwalk and called for Ah See. Jinhai was shocked to have two of the three lawmen pull their revolvers and aim their weapons at him. If he had to urinate, he would have right where he stood.

"Don't shoot him. He is my friend," Ah See said. He spoke to Jinhai in their native language, "It's not a good time, Jinhai. Can we talk later?"

Jinhai held the scroll out towards Ah See. "Read. Hop just brought it to me. Ask them to help my friend."

Ah See took the scroll and read it while taking a deep breath. He spoke to Truet, "This is Jinhai. He works for the pottery shop and is asking you to help his friend. This is from Wu-Pen. I will read it to you.

Jinhai,

You were placed in the company of Lucille for one purpose. That purpose is now due. Plead with her to follow you to your place at five o'clock. We will take her from there. Show her this note, and it explains in English. Act excited to show her your work, and she must come alone with you. No husband or children, or you will fail me. I suggest you do not fail me, Jinhai, or I will destroy them all slowly and you will watch.

Miss Barton,

Jinhai has asked me to invite you over to his store to pick out five items as a gift for you and your store for the grand opening on Monday. It would please him very much if you followed him home at five o'clock. May I ask you to refrain from bringing the family as there are other goods there that are ancient and fragile and very small aisles. Please come. Jinhai is very excited to bless you with choosing the pieces of your choice.

Wu-Pen."

Truet grit his teeth as the fury rose within him. "What does it mean, they'll take her?"

"I do not know," Ah see replied. "But I think like what they did to my sister."

"Does your friend know where Matt is?"

Ah See explained and Jinhai had not known Matt was missing. Ah See answered Truet, "He says if you help Lucille, he will try to help find Matt."

Truet agreed. "William, will you go to the pottery shop and take that family to the hotel for the night? I don't know what is going on, but they are in Wu-Pen's sights too. Let's get them to safety. I'll meet you at the hotel. I'm going to get the sheriff and his deputies to help us find Matt. Give me twenty minutes. After that, maybe you can kill Wu-Pen."

William smiled just a touch. "Gladly."

Nate asked hesitantly, "What about Christine? I don't think she knows about Matt missing yet."

"You're right. Go to the dance hall and bring Christine back to the hotel. If she argues, tell her I said it's non-negotiable. Take the shotgun and pull the damn hammers back before you try shooting it, Nate. I mean it, keep her safe."

27

Matt opened his eyes and blinked a few times to focus on a candle set in front of him. It was a pitch-black room except for the candle set on a stand. His head ached from the ether. He realized with alarm that he was standing upright and tied to a post used to hold the ceiling up. He was disoriented and searched for anything that would identify where he was. There were no windows, only stone walls created with river rock and a ceiling of boards. The scent of freshly dug earth filled his senses and took a moment to understand he was underground. Matt's arms were spread outwards and hanging by his thumbs. He could feel the pressure on the joint of his thumbs from supporting the weight of his arms. A board had been nailed across the beam to act as a cross to hold his arms extended outwards. He tried to reach the board above his hands with his fingers to rest his thumb joints, but a three-inch piece of bamboo slid over his thumbs created a barrier between his hands and the board. A cord made of braided hair was tied to the base of his thumbs below the knuckle and went up through the bamboo to the board it was tied around. He tried to pull and break the string, but it only hurt the thumb joints. Matt was tied to the post with three-inch-wide satin bands around his chest, neck, waist and below his knees, making it impossible to move. For the first time in his life, he was virtually helpless. All the strength, courage and brutality he had become known for could do nothing for him. There was nothing he could do without dislocating his thumbs, and even then, he would not be able to escape where he was. Even the strongest men of courage occasionally get frightened, and with the horrifying memory of what happened to Leroy Haywood coming to mind, it was a very unsettling position to be in. It would be easy for Wu-Pen and his evil guards to do the same thing to him, and there was absolutely nothing Matt could do to stop it. His heart began to beat faster as the fear of the unknown began to take hold. His thumb joints ached and were growing more painful now that he was aware of them.

The temptation to panic was overwhelming, but he forced himself to remain calm and took a deep breath to try to stay reasonable and not start jerking his thumbs and screaming, which might have been a natural reaction. His thumb joints would give long before the braided strings of hair did. No matter what Wu-Pen had planned for him, Matt tried to remind himself that the Lord Jesus

Christ was still in control. He hadn't been reading his Bible lately and he could feel the distance from the Lord that came from not being in the word. There was nothing easier in the world than setting the Bible down, closing the cover, and neglecting to read it for days, which turns into weeks, months, and years for some people. A few days of missing scripture reading dulls the voice of the Holy Spirit while the world's concerns seep in, and before too long praying less soon follows. There is no other book in the world that is easier to set down and not open again, until trouble arises and someone seeks the help of the Lord. It is then when their spirit is refreshed like finding a cool stream in the burning desert that people honestly wonder why they stopped reading the Bible.

Matt learned a secret to avoid that from happening which was to leave his Bible open. Reverend Abraham Ash had said often in his sermons that, "An opened Bible is very inviting. It is the only book in the world that beckons to be read."

How can a God so inviting with his Word be ignored? The Bible penetrates the soul and draws a person closer to Jesus like a magnet. It is also quite strange how knowledge is merely a shell covering the heart and meat of the believer's soul. A man can know the Bible from cover to cover but feel dead inside if he isn't seeking to remain near the Lord in a daily devotion of time in the Word and prayer. Matt had fallen into the busyness of life and neglected to read his Bible for a day, which turned into a few weeks, and it left the feeling of a significant distance from the Lord that was palpable. Danger seemed so much closer to him than the Lord of his life and it was by his own doing that God seemed so distant. The truth is God was still just as near to Matt as he ever had been. Matt took comfort in knowing that the Bible promises God would never leave or forsake him, even when he failed to read his Bible and grow cold in his prayer time.

Matt took a deep breath and slowly released it to help remain calm. He closed his eyes and prayed, "Lord Jesus, before I ask for your help, I need to ask you to forgive me. I haven't been praying or reading your word as I should be. I have sinned in many ways, and I ask you to forgive me. Probably more than anything else, forgive me for not reading your Word. Jesus, I don't know how to say it, except I feel so far away from you. I don't know what Wu-Pen has planned for me, but I ask you to give me the courage to face it and if you will, help me to get out of here. I know I'm not the greatest representation of what a Christian should be or of you. Jesus, you know where I am, and I'm asking for your help. I ask that you will intervene to not allow evil to win..."

He heard Wu-Pen chuckle from behind him. "Oh, Matt, my old friend," Wu-Pen said as he slowly stepped around the front of him with a broad grin. "Look at you! The tough, no nonsense United States Marshal, who has books written about him, is now so helpless that a child could put up more of a fight." He paused and furrowed his brow thoughtfully. "You know, I want to see you cry. Beg me for my forgiveness like you did your god. Do that, and I'll think about letting you go."

Matt peered at Wu-Pen like a cockroach crawling towards his lunch. "You're not going to let me go. I already know that. What's it going to be? Black widows like you did to Leroy, or something new?"

Wu-Pen widened his eyes with excitement. "That was fun for me. Yes, I enjoyed that a lot. I'll admit it now, I did all of it. I even robbed the safe at the Engberg and Penn Assayer's office. But for you, black widows are a bit too quick." His expression turned cold. "Because of you, I may have to leave town. As you Americans say, I must close my shop and go somewhere else where I am not known. I may even have to change my name, and that is your fault!" He paused to yawn. Like Matt, he had been up most of the night as well.

"That would be too bad," Matt said with spite.

"Yes, it would. I tried to be your friend, Matt. All I wanted was for you to turn the other way here and there. I would never make you look bad, just like when I helped you solve a crime by giving you Izu and Wang. You solved a horrible crime and received high praise from this community. I could have made you far more famous. I could have made you rich, very rich, if you had been my friend and just left me alone. I help you; you help me. We could have had a wonderful friendship, you and me. Now that we can talk openly and understand each other, I am curious. You see, I don't want to leave this town. I like it here. What if I was to offer you a chance to start over again as my friend. We could work together and become very, very wealthy. Will you work with me if I let you go, and we forget all about this? I am willing to let the past go, if you are. Will you agree to work with me?"

It would be easy to agree if he trusted Wu-Pen would set him free. Matt had never taken a bribe to overlook a crime or a criminal, and he refused to be bought now. He was a lawman, and he had sworn to do his duties to the best of his integrity. Matt answered plainly, "No."

Wu-Pen was disappointed. "You do understand that you are forcing me to leave here. If I have to leave, I will not leave you here alive. You do understand that. Yes?"

Matt's throat contracted anxiously. "The Bible says, you can only kill my body, but you cannot kill me. I'll be in heaven for eternity. I can't say the same thing for you," Matt said, looking in Wu-Pen's cold dark eyes.

Wu-Pen smiled slowly. "Look around you, Matt. You are underground in a small room that I can have walled up in a few short hours and leave you with one candle burning until it burns out. You would have the pleasure of being buried in pitch blackness just as you are until you are found a hundred years from now. No one would ever know what happened to you. I suppose I should remind you that if you are not here, who would protect Christine? If I must do away with you, I will take her as my property as a departing gift from you. She will work off the debt you cost me by leaving here. The profit from her would be a hundred times over that of the other women I own. But even so, the debt is great and will take a good portion her life to settle."

Matt's fury brought a snarl to his lips. "I'll kill you!"

Wu-Pen softly laughed at him. "No, you won't." He patted Matt's cheek lovingly. "I suppose if you don't work with me, then I'll be forced to take Christine and Lucille with me. However, if you would work with me, they could live freely. You could marry Christine and become rich and live a beautiful life. Of course, the only cost you would pay is looking the other way here and there and perhaps a little mistake while investigating when needed. I'm offering you heaven on earth over slowly dying of dehydration in the dark while wondering what kind of life your decision has committed Christine and Lucille to." He chortled a small laugh. "Just imagine the gossip. Your name will always be a mystery as the man who disappeared with the two most beautiful ladies in town. You should think about that for a little while before I have them seal up the wall. Your thumbs will become unbearable soon but bearing the unbearable is torture of its own. Your spirit will break when the pain is too much, and you will decide to be my friend. Or your pride will cost you everything when you could have had anything you and Christine desired. Keep praying to your god. Pray harder even; maybe an angel will appear and set you free," he laughed. "I won't pack my things just yet. I'll be back in an hour or two for your final decision."

Matt was frightened, angry, and desperate to break free at the same time. He could not break the binds that held him and there was nothing he could do except pray to the very God Wu-Pen mocked. He looked towards the wood plank ceiling. "Jesus, you heard Wu-Pen. You know the intentions of his heart as well. Please do not let him get away with what he has planned and protect your children from him. I'll accept what happens to me if it's your will, but I will not bow down to him. Jesus, please protect Christine and Lucille from the evil of his reach. And if you're willing, help me to get out of here to stop him myself."

Luther Fasana could not climb the hotel stairs with his injured knee. There were no rooms on the first floor of the Monarch Hotel, except for William's, which was near the courtesy desk across from the grand stairway in the lobby. William let his uncle take his room while he stayed in another. Luther wasn't used to being idle. Staying in bed for any length of time reading led to heavy eye lids and falling asleep. He had slept for a few hours before waking up and using his crutches to approach the courtesy desk to chit-chat with Pamela Collins and the Hotel Manager, Roger King.

"William said he'd clean the room before I stayed in there, but I haven't noticed a single crumb or dirty dish being removed yet. I do thank you for having that young lady change the bed sheets, though."

Roger King explained, "William's room is not on the housecleaning list. As an employee, he gets to clean his own room. I can have it cleaned tomorrow morning at eight o'clock sharp."

"I hope to go home tomorrow, but if not, I'd appreciate it." Luther received his meals, bath, laundry and anything he wanted at no charge, but he wanted to go back to his house and sleep in his bed. He missed his dog Red too.

Pamela offered, "We tell William to keep his room's door closed at all times, so guests don't think we have shoddy housekeeping. I've also had to tell him to clean his room a few times when the stench starts creeping out here."

Luther said through a humored smile, "For a young man who grooms his hair and clothes with a fine-toothed comb, I think my hogs have more sense about keeping a clean pen than my nephew does."

Pamela laughed. "I'm sure they do."

The entrance door opened, and Joe Thorn was surprised to see Luther standing at the courtesy desk holding crutches. He asked cautiously, "Is Billy Jo here?"

Luther's countenance had gone from friendly to hostile by the time the door closed behind Joe. "You're not talking to my daughter. You might as well turn around and walk out before I slam one of these crutches up against your head! It's over and it needs to stay over."

Joe's attention shifted to Pamela and Roger with a touch of humiliation before shifting back to Luther. "I want to marry your daughter."

Luther tossed a crutch up in the air and grabbed the narrow foot of it to have a harder swing. He hobbled one awkward step closer to Joe with his other crutch determined to hit Joe with a crutch.

Joe explained quickly, "Luther, I know you're thinking this is going to happen again and again. But I assure you, Billy Jo and I were getting along better than ever until I found out about Wes and her. It infuriated me. Certainly, you can understand that. Billy Jo told me about your first wife running away with another man. I don't want to be hit with your crutch, Luther, but I might deserve it after what I said and did to Billy Jo. I came here to apologize."

Luther was unsympathetic. His voice rose, "Get your scrawny woman-beating ass out of my sight or I will bust your head open right now. Don't come in here and tell me you're sorry. I've heard it too many times to believe a word of it, and I will not let you see Billy Jo. I'm taking her away from here when my knee heals, and I'm not bringing her back. I would rather not see my daughter or my grandsons than have you in their lives. You're poison, Joe. That's all you are."

Joe pleaded softly, "You can't take her away from here. We have children together."

"I will! And I won't tell you where."

The threat of Billy Jo leaving with his boys scared him. For all these years, he had taken them for granted, and now that he appreciated what he had, he couldn't stand the idea of losing his family. "Luther, that's my family, whether you like it or not. Your boys ran away from here as soon as their mama wrote, so you know what it's like to lose part of your family. I'm trying to be a better father like you are. All I need is another chance to prove myself."

Luther's usually friendly face transformed to cold and mean. "Your boys watched you try to throw their mother into a sewer pit! Do you think they want anything to do with you? You are poison to their souls. I will not stand by a moment longer and let you tear those boys up any more than you have! Get the hell out of here and don't come back. Billy Jo is my daughter, and those boys are my grandsons. You are not going to cause them any more heartbreaks. I promise you that! I want my daughter to marry a Christian man, not a horse's ass."

"Thankfully, the boys didn't see that," he said remorsefully. "Billy Jo is old enough to make up her own mind. I'm sorry, but I don't need your approval to marry her, let alone talk to her. What room is she in?" He asked Pamela. "You better tell me before I go bang on every door in this place."

Luther rammed the crutch forward and the broader end connected with Joe's chest hard enough to knock him two steps back. Luther raised the crutch back at shoulder height. "The next swing will crack your head wide open!" he warned.

Joe rubbed the pain away on his chest where the crutch hit him. Luther may have been an old man, but he was the stoutest old man Joe would ever meet. There were many toughs in the silver mine, timber industry, and around the Branson saloons, but the one man Joe never wanted to tangle with was Luther. It wasn't just the fact that Luther was Billy Jo's father. For a long time, he didn't care about that. Luther was a friendly and gentle man who was as big and powerful as a bear. There was a saying that if you poked the bear, you might get clawed. The blow to the chest was a mere growl, and any further conversation could bring out the claws and snarling bite. The gentlest man in the room may well be the most dangerous, and when it came to Luther, Joe believed it to be true. The warning was heeded. "Just tell her and my sons that I love them, please." He opened the door to leave but instead held it open for Nate Robertson and Christine Knapp as they stepped into the Monarch Hotel. Christine appeared upset.

"Thank you, Joe," Nate said.

Luther frowned when he saw Christine's somber expression. "Christine, sweetheart, you look troubled. Are you okay?"

She shook her head worriedly. "I will be when I know Matt's okay," she said emotionally.

"Is something wrong? Did he get hurt?" Luther asked with concern.

Nate answered, "He's missing, Luther. We know Wu-Pen has him."

"Missing?" The alarm showed on Luther's bearded face. "Does the family know? Did you send a wire to the Big Z? Adam and Charlie will come to help look for him."

"We don't have time. We're going into Chinatown as soon as I get back to the office. They're waiting for me." He spoke to Roger King, "Roger, we need to check Christine into the hotel for the night."

Joe Thorn stood holding the door open, listening. "The Chinese took Matt?"

Luther rested the crutch he hit Joe with against

the courtesy desk. "Christine, come here." He held an arm out to invite a comforting hug. She went to him like a little girl to her loving father. He wrapped his large arm around her and held her softly. "He'll come out of this just fine. The Lord will see to that. Let's pray. Roger, Pamela, Nate, let's pray with Christine for Matt's safety."

Joe Thorn's question had been ignored. He was left out of the prayer circle as the others held hands and prayed to Jesus for Matt's safety. For a moment, he longed to be invited to take part in it. He quietly stepped into the entry and closed the door softly so it would not interrupt their praying. It was the least he could do.

The idea of Billy Jo taking the boys and leaving town left a frightening and hollow hole in his chest that brought an urgent desperation to reach out to her as quickly as possible. She needed to know he was sorry, he loved her, and he would forgive her. She needed to know he wanted to marry her. He walked past a mercantile and stopped. An idea came to mind, and he went inside. It took him a moment to pick out a sheet of stationery and borrowed a pen to write a letter. He bought a small hinged-top wood box not much bigger than a gun holster and placed the letter and her wedding ring inside of it. He had used a garden hoe to dig the ring out of the community privy and washed it in a creek. He had the lady behind the counter tie a red ribbon around the box to hold the lid closed. He carried the box back to the hotel and was pleased to find Pamela alone behind the courtesy desk. "Miss, will you do me a favor and give this box to Billy Jo? It would mean a lot to me."

Pamela took hold of the box. "I suppose I could, sure."

"Thank you so much. And don't mention this to Luther. I love his daughter, but he'll throw it away."

"I'll make sure she gets it," Pamela said with a pleasant smile.

"That's all I can ask. Thank you." He hoped the letter would explain his heart and desire to marry her.

29

Bing Jue was in Wu-Pen's apartment watching Ling rub his feet after washing them. She sat on a small stool with his leg resting over her lap while she expertly massaged his foot. Wu-Pen was confident Matt would eventually clear his mind of the foolishness of integrity and come around to seeing the benefits of compromise. A life of wealth is better than a life without and certainly given a choice; it was better than no life at all. Wu-Pen had a goal to be the most powerful man in Branson. A man didn't need to own land to be powerful. He only needed to have persuasion, influence and control of others. All of which could be gained by blackmail and intimidation. Mutual respect was always the best way to negotiate a friendship, but the threat of violence being made clear had a way of securing deals. It was good to be nice and remain friendly, to smile at children and open doors for the ladies, but at the same time, business was business, and extortion and percentages were part of the game. Every company he wanted a partnership in could be accomplished either above ground as friends or underground in his secret room that he referred to as the dungeon. The room wasn't completed yet. He wanted more implements to get his message through loud and clear so that no man could tolerate the means and fear the consequences if they betrayed him.

Unfortunately, the one problem he had was Matt Bannister. The man was hard-headed, stubborn, and fixated on a word with little meaning to Wu-Pen: integrity. The word itself meant moral incorruptibility, soundness, firm adherence to values and, in essence, doing what is right no matter the cost. In short, it meant becoming a thorn in Wu-Pen's side. He liked Matt, he liked him a lot and did not want to kill him, but he would if Matt did not adjust, conform and accept the conditions of the friendship Wu-Pen was offering. It was just that simple. Conform to Wu-Pen's idea of integrity and become wealthy or die. There was no other option of colors outside of black and white. Matt had no choice. Soon, Jinhai would bring Lucille Barton to his small store, and they would take control of her and prove to Matt that Wu-Pen's words could be trusted. Manipulating Christine and taking her would be nearly as easy. Matt would conform. He had no choice if he valued the lives of the two ladies.

The tragic loss of Uang Yang the night before could be overlooked. There was no intent to harm anyone other than Ah See. Matt would have to understand that and so would Lee. Deception was a strategic part of the game of chess. It was no different in the game of life. To win, one must protect the king and all costs, and Wu-Pen was the king. Ah See was a mere pawn, but even a pawn can bring down the king. He needed to be eliminated, and in the process of doing so, Wu-Pen lost a strong knight. It was a fair game, and he accepted the loss of Uang. In truth, he may have had Uang killed for waking up Lee. It was supposed to be done in silence like everything they did was supposed to be. Now that Uang had been killed breaking into a city leader's home, he would have to explain Uang and Heop were rogue Chinese and rightfully were killed by the homeowner. Wu-Pen had to protect the public image of himself at all costs.

He hoped Matt would come to his senses and become a willing partner in his business endeavors. To encourage Matt to make the right choice, Wu-Pen chose to use a slow and gradual method of torture that would not immediately cause damage but could if he hung by his thumbs long enough. In China, he may have been lifted to his toes to create permanent damage or chains placed under his knees while his arms hung by his thumbs to increase the pain tenfold. It was not Wu-Pen's plan to hurt Matt permanently. He wanted him to act as a protective shield of authority while taking specific percentages from every business in town. Enduring the gradual growth of pain and the anguish of knowing what would happen to his dearest Christine if he refused to abandon his values was more than a man could stand. Matt would be broken, but he would swear allegiance to Wu-Pen. However, time was short to get that sworn allegiance because the town would not tolerate the marshal being taken by the Chinese. If Matt refused once more to join into a partnership, more weight would be added to his arms, and soon he would beg to have the strings of braided hair removed from his thumbs to stop the pain. He would become Wu-Pen's pet dog to order around and reward with a pet's treat of money. A behaved dog never bites the hand that feeds it, nor does the master kick a content dog. Once they had an agreement, their friendship could be sealed.

He had heard that the deputy Truet had arrested his road leveling crew and killed one of the men that tried to run away. Wu-Pen had not expected that move, but he was not concerned because all of them knew if they spoke a single word about what had happened, they and their families would die. Where there was no evidence, there was no proof, and accusations without evidence were merely gossip.

Bing Jue asked, "When do we go check on the marshal?"

"After Jinhai brings Lucille. In half an hour, when his workday is done, she will be at Jinhai's. The marshal should be grimacing and groaning by then. If not, we will increase the weight every hour until he does."

Bing spoke with an impatient tension to his voice, "If I may say, I think keeping him alive is a mistake. You should let me go down there and drive a blade through his heart as his brother did to

Uang. Uang was nearest to a brother to me."

Wu-Pen snapped loudly, "Uang was a fool! Do not let your emotions control your thinking, Bing. Matt is most valuable if he is alive and conformed to our thinking. There is not another lawman like him or with his power. He will be our best and greatest ally and a weapon for us to use against our enemies. No man can endure what he will and not break. He will break by tonight, and once healed, he will know there is nothing he can do without the consequences being more than he can stomach. He will be loyal to you and me."

"What about his woman if he does not conform? Are you really going to offer her to the commoners?" he questioned.

"No. Christine will be my consort along with Lucille at first. They are beautiful women, don't you think, Bing?"

"Yes."

Wu-Pen glanced at his lady, Ling, and smiled. She was a wise young woman. "Bing, if you bring me the head of Ah See, I will give you his sister, Meili, as your bride."

Bing's lips rose with a hint of a smile. "After darkness comes, I will find him and do just that."

A slight sound of yelling downstairs caught their attention, and then a gunshot sounded in the temple. Time was shorter than expected, and the need was urgent to hide Wu-Pen.

"In the stairway, now!" Bing sputtered. Wu-Pen and Bing hurried into his office and opened the secret panel doorway that opened into a stairway that led to the store below. Wu-Pen wasn't surprised by the invasion of lawmen, but it did come much sooner than he expected. He could hear the lawmen in the store breaking items and tipping over shelves of displays onto the floor while yelling at Wu-Pen's loyal servant while they beat on him. Having lawmen at the bottom of the hidden stairway and the top also left them trapped in the false wall trying to listen to what was being said at both ends. Wu-Pen was tempted to send Bing out to kill the lawmen that were beating on the store owner, but he risked exposure and losing his primary source of protection because there were several lawmen in the store. Wu-Pen would remain hidden and hope the lawmen left soon so they could escape into the tunnel.

30

Truet stood on Rose Street with his fellow deputy marshal, Nate Robertson, occasional deputy marshal William Fasana, Branson Sheriff Tim Wright, and four deputies. Lee Bannister refused to be left out of the search for Matt and joined them. All the men wore gun belts while the two youngest sheriff deputies, Alan Garrison and Mark Thiesen carried shotguns. Ah See was staying temporarily in the Monarch Hotel until they had completed searching for Matt. Any suspicious Chinese were to be shackled or tied and taken immediately to the U.S. Marshal's Office where Phillip was waiting. All the men had three twelve-inch lengths of strong twine for tying wrists together, if iron shackles were not available. In preparation for new prisoners, the entire road crew of Chinese men were moved to the city sheriff's jail cells for holding.

Truet spoke to Sheriff Tim Wright, "William, Lee, Nate and I will search the temple and upstairs where Wu-Pen's office is. You and your deputies search the store next to it. We will keep going down the line like that, one building after another. Keep in mind that Matt is probably underground somewhere, so we have to find those tunnel access points. So, move rugs and find those openings. We will search underground when we find a tunnel. Lee killed Uang and another man last night, Bing Jue is still there somewhere. Don't take any chances, and stick together with your guns handy. If you find Matt and he's injured, get him to the doctor's. If you find Wu-Pen, try to arrest him, but I promise Bing Jue will try to fight, so kill him first. Let's go find Matt."

Truet opened the red door of the temple and entered, stepping on the clean and waxed oak floor with his boots on. William, Lee and Nate followed right behind him, careless of removing their boots or staying on a narrow red carpet that ran along the wall and stretched the length of the large room. It was added recently for Americans to walk on when they came to visit Wu-Pen. Originally the access to the stairway was through an unnoticeable concealed door just like the stairway from Wu-Pen's office to the store below. With business growing with more Americans, Wu-Pen had the concealed doorway removed to create a more welcoming environment for the Americans that came to see him.

"Hey, you, look who's here?" William announced himself loudly to a temple priest wearing an orange robe as they entered. The priest was an old man with the front half of his head shaved and a long queue on the back. The priest was infuriated to see the men walk with their dirty boots on his temple floor. He began speaking irately in Chinese while pointing at their feet and then the red carpet. His intent was clearly understood, and he moved quickly to stop them by putting his hand on Truet's chest.

"Shut up!" Truet snapped and shot his left hand to the man's mouth with a quick, solid jab. The priest's head snapped back with his top lip split open. His eyes burned into Truet, but he politely bowed as a drop of blood dripped to the floor. He stepped out of their way to let them pass.

Truet was set on getting to the stairs with Lee and Nate following him. William paused to look curiously around the temple. He had never been inside a Chinese temple and was surprised to see a large room decorated in vibrant colors of silk banners with gold dragons and lions encircling the room's high ceiling. At the far end of the temple was the altar, and a large brass gong in an ornamented painted red frame, a golden bowl of incense smoked lightly, revealing a strong aroma of a sweet fragrance. Multiple figurines of various kinds and sizes set about, such as a pair of large golden lions and some creatures that appeared to be dogs but had the head of snarling dragons. Two vertical columns appeared to be circular black bars with eight large sharp points directed upwards towards the sky on either side of the altar. The columns' relevance came quickly when the priest grabbed one of the columns black bars and pulled out a seven-foot-long spear with a painted black spearhead. The decorative circular columns were merely standing black spears placed in a decorative stand made to hold them. The priest raised the weapon and took a short hop before bracing his legs to throw the spear at Truet.

William's right hand went to his reversed handle revolver on his left hip and pulled it quickly, aimed and fired just as the priest's arm came forward. The bullet entered the priest's ear and blew out the other side of his head. His body crumbled to the floor as the spear flew just far enough to hit the side of the wall harmlessly, and bounce to the floor a few feet in front of Truet.

William was relieved to had been quick enough and accurate enough to save his friend. He mimicked a deeper authoritative voice that only Lee would recognize, "I believe we are in hostile territory, boys. Prepare for battle." He asked Lee, "Remember Uncle James always saying that about the time we knew we were trouble? Like after we were ambushed!" He referred to their uncle, Colonel James Ziegler, during the Snake War against the Paiute, Bannock and Western Shoshone.

Lee nodded quietly. He was in no mood to smile.

"Nice shot," Truet said, glancing at the dead priest and the spear on the ground in front of him. "There's more of them, so stay alert. There are four doors up here on the right. Lee, you and William check those rooms. Wu-Pen's woman is probably up here if he's not. Watch out for Bing Jue. He is fast and lethal. Don't hesitate to shoot him," he emphasized to Nate.

The stairs ended in a hallway, just as Truet explained. There were six doors before Wu-Pen's office at the end of the hallway. Candles on-wall-mounted holders covered by glass lit the corridor. It was dead silent and there was no telling what they would find behind any one of the doors.

Lee held his revolver with the hammer pulled back before he opened the first door. It contained a small mat on the floor and weapons of various kinds on the wall. He closed the door and went to the next room as Truet opened the office door and found it empty.

Nate opened the first door on the left and entered. William came up the stairs and followed Nate into the room. It was a small room that had to be a woman's room by the aroma of an arousing perfume, jewelry, makeup and the clothing hanging in an opened armoire. William flipped through the woman's clothing, feeling the silk fabric. "Dog-gone, Maggie would sure like these. I'm going to Portland to see her in a couple of weeks, you know," he offered to Nate with a desire to take the dresses clearly evident in his tone. "I don't know if they'd fit her or not, but she'd like them."

"This room's empty. Let's check the next," Nate said professionally.

"In a minute. Nate, wait. Hey...I just named your first child. Do you know why the Chinese keep their women hidden?" William asked as he opened a drawer of a cabinet and flipped through it curiously.

"No, I don't," Nate said impatiently while opening the door to leave.

"To keep them away from me! I have a certain knack for winning women from the orient's hearts. If they let their women run free, why, I'd have a harem. It's self-preservation on their part; it's my pretty blond hair and curls that drive them wild. Have you ever seen a Chinese man with blond hair? Well, their women haven't either, and that's why they love me. I'm like a Greek goddess or something to them. If I weren't here, you'd have pretty good luck stealing Wu-Pen's woman away from him with your blond hair, but mine's long and yours isn't. So, you're out of luck, unless she's old and ugly. Your tragic love life might just be resurrected today if she's ugly," William said with a thumbs-up gesture.

Nate gazed at William with a dumbfounded expression. "I can't believe you're related to Matt. You don't act like you're concerned about him at all. Is everything always a joke to you? Matt could be dead for all we know, and you want to talk about your blond hair?" Nate questioned irritably. "We have to search the next room."

William paused and stared at Nate seriously. "It's how I deal with things, okay? I am very worried for my cousin, more than you are. I can't explain why but even in the worst of fighting and death looked me right in the eyes, I said whatever came to mind. It keeps me from panicking; you ought to try it. I may not act scared to death, but that doesn't mean I'm not. And it sure as well doesn't mean I don't care for my cousin."

Lee had checked the four rooms, and the last three were empty bedrooms. Truet had taken a moment to search Wu-Pen's desk for anything that would help him find Matt. There was nothing obvious that stood out other than the broken window from the day before. Truet turned the knob to Wu-Pen's apartment, but the door was locked. He stepped back and kicked the door with enough force to bust the lock, and the door flew open to a startled scream of a woman. Ling Tseng ran across the room, opened the door leading to her apartment, and disappeared into her room.

William having just finished his conversation with Nate was surprised to see a false wall door open with a young Chinese lady bursting through the room. He caught her arm as she tried to run past him and spun her around, forcing her face down on her mattress on the floor. He followed her down and placed a knee across her lower back to pin her down. He laughed while she screamed and cursed him bitterly in Chinese with fury scrolled across her attractive face.

He asked through a wide grin, "What did I tell you, Nate?" William was humored by her blatant dislike for him. "These Chinese women come running out of nowhere to me every chance they get! I'm irresistible to them. Have you got a pair of shackles handy?" he asked as he pulled her wrists behind her back. "I'm assuming Truet wants this one arrested."

Truet stepped into Ling's room from the connecting door to Wu-Pen's and nodded with approval. "I do. There is no sign of Wu-Pen or Bing Jue.

Let's go next door and see what Tim and his boys found, if anything. Nate, take her back to the jail and come back to join us. I want to find an access way into those tunnels Ah See talked about."

Nate took Ling towards the jail while Truet and the others went next door to the store to check in with Tim Wright and his deputies. They found the store had been obliterated with overturned tables and bookshelves with various goods on them. Mirrors had been broken and the store windows as well. Worse, the store owner had been beaten up and was sitting against the wall, bruised and bleeding from various places on his face.

Truet was furious. "Who did this?"

Tim answered with a smirk, "Bob was looking for a tunnel access and apparently, the man didn't answer his questions very clearly."

"Tim, do you think this is a joke?" Truet asked, holding back a floodgate of frustration.

"No. That's why we need answers. Matt could tell you himself that sometimes force is the quickest way to get answers."

"Do you speak Chinese?" Truet's hardened gaze went to the injured Chinese man who had done nothing wrong other than not speak English.

"No!" Tim scoffed at the idea of speaking Chinese.

The floodgates opened, and Truet yelled, "Then how could you expect to ask him anything? Listen, all of you, we are not here to terrorize anyone. We are here to find Matt. If you can't find him, move on! You don't lay your hands on anyone again unless you have to." He could not hide his disapproval of the Branson deputy Bob Ewing. "And you do not destroy their businesses! This man did not take Matt! He may know nothing about Matt at all."

"He's Chinese," Bob explained with a careless shrug.

"Not when you're working for me, he's not," Truet answered with a cold stare. "These are men just like any others, and you will treat them as such, or you can leave and go back to your office. Leave them be! Just search their property and move on. If anything happens like this again, Bob, I'll leave you in much worse shape right where you stand!"

"I don't work for you," Bob stated with a smug, uncaring expression.

Lee Bannister's patience ran out. "Then I will beat you to the brink of death myself! My brother is missing. I don't want to hear any arguing. Just do what you're told and keep your mouth shut!" He caught a glimpse of the edge of a red rug under a sizeable solid shelving unit Bob had pulled over that had stored a collection of dishware. Broken glass, clay and ceramic dishware were scattered across the floor and piled under the shelf. "Did you look under that rug?"

"What rug?" Tim asked.

"The one under the bookshelf or whatever it is, that your deputy pulled over! Do you see it right there? Did anyone check under it?" Lee shouted.

Tim shrugged innocently. "I don't know. Bob, did you pull that rug up before you pulled that cabinet over?"

Lee didn't wait for Bob to answer. "Did you bother to look under the rug, Bob? Or did you just start terrorizing this man?" Lee knew Bob's character well enough to know looking wasn't Bob's intention for demolishing the store. "I heard Truet tell you to look under any rugs. But you didn't, did you? You just started tearing this place apart and beating on him, didn't you?" Lee demanded to know.

Bob scowled with disgust. "Don't you talk to me like that, Lee. You're not a lawman. You shouldn't even be here."

William stepped forward and brought a hard swift kick into Bob's groin. Bob dropped immediately to his knees while holding his hands over his groin. He couldn't get a breath for a moment. William grabbed a handful of hair and jerked Bob's head back and brought his knife to the edge of his scalp. William's blue eyes were as hard and dangerous as the steel blade of his knife. "I am sworn in and deputized. Lee's brother is missing, which gives him more of a right to be here than you. Now answer his damn question before I take just enough of your scalp to patch the hole I'm going to put in your chest, if you don't start helping us find Matt!"

"I didn't look," he answered through short breaths as the agony of the blow had not subsided.

Truet cursed irritably and lifted the shelving unit while Lee pulled the rug covered with broken dishware across the floor, revealing a plank door. Tim pulled the door open revealing a wood stairway that led down into a dark tunnel lined with river rock walls and a plank ceiling overhead.

Unlike a mine, the tunnel appeared safe and secure from caving in.

William didn't hesitate to walk down the staircase, with a revolver in each hand pointing in both directions as he descended. "It looks like a maze, but it's lit. Let's split up and find Matt."

"Come find us next door when you're ready, Bob," Sheriff Tim Wright said quickly. He explained to Truet, "I think me and my boys will keep looking above ground in case Matt is in a room somewhere." He had no interest in going underground.

31

Bob Ewing stayed on his knees and took some deep breaths as the pain resided slowly. William's kick had taken every ounce of fight and strength out of him. Bob heard a strange click, and a part of the wall near the counter opened. Bob's stomach dropped into his bowels when Bing Jue stepped out of the wall, followed by Wu-Pen. He tried to pull his revolver, but he had reacted too quickly and neglected to remove the trigger guard that held it in the holster. He stood as Bing promptly moved towards him. Bob heard Wu-Pen speak in Chinese urgently, while his fumbling fingers removed the leather thong and jerked his revolver out of the holster. He had no sooner freed his gun when Bing delivered a quick kick to Bob's groin, doubling the sickening pain that reached up into his stomach. The revolver slipped from his fingers as Bob dropped to his knees and fell forward, hitting his face on the floor. He held his groin in agony. His body heaved to get a breath, but the misery was overbearing. Bing grabbed him and pulled him to the edge of the stairs leading into the tunnel and pushed him over the edge. Bob hit the stairs with his back and rolled to the packed earth with a hard landing. He got to his hands and knees and began vomiting.

Wu-Pen kicked Bob's revolver down to him. "Let Truet know this south tunnel is a dead end with nothing in it. He will not find Matt down there, and this is the only way in or out. The candles will burn out soon. You will be trapped in the dark, and no one will answer your cries for help. Enjoy the darkness." Bing reached down and slammed the access door closed. He then pulled the heavy shelf unit that Truet had stood up, back down across the tunnel entrance.

Wu-Pen's words were not exactly true. Matt was in the south tunnel, but they could walk past the door he was behind a thousand times and never know it. The tunnels were connected as well, but only one narrow passageway connected the north from south tunnels. The north section of the tunnels contained the opium den, brothel and gambling houses that would make the American's uneasy if they were on Flower Lane. Wu-Pen wanted to have an inclusive Chinatown where the citizens of Branson could shop, eat and enjoy their day without knowing there was a darker side of town under their feet.

To minimize the risk of the underground activities being discovered by the Americans, precautions were made. Investments had to be protected, and although it was not completed, Wu-Pen's plans of an entire city underground were vast and would help make him a wealthy man. Any trespasser who discovered the secrets became a threat to Wu-Pen's kingdom. Deception, fake walls, escape routes, trick doors, rules and alarm bells, code words and consequences were all taken seriously and prepared. What should never be known would never be if all that was discovered were just empty tunnels.

The south tunnel was empty except for the room where Matt was hidden. There were many things Wu-Pen was proud of, but the one he was most excited about was his dungeon. It had taken an architect, skilled laborers and much work to finish. The room was twelve feet beneath the south tunnel, which was conveniently under the temple. A stairway had to be dug in two tiers to a space carved out of the ground. Secured with mortar and rock walls, stone floors, and heavy beam supports for the ceiling, the dungeon had become a secret that was never meant to be found. To conceal it was trouble all its own. However, every problem has an answer and a hidden door had been carefully designed to remain invisible. A door on hinges needed one-eighth of an inch to open and close correctly. One-eighth of an inch isn't much space but becomes quite recognizable to the eye as a door when seen along a wall. To conceal the door, a twenty-foot-long section of wall was constructed on both sides of the main tunnel with six-foot vertical boards evenly spaced one-eighth of an inch between boards to match the door frame. One had to know which knot hole to put a finger in and hook a lever to pull and release the lock to open the door. Without that knowledge, no one would ever know there was a door to a hidden room right in front of them. Truet and his group of men could walk past it thirty times and never realize Matt was right under their feet, hanging by his thumbs. Even if Matt screamed, a custom-made door four inches thick filled with dirt at the room's entrance and the multiple feet of soil between him and the main tunnel muffled most of the sound.

Wu-Pen was not concerned about Truet and his deputies finding Matt, even though they were near him. He was confident his deceptive designs would not be discovered anytime soon. He had overheard Truet and the others talking about Ah See telling them about the tunnels. It aggravated him a great deal because it was supposed to be kept secret. Inside of him, a candle burned with desire, and he could not wait to take Ah See into the dungeon.

Now that the secret of the tunnels was known, it would be a good time to test his people in the north tunnel system and play a little game with the lawmen. A man who prepares for the most un- likely of circumstances is never caught off guard, and an occasional test for those unprepared pre- pares them for next time. He could not lose by inviting Truet and his deputies to investigate the north tunnel system. It was ready. Any entrances that the lawmen found would have to be sealed once they left, and new ones designed that were much harder to locate.

Wu-Pen spoke to Bing, "Come, Lucille will be at Jinhai's soon. We will go out the back and stay out of sight."

Bob Ewing got his breath back and observed his surroundings. He could not see anyone and wasn't sure which way Truet had gone. He picked up his revolver and climbed the stairs to push the trap door open. He could not budge it, which brought a fit of anxiety that began to take root, of being trapped in the dark. The candles were the only source of light and if they burnt out, he would be trapped in pitch blackness. He aimed his gun at the door and pulled the trigger. The percussion echoed loudly through the tunnel. He fired again. "Let me out of here!" he shouted.

Nate Robertson could hear shooting and went into the store with his gun drawn. The merchant who had been beaten up was standing near the fallen shelf unit, looking at the covered hole. A knife was in his hand.

Nate could hear Bob's muffled yells coming from below the floor. "Bob?" Nate questioned.

The merchant turned towards him, and with a cry of outrage ran towards Nate while gripping the knife tightly.

Nate had no time to react except for raising his gun quickly and firing. The first shot missed, but the second shot of his double-action .44 hit the man dead center in the chest. The man fell to his back and moved momentarily, sputtering out droplets of blood before his last breath was exhaled. Nate stayed in place, staring at the man's body for a few moments. It was the first life Nate had ever taken. It did not feel good. He was numb, angry and sorrowful all at once as a heavy cloud of bewilderment settled over him. He had no intention of killing the man until he had to.

After hearing the shot, Tim Wright and his two deputies, Alan Garrison and Mark Thiesen came into the store to see what had happened. "You killed him? Where's Bob?" Tim asked, looking around.

"Let me out of here!" Bob's voice rose from the floor.

Tim and his deputies lifted the heavy shelving unit and pulled the door open. Below, Bob was telling Truet and the others what had happened to him. Truet came running up the stairs, followed by Lee and William.

"Wu-Pen is up here somewhere. He told Bob we're looking in the wrong tunnel by the sound of it. We will check the temple again and then go to the north side and look for another tunnel access. You men keep searching the buildings from here, and we'll meet in the middle. Matt's got to be somewhere." He looked at the dead Chinese man and then at Nate. "Are you okay?"

"Yeah," he said with a slightly troubled voice.

William put a hand on Nate's shoulder approvingly. "You shot him, right?" he asked.

Nate nodded. "He came at me with a knife."

"Your virgin kill, huh? It gets easier to stomach. You can't feel sorry for him. It was your life or his. It's a well-placed shot, Nate. You did what you had to. You don't have time to stand here and contemplate how you're feeling. We have a job to do." William patted Nate's stomach reassuringly and waved for him to follow them.

The temple was empty, so they separated in pairs to search two buildings at once on the north side of Chinatown. Lee and William were searching the restaurant when William found a hatch door under one of the tables with a long tablecloth that touched the floor. They moved the table and opened the hatch. A wooden ladder allowed them to descend into the tunnel. Like the other tunnel, it was lined with rock, and sections of the wall were brick. It was brighter with lanterns hanging from the ceiling. They walked south and spotted a Chinese man walk around a corner twenty yards away from them. The man spotted them and ran back the other way, yelling in Chinese.

"He knows something!" William said, and he and Lee ran after him. They hurried around a corner the man had turned into and were suddenly in a smaller passageway blocked by a single white wooden door. William grabbed the handle and discovered the door was locked. "This must be where they are keeping Matt. Stand back, and I'll break it down!"

Lee stepped back while William positioned himself to kick the door as hard as he could. He took two steps forward and kicked the door near the handle, his foot slid along the door as the top of the door rotated down and the bottom half of the door flew upwards, cracking against his groin between his legs before lifting his leg higher and dropping him to the ground. The bottom of the door dropped back down and swayed just a bit before the door was still and looked like any other door.

"What the...?" Lee asked and slowly grinned at his cousin, who was on the ground groaning in pain.

William held his jewels. "It's not funny," he spoke through gritted teeth.

Lee asked through his laughter. "Are you going to get the door open, or do I have to?"

"No," William grunted as he stood up slowly. "I will. I won't be beaten by a door!" Furious, he kicked the bottom of the door as hard as he could, and the bottom of the door swung inward while the top of the door spun down and hit the top of William's head with the same amount of force that he had kicked with. The blow knocked him flat on his butt, leaving him stunned and a bit confused about what happened.

Lee was worried about his brother, and the seriousness of it was no laughing matter, but Lee couldn't help but bend over laughing at his cousin.

"Damn it, it's not funny!" William shouted. He remained on the ground, rubbing his head.

"You have to be smarter than the door," Lee laughed. "Let me try." Lee stepped around William and pushed the top lightly. The door was on a steel rod plumbed through its center that allowed the door to swing freely. Lee got on his hands and knees and crawled through the bottom half of the door and let it close behind him. "They drilled holes in the bottom of the door and melted lead to weigh it down to stop it from swaying back and forth. Brilliant."

William rubbed the knot on top of his head. He answered bitterly, "I'm beginning to hate these people. I'm glad you appreciate it."

The tunnel narrowed to about sixteen inches wide and they had to stand sideways and take sidesteps to maneuver through it. An iron bar was set across the passageway at waist level creating a barrier that caused them to scratch their heads for a moment to consider how to get around the bar in the narrow space. The only options were either crawl underneath on their side or tumble over the top and take the possible head-first landing. Intent on knowing where the tunnel led, Lee removed his gun belt and crawled under the bar on his side to get past it. William watched Lee struggle to shimmy underneath and chose tumbling over the top. For both men getting back on their feet in the narrow passageway was a difficult task without room to brace a foot for leverage. Once back on their feet, the tunnel widened just enough for them to walk straight forward at a normal rate, but it was interrupted by another bar as they turned a corner at shin level. Lee racked his leg into it and fell forward with multiple curses coming from his lips. They could see another white door at the tunnel's end, but before they could reach it, the tunnel narrowed to sixteen inches wide again with a bar at waist level to maneuver over or under in the faintly lit tunnel. It took time to contort one's body in a narrow corridor where there was barely enough room to bend their knees. The passageway wasn't that long but had multiple barriers to cross. At the end, Lee tapped the door , and it swayed outward. They got on their hands and knees and crawl under the door. When they stood up, they were in the same tunnel they had initially been in. They were twenty-five feet or so from the original white door.

"William, we were just suckered," Lee said irritably as he rubbed his shin. "That guy disappeared."

The door had made William mad, but the narrow tunnel had infuriated him. "I'm going to kill that little Chinaman when I see him again. What kind of a playhouse is this? Is that supposed to be fun?" he asked bitterly.

It didn't take long to discover why the man had run. The man's warning emptied the tunnels of customers. They found what appeared to be a saloon by the gambling tables and bar, but there was no trace of drinks or bottles of liquor. Not too far away, a blue painted door led to a room with cots where a few men slept soundly, but there was nothing else to be seen. William believed it was an opium den by a lingering scent in the air, but no evidence could be seen. Most all the walls were stone, except one wall with vertical boards. They left the men to sleep and walked past various dugout areas still being constructed. They came to a green-painted door and went inside another room with eight mattresses on the floor. There was no explanation nor person in sight. Again, the walls were stone or brick except for one wall with vertical boards.

Lee noticed a bell on the ceiling connected to a

string that led to a bamboo shoot going through the wall. He followed the string outside and saw it was tied to the main rope that went the entire corridor. They went back to the room with the blue door and found the saloon as well had the same bell system tied above the fabricated bar. It had become clear that a rope could be pulled at various places spread out along the tunnel system, and it would ring all the bells. By pink ribbons tied periodically along the mainline, the pull would notify the patrons of what direction the warning was coming from and to disperse in the other direction.

"William, I'll bet people were down here having a good time when we spotted that man. He led us on a wild goose chase through that door," he chuckled at the memory. "Someone heard him yelling and pulled the string and notified everyone to leave. I don't know what they would be afraid of, but they scattered like cockroaches. There is nothing down here."

William exhaled. "I'm getting worried. I thought for sure we would find Matt down here."

"Me too. Let's find Truet and let him know there is nothing to see down here. Not unless we are missing something. They must have Matt in one of the buildings. They are a tricky bunch, we figured out, so I guess we look for anything that's not normal," Lee suggested.

"Nothing is normal here!" William exclaimed. "Everything is suspicious. Colored coded doors, mats and cots and Chinese bar and tunnel games. Why do they have funny doors and an alarm system of bells to get drunk and gamble? No, I bet that was an opium den and the other one, I don't know, a bunkhouse maybe?"

Lee agreed. "We need Ah See to come down here and translate. We will never find Matt alive if we don't bring him here and force these people to talk. Time's running out."

William widened his eyes questionably and exclaimed, "You have to find the people first! They're just gone. Vanished."

32

Wu-Pen's tone asked dangerously, "What do you mean she isn't coming? I told you in my note to make sure she follows you here. Why is she not here, Jinhai? I gave you one simple order to follow, and you could not accomplish it?"

Nervousness plagued Jinhai's expression. Wu-Pen had proven repeatedly to the people under his authority that failing him came at a cost. Sometimes it was financial, sometimes painful and on two occasions that he knew of it cost the lives of loved ones back at home. Obedience was accomplished through fear. That fear was evident in Jinhai's eyes and quivering hands. "I tried. Trust me, I tried. But Lucille is not feeling well. She is stricken with a sour stomach and has been urgently running to the privy all day. She is not herself today. Tomorrow perhaps, she will feel better. But today she is not well. I know she wants to come to see what I can give her, but not today," Jinhai lied. He had refused to show her the note Wu-Pen had written. He had no intention of being a part of causing her harm. He wasn't only afraid of Wu-Pen. He was scared of betraying Wu-Pen. He had Ah See tell the deputy Truet where and when Wu-Pen expected to meet Lucille. Jinhai was anxiously waiting for the American lawmen to enter his room, arrest Wu-Pen and Bing Jue, and free the Chinese community from him.

Wu-Pen was frustrated. "Tomorrow then! Do not fail me again, Jinhai. It won't be good for you if she is not here." His glaring eyes held no mercy. "Come, Bing, we must go ask the marshal if he chooses to be our friend or not."

When they left his room, Jinhai sat down on his raised bed with a heavy sigh. His room was one of many crammed together in a two-story bunkhouse. The rooms like his were small but had thin walls to give some privacy. An ample open space upstairs had no privacy and had three-tiered bunk beds lined up in four rows filling the room with nothing except beds. Jinhai was given a room when Wu-Pen chose him to work with Lucille at the pottery shop. Before that, he slept in a bunk upstairs. Jinhai's hands began to shake. He had controlled his fear to the best of his ability while speaking to Wu-Pen, but now he was starting to panic. The Americans had not shown up as planned, and if Wu-Pen discovered the intent to betray him, Jinhai would suffer the consequences and perhaps his remaining family in China. Even so, he would refuse to deceive Lucille into coming to Chinatown. He knew Wu-Pen had no good things planned for her. If his attempted betrayal was not discovered, he had one day to live; Wu-Pen's warning was made clear. However, if one of the five men in Chinatown mentioned the planned betrayal to a loyal servant of Wu-Pen's, he would not live to see the sunrise.

He and Ah See had told five of their friends, who had come to Branson long before Wu-Pen had taken control of Chinatown, about the betrayal. They were five friends that knew what life was like before the Chinese Benevolence Association took over the community. The title was changed to the Chinese Benevolence Society to sound more empathetic to the Americans and less like an organized group. Either way, it was a deceiving title. Under the installed Chinese Benevolence Society's rule, all Chinese were forced to labor and report any income and personal valuables. All spouses, children and relatives had to be named, and locations were required information by the Benevolence Society. It was collected with good intentions of notifying family members of any deaths or emergencies and mailing letters and finances to and from family for the men who could not write. As some men discovered, the information was used for far darker purposes, such as Ah See's young sister being kidnapped and brought to Branson. It was only one example of how powerful Wu-Pen was and his control over a community.

All of them came to America to escape the poverty of China and earn enough money to support their families and make a better life for themselves.

Life was hard enough without a good portion of their earnings being taken under threat of harm to pay the Chinese Benevolence Society a tax and added fees. The right to work in America was given freely, but in Chinatown, the right to work went through Wu-Pen and his taxes. There was only one driving force behind the community's submission to his power, and that was fear; fear of The Six Companies, fear of being murdered and fear of Wu-Pen and his loyal men.

The recent deaths of Izu and Wang Chee for the sins of Wu-Pen showed them all how little value they were. Any Chinese man could have been Izu, and any relative of a man chosen could have been Wang. Very few were loyal to Wu-Pen. Most men were afraid to disobey the rules, and lived with contentment as best they could. Those who came after Wu-Pen's arrival knew nothing different, but those who were here before knew how good being free, even as a Chinese man in America could be. It was one thing to be separated by Americans with laws forbidding owning land and going outside after dark. It was another thing to be controlled by a madman who would destroy all of them if the marshal was not returned alive. To not think the American citizens would burn down Chinatown and shoot every Chinese man they could find in retaliation was insane. Wu-Pen had come to believe he owned Chinatown and everyone in it. Jinhai had no doubt it would not bother Wu-Pen if they were all killed as long as he survived and took his gold and money with him. As Ah See had said to him and the others, it was time to gather some courage and help fight against their self-proclaimed leader. They were a group of men who did not want an evil man to rule over them anymore.

Jinhai did not know why the deputy marshal Truet did not come as expected, but he could sit and wait to die or stand up and try to do what was right. He could not hide in fear while Wu-Pen sabotaged the Chinese community by killing the lawman. No one knew where Marshal Matt Bannister was, and Jinhai did not know the tunnels, but he knew many of the men that did. The risk was not knowing who was loyal to Wu-Pen.

33

Matt took a deep breath in through his nose and slowly exhaled. He reminded himself to remain calm. He had felt helpless from time to time in certain situations, but Matt could not think of a time when he was physically helpless. He had always been curious how anyone could subdue a man as big, hardened and mean as Leroy Haywood and contain him well enough to kill him with spider bites. The ingenuity of the Chinese was simple but brilliant at the same time. Braided strands of human hair held his thumbs in bamboo shoots that kept his hands immobile. A man wouldn't think his arms weighed very much, but the weight of his arms over time increased the slight aching of his thumb joints into a throbbing pain that promised only to get worse. It was a humbling experience to know there was nothing he could do to end it. The only thing he could do to help himself and minimize further damage to his thumbs was to remain calm and endure it. Trying to break free would only dislocate his thumbs long before it broke the braided cord of hair.

His thumbs weren't the only thing hurting, though. His shoulders ached from being out-stretched for an extended time. He had been there for hours, and the muscles around his shoulder blades burned miserably. The slow torture gave him little comfort to think of anything other than the discomfort and throbbing of his thumbs and burning shoulders. However, like a fifty-pound stone in his chest, Christine's heartbroken expression leaving the restaurant that morning haunted him. If he never left the room he was in, the one thing he would regret before he went to heaven was breaking Christine's heart. Bella's words rang deep within him like a church bell on Sunday morning echoing through a long valley. He was a danger to her. It was proven once again now that Wu-Pen planned on abducting her. Matt would gladly suf-fer for weeks on end if it saved Christine from any harm. Some men treated their women with discon-tent and bitterness, but to Matt, spending the rest of his life with Christine was the closest to paradise he would ever find on earth. She was his best friend, and their love was based upon that friendship and not built on lust or infatuation. Earthquakes, Matt heard, can break solid ground in two, leaving vast cracks in the ground. With his hands outspread and pain running through his body, the most an-guished part of him was his heart being ripped away as he sacrificed his love to let her go. Bella had a point; he was the link to all her misfortune thus far and the danger she was in presently. Being responsible for any harm that came to her was far heavier than his arms on his thumbs. The physical agony would eventually cease one way or another, but the sorrow of being blamed for Christine's fate was far more unbearable. She deserved to live her life in safety. She deserved a life with someone else that would love and provide for her without inviting criminal elements into her life.

The sound of the door opening pulled his attention away from Christine. Wu-Pen Tseng stepped in front of Matt and smiled contently. "Your thumbs must be sore by now. How are you feeling?"

"Like a rock," Matt replied dryly. The misery was not hidden from his expression.

Wu-Pen was humored. "You might think you are an unbreakable stone, but I assure you, you are not. A man can tolerate only so much pain, and you will reach your limit soon enough. Fortunately for you, I am willing to end this and will right now, but the decision is yours to make. Let me explain what I want in exchange for cutting you loose and having our doctor heal your thumbs and muscles. I want you to partner with me. It is as simple as that."

"A partner in what? Murder? Extortion? Kidnapping?"

"Please listen. We could run this whole county together and become richer than you or I ever dreamed. You could marry Christine and provide the best of everything for her, and in a few years, five I'd say, you could retire your badge and raise your children without a single concern. Think of it; the good life could be yours for free. You and Christine could travel across the great land of America, the world for that matter, and not waste a moment wondering how your bank account is doing because you would own some of the biggest businesses around here.

"Do you not know William Slater is starting a copper mine up north and other mines as well? We could take over his entire company and use Chinese labor nearly for free. Imagine the possibilities. It is a dream come true, and I can make it happen, but I need your help. All I ask is for you to work with me. I will do the hard work. All you have to do is agree to look the other way and allow me to provide any guilty parties needed for any crimes that arise. Our partnership will never be known to anyone outside of this room. And I swear never to wrong you or any one of your family or friends. Our brotherhood would share the success and the protection of my authority over your family as well. That means if you have to leave town, your wife and children will be protected by Bing or whichever one of his students I choose to replace Uang. Security in every way will be yours and every member of your family from this day forward. I will make you rich, famous and compensate you for every compromise of your principles. That, I promise you. I will cut the cords and set you free right now if you give me your word that we can be partners."

"How do you know I won't come back and shoot you?" Matt asked.

"Why would you? I'm offering you a life where all of your dreams can come true for nothing more than..." he dramatized the action of slowly turning his face away from Matt, "simply looking away."

Being bribed to "look away" from a crime by wealthy people was not uncommon in the law enforcement business; it happened every day in some places, including Branson. The pain could be finally ended in his body. Christine's immediate threat would become nonexistent, and perhaps he could buy the hill Christine wanted to build her dream house on and make her dream home a reality long before they were old. There was little doubt in Matt's mind that Wu-Pen could convince the Slater family to sign over their entire mining company to Wu-Pen in some warped manner. Matt did not like the Slater family, and it would be easy to close his eyes and turn his back to certain things. But a man doesn't have to like someone to do what is right. The temptation to agree was strong for immediate reasons that he was suffering and the promised wealth, but it was not right. Matt licked his dry lips and answered, "The Bible says, *'What good is it to own the whole world and yet lose your soul?'* I won't do what you want."

Wu-Pen clicked his tongue with disappointment. "Well, that is too bad. I hoped we could be friends. Your Bible talks about forgiveness, right? Well, you could always ask for forgiveness for your trespasses of conscious. I don't want you to suffer. I don't want to make Christine suffer, but I definitely will. I am a businessman. If you will not agree to help me, then

301

I must profit in other ways. I understand there are men right here in Branson who would pay good money to spend time with Christine." His dark eyes turned cold and menacing as he explained ruthlessly, "I could set a cot right over there and let you slowly starve to death as you watch me take their money. You think you are a rock? You could not stop that from happening right here in front of you!" His expression and voice returned to normal. "If you love her, you will never allow that to happen."

Matt squeezed his eyes shut and focused on trying not to pull his arms loose from their binds to kill Wu-Pen right then and there. His wrath alone would be enough to kill the man with his bare hands. His breathing became erratic. "I will kill you!" Matt blurted through his gritted teeth.

Wu-Pen slapped the side of Matt's face with a loud stinging blow. "Do it right now!" He mocked. "You are merely a pet fish in a small bowl. Don't be a fool. All I'm asking you to do is turn your head and work with me on occasion, and you and Christine can live a very long and beautiful life together. Don't make me harm her or your family and friends. I will go right down the line one by one until you agree or die of starvation, whichever comes first. But you will never leave this room until I know I have your full allegiance and partnership."

Matt gasped, "You don't know what you're asking me to do."

Wu-Pen nodded empathetically. "Yes, I do. You are a man of principles and conviction. That is precisely the kind of man I need to partner with. The sheriff could do what I need, but he is bought and sold a dozen times over. He cannot be trusted. You can once I have your word. I know you think I am untrustworthy, but I assure you that you have my allegiance and will never harm you or your family. You and I can be brothers. I will cut my hand and yours, and we will seal the deal in blood. No harm shall come between us. It will be a good partnership."

Matt's lips tightened emotionally, but he did not speak. He lowered his head in silent, but anguished prayer to the Lord.

"You must think about it, yes? I will have supper and come back in a couple of hours. You think about it carefully. Your yes, must be a yes, all the way through because if you did try to betray me, everything you love will die. And you will suffer far more painfully than you are now. This…" he waved at Matt's arms, "is mild compared to the pain I could inflict. Am I understood?"

Matt lifted his head to meet Wu-Pen's gaze. "Yes. That is understood."

Wu-Pen tapped Matt's cheek like a pleased parent. "Very good. I will be back in a couple of hours, but first, let me encourage your submission. Bing," he said and held out his hand. Bing held two large potatoes with a string punctured through them. Wu-Pen tied one to Matt's right elbow, and then the other to his left. He lifted Matt's chin to look in him in the yes. "A potato by itself does not weigh a lot, but on your thumbs, it will feel quite heavy. You will give me a final answer in two hours before I tie another potato to your wrists. Please make no mistake about it, Matt; I can take whoever I want to take. I got you here and you should have been the hardest of them all. I have all night and there are many more potatoes. However, I would like to avoid that. I really do not want to harm you. I want to be your friend, but friendships need to go both ways. That is up to you. Keep in mind, the sooner you agree, the better the chances are of you having working thumbs."

Matt heard the door close behind him, and he exhaled from the agony of his thumbs from the added pressure of one simple potato tied to each elbow. He was being given no choice but to conform to Wu-Pen's plans. He could live with sacrificing himself for the sake of his belief in the Lord and what was right and wrong. There was no question about that. But were his moral objections worth the cost to everyone he loved? Could he live with the shame of being compromised in his principles if it gained him the wealth, power and life he wanted with Christine? A more important question was if he had all he ever dreamed of having could he look at himself in the mirror and not be ashamed of how he got it?

Matt had been scared before. He had faced desperate times in the past, but in hindsight, the Lord had always been faithful to carry him through the darkest times. There is a vast difference between helpless and hopeless. To depend on men can be hopeless sometimes, but with Jesus, there is always hope. The candle that lit the room was small, dim and fragile to the slightest breeze that caused it to flicker when the door was opened. Yet, that tiny bit of flame could start a raging forest fire that could burn the entire city to the ground. Jesus said he was the light of the world. The world was as cold, dark and hopeless as the dungeon walls. Evil runs boldly in the dark where people think their crimes will never be discovered. The world is full of evil actions, loneliness, sickness, sorrow, and hopelessness in a lifetime of dead ends for so many. People cannot be trusted, and hurt hearts reign in the lives of many. To gaze into the darkness is an endless void of nothingness, but a single candle can brighten a dark room just as Jesus can brighten the spirit and heart of the hopeless. There is hope and that hope is only found in Jesus. He is the light of our lives and the only hope we have in any and every circumstance we face, even when it seems hopeless. Matt focused on the candle; it was small, faint and fragile, but it represented the greatest promise in life and that is Jesus does not give up on anyone. He will not ever abandon anyone that comes to him, even if the person, like Matt, feels a thousand miles away from the Lord.

In the silence of the room, Matt had time to think, and one of his earliest memories from his childhood came to mind. He was very young, and his parents had taken him to Branson and stopped by the Modoc River on a hot day. While his brothers swam, Matt wandered out too far into the current and lost his footing. He was being swept away with no hope of getting back on his feet. He remembered being underwater and watching the rocks pass by him as the current pulled him further from the safety of his family. He was helpless to fight the current, but the loving arms of his mother pulled him out of the river and embraced him comfortingly. He remembered she thanked the Lord that she was near to him. He certainly would have drowned that day if she was not watching over him. In the same way, the Lord is always near watching over his children, even when they wander into depths that can sweep them away. Sometimes he leads his children out of the danger without them knowing like a shepherd, and other times he waits to hear those words that Peter cried out when he sank in the Sea of Galilee, *"Lord, save me!"* Jesus immediately took Peter's hand. Jesus is just as powerful today as he was then and still willing to take the hand of anyone who calls to him to save them from the dark and hopeless situations of life.

The candle revealed stone walls built underground and Matt could not help but to think of the story of Daniel in the lion's den. Whether it was a cave system, or a pit dug into the ground, Daniel was thrown into a hole where lions were kept intentionally to kill and eat whoever was thrown in. Daniel was an uncorruptible and righteous administrator in King Darius' reign in Babylon who served his God full heartedly. Other administrators could not compete with Daniel's reputation and service. Growing jealous and resentful as people sometimes do, they conspired to get him fired, in modern terms, but they couldn't find a reason to. What they did know was Daniel served his god faithfully. They intended to use that knowledge against Daniel by approaching the king about making a decree to make it illegal to pray to any god or man except King Darius for thirty days. It was a short-term ploy to have Daniel killed, and it worked as Daniel refused to stop praying to God. He was thrown into a dark hole with multiple lions and the next morning the seal was removed, and Daniel came out unharmed and untouched *because he had trusted in his God*, as the Bible says.

Matt had an opportunity to end his troubles and perhaps become wealthy enough to make every dream he and Christine ever wanted to come true. He had the opportunity to build the house on the hill with a wraparound porch where he could watch the sun set in the west and hold his beautiful lady until they watched sun rise in the east. To never have to work again and just enjoy his bride and children doing whatever, whenever they wanted to. It was a dream come true to just about anyone and it was right at his fingertips. All he had to do was say one little three letter word: yes.

It didn't take more than a moment for a verse in the book of Proverbs to cross his mind.

> *Better a poor man whose walk is blameless*
> *than a rich man whose ways are perverse.*

Daniel was thrown in a lion's den for his integrity and faith. Matt was being held not because of his faith but his life depended upon compromising his faith. His answer would be no. Thousands of martyrs suffered and died willingly for their Christian faith and he would not back down when his time came. He was a Christian. He would walk the Christian walk and could not be bought or sold. A Christian trusted Jesus with their life whether it was leading a lamb to the slaughter or opening the door to fight like a ferocious lion. Matt had made his requests known to the Lord. There was nothing more he could except wait. He thought of a verse in the book of Daniel that held a great Biblical truth.

We do not make requests of you because we are
righteous,
but because of your great mercy.

An hour later, Matt heard the door open, and three men entered the room. Matt did not recognize the Chinese men, but they smiled comfortingly at him and cut the bonds that held him in place. One old man, who looked slightly familiar, carefully cut the cord of hair tied around his thumb joints and then pressed gently to massage the soft tissues around the joints. Matt recognized him as the Chinese doctor that had been at the silver mine when Oscar Belding died of an apparent heart attack. Matt was physically turned towards the door and saw Jinhai, the old man from the pottery shop, standing at the door, beckoning Matt to follow him. "Come," he said in broken English, "Come." He led Matt up two flights of stairs cut into the ground and into a tunnel. He followed as they led him through a tunnel and came to a door where they stopped. Jinhai pulled a string ringing some distant bells and waited for a moment and then opened the door and continued through a brighter lit tunnel with doorways of different colors and past what appeared to be an empty gambling parlor. Faint scents of incense and perfumes mixed in the air. Eventually, the tunnels led to a stairway that opened inside of a barn. The hatch door had been covered in straw for the mules. The barn was where the wagons, carts and mules were stored for the men working on the streets. It became clear by a pulley system overhead with four ropes with hooks and the specially designed tarps with metal ringed corners that a larger hatch opened where the dirt was pulled up from the tunnels.

"Come," Jinhai said as he peeked carefully out the door and then waved Matt to follow. The morning daylight Matt had last seen had faded to the last twilights of the sun as darkness quickly approached. Even so, the first breath of the fresh evening air was like a new breath of life. The other three Chinese men followed as Jinhai led Matt to the safety of the Monarch Hotel.

To his great relief Christine was first person he saw as he walked by the restaurant's bay windows and he rushed to reach her. She dropped her fork to her plate and hurried to meet him at the door. The jolt of her body hitting against his as she launched herself into him jarred his burning shoulders and aching thumbs. He wrapped his arms around her and used his wrists to hold her tightly.

"Where have you been?" she wept. "I love you so much. Don't you ever listen to anyone again when it comes to me. You talk to me, not Bella." She grabbed his cheeks and held his face to look into his eyes. "Bella had no right say what she did! I am the one that decides my future, not her! We decided to trust the Lord, remember? I won't be scared away by anything or anyone; that's my commitment to you. I love you, Matt. Life is always a risk, but I want to risk spending my life with you. Don't let a drunk woman's foolish words ruin what we have. Please."

His body jolted with a compressed sob that he refused to give in to. He held her close and closed his eyes with the comfort of her in his arms. They were joined by his family, whose expressions revealed their concern and relief all at once. The questions came fast, but all he wanted to do was hold Christine. He buried his face in her hair and allowed a silent tear to fall. He whispered in her ear, "I love you. I love you so much." He refused to let her go. She was safe in his arms.

34

Wu-Pen was furious to find Matt was gone. The cords of hair and the silk bands that held him were sliced with a sharp blade. Only a few men knew Matt was being kept in the lower dungeon, gossip could have spread quickly, but few would have the courage to undermine Wu-Pen. A quick interrogation of the people gathering in the tunnel brothel, fan-tan tables and saloon revealed someone had pulled the alarm bells, and everyone scattered, fearing the deputy marshal was in the tunnel again. There was a strict policy of never pulling the alarm bells except when intruders entered the tunnel. It was a means of security for all of them to hide the illegal activities they enjoyed. Whoever helped Matt escape had used the alarm bell to lead him out of the tunnel unseen. Only a Chinese man would know to do that. There were five exits they could have left the tunnels from, and it was hard to determine precisely where or who had committed such a brazen and deadly crime. Whoever had done it would pay the price with their life. A house-to-house and bed-by-bed census was taken of every man and woman in Chinatown. A handful of five men were unaccounted for, including Jinhai, the doctor and the carpenter who installed the door to the dungeon. A few others of no real account were also missing. There was no trace of them present in all of Chinatown, which only meant they were the ones that helped Matt. It infuriated Wu-Pen, even more to realize Jinhai had lied to him about Lucille. Knowing the marshal was back with his people became a threat to everything Wu-Pen had planned.

It was unlikely the Americans would welcome the missing Chinese men and they'd come back with a corroborated lie. Wu-Pen had some men waiting to tell him when they returned, but it was getting late, and despite his worries, sleep was a needed thing to keep a man's brain thinking clearly.

There was a lot to think about now that his plans were ruined, and he could not stay any longer in Branson. He was right on the verge of creating a world of dreams if Matt would have broken and he almost was. Everything Wu-Pen worked for was endangered by his arrest, but a desperate move to kidnap Matt and break his spirit had renewed that hope. It had always been the plan to win Matt's favor and weave him into the details slowly as a trusted friend. Unfortunately, Matt was slow to trust and as stubborn as a bad mule. Matt's faith in his God ran deep and strong, stronger than a bribe or friendship could bend. Wu-Pen called himself a high priest, and the temple was a cover for his coming to Branson, but the truth was it was all business. He had accomplished much in Branson, but it was over.

He needed to disappear, but it would take some planning to escape unnoticed. He only needed to cross over the mountains to reach the nearest Chinatown, and there he could hide until he found a new prospering place to call home. Changes were inevitable, but this one hurt. He would have to hide until he left town but did have the night to pack up his valuables because he expected to be raided by the lawmen in the morning. Matt's hands would be too sore tonight for him to think about anything else other than the pain. Wu-Pen posted guards on the roof of the temple and two out front of the temple's door. He was safe for now and would take advantage of it. He would get up early and write a note stating he had left and was never coming back. The scent of his departure might send the bloodhound deputies off in various directions, trying to find him while he remained right where he was for a few days to plan. They would no doubt search his belongings, and anything of value had to be packed up. Everything else could be found.

The guards were given instructions to not let anyone into the temple, especially not Americans. It was unlikely, but if any trouble occurred, they were to notify Wu-Pen immediately by shouting, and a guard inside the temple would beat on the gong. It would give Wu-Pen a few moments to grab his bag of valuables and disappear into the stairway leading to the store where he had hidden before.

Wu-Pen entered his home and closed the door. He turned up the lantern and sat down in his favorite chair. He stared at a chess set on a table in front of his chair and cursed. He swept his hand across the table, knocking all the jade and onyx pieces off the table onto the floor. His game was over. He took a deep breath and exhaled to relax for a couple of hours before he packed his treasures and moved into his dungeon for a few days. He could organize safe passage out of Branson from there. A click of Ling's door opening caught his attention.

"Ling?" he asked with excitement. He stood and turned around to greet her. His eyes widened in horror to see Matt Bannister standing in his apartment holding a silver-plated revolver in his right hand. His hand and thumbs were wrapped in gauze, but he held the revolver's grip with his three lower fingers and his index finger on the trigger. The gun was at hip level and pointed directly at Wu-Pen.

"Shh," Matt said, stepping forward. "You look surprised. You shouldn't be. You should have known I'd be coming for you."

Wu-Pen was dumbstruck. For the first time, no words came to mind. Only the thin streak of terror that ran down his spine. "You, ah…"

"Yeah, my thumbs hurt. But luckily, I'm not using my revolver; I'm using William's double Action Colt .45 with a lightened trigger. It will shoot as fast as I can pull the trigger. I see my gun is on your wall as a trophy. Grab it, and let's see how you do. Go on, Wu-Pen. Give me a reason to shoot you here and now!"

Wu-Pen glanced towards the door; he wanted to shout for Bing Jue and his guards to distract Matt, while he escaped. He wanted to, but his mouth was dry. "How did you get in? The doors were locked, and priests are downstairs."

"I used your tunnel into the store and your tricky staircase up to here. It was quite handy getting past your guards." Matt offered a slow smile. "Your carpenter was very helpful. Your people have turned against you, and now you are under arrest."

"I have gold, a lot of gold and money. Take it. I'll leave town and you will never see or hear of me again," he pleaded nervously.

There was no change of expression on Matt's face. It was as hard and cold as a block of granite. "As I said earlier, what good is it to own the world and lose your own soul? Your deeds have caught up with you and you will hang for them. There is nothing you can offer me that's going to change that. Nothing at all."

Wu-Pen's nervous eyes shifted to the door again. "I can call Bing," he said in a louder voice. "Okay, you got me," he said, trying to raise his voice to be heard across the hall.

"Go ahead and call him," Matt challenged. "It's just me here. I'd say you'd have a fifty-fifty chance of defeating me. I'm not sure I can hold this gun once it's fired, but I'll try. Call him."

A glimmer of light flickered in Wu-Pen's eyes. He shouted in Chinese, "Bing, the marshal's here with a gun. Come in through Ling's room!"

Truet was waiting in the doorway of Wu-Pen's office with a shotgun leveled on his shoulder, waiting for Bing Jue to come out of his room. When Bing's door opened, he stepped into the hallway and noticed Truet just a moment too late. Truet pulled both triggers, and the two rounds ripped into Bing's chest, killing him before his body hit the corridor floor. Truet set the shotgun down and pulled his revolver, expecting the two guards from inside the temple to come upstairs. He could hear the footsteps ascending the stairs. A man wearing an orange robe started running towards Truet with a dagger in his hand. Truet aimed his revolver and fired, hitting the man in the chest. The priest fell quickly. The other man in orange reached the top of the stairs, and Truet wasted no time sending a bullet in and out of the man's head. He tumbled partway down the stairs.

Outside, four or five rifle shots could be heard being fired from Lee Bannister and William Fasana while they killed the two guards in front of the temple and the two guards with bows and arrows on the roof. Truet waited for any more unexpected guards to reveal themselves.

Wu-Pen was startled by all the shooting. "You said you were alone!"

Matt smiled just enough to show he enjoyed seeing the surprised, yet horrified expression on Wu-Pen's face. "I am in here alone. Bing and your other guards are dead. Like I said, your carpenter and others were very helpful. I knew your whole setup before I came here. You are now alone."

"Bing was my nephew," Wu-Pen said softly.

"You should've been a better uncle," Matt answered simply. "Now, you are the pet fish in a bowl, and I am the one who is going to shatter that bowl and watch you die. I've met a lot of bad men, but I don't know if I ever met anyone as evil as you. It will be my pleasure to see you hang." Matt shouted, "Truet, come shackle him good and tight."

The door opened, and Truet entered, holding a shotgun in his hands. He set it down and pulled a pair of iron wrist shackles out of his coat pocket. He spoke to Wu-Pen, "Bing's not feeling so good right now. He's just laying out there like a dead fish."

Matt lowered the gun with a growing grin. "You heard me talking, didn't you?"

Truet nodded. "I did."

"Matt, Truet, we're coming up. Don't shoot us," Lee yelled before he and William approached the apartment.

Wu-Pen stared at the shackles in Truet's hands, with the terror evident in his face. He shook his head with an attempt to plead for his life and then wordlessly turned and without warning, ran towards the door that opened into his office. He ran straight towards the broken window and dove headfirst out it, expecting the canvas awning to be there to catch his fall. He was horrified to remember too late that Uang Yang had broken the awning when he jumped out of the window. Wu-Pen could see the stone walkway two stories below him approaching fast. Not ignorant of how to roll through a fall, he tucked his head and attempted to turn his body to land on his shoulder and roll through the landing, but his body was vertical, and his time to react was too limited. He lowered an arm to absorb his fall. It snapped like a twig on impact against a stone, forcing the shattered bone to burst through his skin, creating a compound fracture. He hit hard with just enough torque in his attempt to roll through the fall to roll onto the dirt street. Pain racked through his body from hitting the stone pathway. His back, legs and even his ankle hurt tremendously. He groaned in agony but knew his life was dependent upon reaching the tunnels before the marshal and his deputies could get downstairs. Pure will of desperation put him on his good hand and knees and forced himself to stand uneasily. A head wound bled profusely over his face, and down his arm from the broken bone. He looked upwards at the window and saw Matt and Truet staring down at him. Matt's cousin and Lee quickly joined them. Truet immediately left the window to run downstairs, followed by Lee.

William shouted out the window, "You jackass, you should have taken the stairs!" he laughed softly, as he held his rifle bead on Wu-Pen. "Go ahead and try to run. You won't get one step before I put one right through your knee, just to make sure we get to see you hanging like a dead buck."

Wu-Pen could see the shadow of several Chinese men standing inside of the store below his office, where they brought Matt up through the tunnel. "Help me," he begged in their native tongue while reaching out to them with his good arm. "Help me.

I'll reward you all with a pound of gold. Hurry!"

Ah See stepped onto the street and hollered at the men in the window, "Don't shoot us," he said in English while motioning the others in the store to stay back. "Matt, Wu-Pen threatened your woman, but he took my sister from my family and brought her here. He sold Hui-Cao's wife to another tong for prostitution because he lost a game of chess! And the same would happen to your wives. He killed our friends and took all that we labor for. You want justice for the crimes committed against Americans, and we want justice too—Chinese justice without being shot. Hui-Cao and others, myself, too, ask for your permission to allow us our justice. Because if it were not for those men, you would not ever be found. They saved you so that you do not have to live with the rage Hui-Cao lives with every day. We only ask for justice, *our* justice."

Wu-Pen spoke in Chinese, "Ah See, I'll forgive your betrayal. Help me into the tunnel. Hurry," Wu-Pen pleaded. His eyes widened with hope when he noticed a lantern brighten the store's broken windows. He watched Hui-Cao bend over to pick up the knife the store owner held earlier, off the floor. Wu-Pen had understood every word Ah See had spoken to Matt and realized his own people intended to kill him. Wu-Pen pleaded with Matt with a fearful expression, "Matt, help me!" He locked eyes with Matt and saw the cold stare of a man considering Ah See's words carefully. "Don't let them kill me! Take me to your jail. Please," he pleaded.

Ah See held out his hands questionably. "He has

loyal servants who will help him escape at the cost of many more lives, ours and yours."

Truet and Lee stepped out of the temple door and approached Wu-Pen.

"Matt?" Ah See questioned.

"Stop, Truet. Stand back," Matt called from the window.

"What?" Truet asked dismayed.

Wu-Pen begged in English, "No! No. Take me to jail. You can't let them kill me here. This is America, not China. I have a right to a trial. Please, you have to save me! You're a lawman!" he shouted.

Matt raised his hands, showing his wrapped-up thumbs. "You're right, Wu-Pen. This is America, and I am a lawman that must obey the law. You do deserve a trial where your good city lawyer can get the trial moved to Portland and have the charges dropped, which you bragged about in my jail. You have no idea how heartbroken I am, Wu-Pen, to have to say, back away from him, Truet. Wu-Pen reminded me once that we are out of our legal jurisdiction. There is nothing I can do to help you."

"No! No! No," Wu-Pen cried and began to shake with fear.

Ah See waved his arm and five men quickly approached Wu-Pen and stopped him from trying to hobble away. They grabbed his arms and held him while the man with the knife shouted in Chinese, "This is for my wife! You had no right!" He plunged the knife into Wu-Pen's belly with all the anguish he felt forced into the blow. He yanked the knife out and plunged it in again and again while a sickening growl of rage escaped from the deepest part of him.

Wu-Pen was allowed to drop to the ground, and the group of men began stomping and kicking him repeatedly. Others shortly joined them as they came out of their homes and businesses bringing clubs, and one carried a pitchfork. Wu-Pen's body had stopped moving, but they still kicked, pounded, beat and stabbed at him with whatever they had.

William took a deep breath as he watched. "I don't think he's going to survive that."

Matt watched the ordinarily peaceful and humble Chinese crowd grow one by one like angry yellowjackets when a nest is disturbed. "I don't think so," he said as he watched a man drive a pitchfork through Wu-Pen's chest another hit his head with a wooden club.

Truet and Lee returned upstairs. Truet asked curiously, "You don't think we should have arrested him and to face a court of law? There might be some people who disagree with allowing this to happen."

Matt watched a Chinese man tie a rope around Wu-Pen's feet before they dragged his body away to hang somewhere. There was no question by the condition of Wu-Pen's body that he was dead.

Matt turned away from the window to face Truet. "We tried. Unfortunately, he dove out the window. We never recovered the keys to our jail. Who is to say his people wouldn't kill Phillip or Nate or whoever I have watching the jail, to release Wu-Pen? That's not a risk I want to take. If we had arrested him and it went to trial, Wu-Pen would plead not guilty. His Portland lawyer would get the trial moved to Portland where a less partial jury might be found and gotten Wu-Pen released because officially, according to city and county ordinances, there could be an argument about our legal jurisdiction because it's right on the borderline. He knew that because he told me about it. That little technicality could release that beast on the public."

"I won't argue that. I'm just saying some folks aren't going to approve of what we did."

Matt took a deep breath before continuing, "This is not how justice is supposed to work. But under the circumstances and the risk to those we love, justice was done. There is no doubt of his guilt in just what we know of. By the rage of that crowd and the sound of the celebration starting, there is a lot more we don't know. I do not believe one person in this entire county would convict any one of those men outside for what they just did if all the facts were known. If Sheriff Wright wants to arrest them, he can go for it, but personally, I saw nothing. What about you?"

Truet answered, "No. What was that word he used when questioned about Leroy's murder? Karma?"

William watched the men outside cheerfully dragging the body down the street. "Well, if asked, the fall killed him." He shrugged.

"Yep," Lee agreed. He noticed the small plates of gold on a shelf. They were stacked together and weighed about a pound apiece. "You're not going to leave anything valuable here for the vultures, are you?" He asked Matt. "These are solid gold plates."

"Can I have one?" William asked with interest. "I say we take what we can. Those have to be worth a fortune."

"No. You cannot have them," Matt answered. "Let's start searching the apartments and temple for any gold, money, weapons or anything of greater value, so they aren't stolen."

35

The Grand Opening of Barton's Pottery Shop had been good for Lucille and Lawrence. There was a lot of interest and even those who did not make a purchase had been very impressed. One of the most unexpected things to happen was Lucille had created a unique coffee mug for Lee Bannister as a gift of appreciation. It was a cream-colored mug with an image of the Monarch Hotel painted on the side. Lee was so impressed; he ordered twenty-five more with the possibility to keep a permanent order if they sold well among the guests. It was Lee's idea to set the mug on the counter next to the cash register with a note stating they could personalize any business. That small token of goodwill had led to two more people wanting mugs with their businesses being advertised. It was creating orders, and that meant business for Lucille and Lawrence.

John Briggs owned the Thirsty Toad Saloon. He wanted to order coffee cups and beer steins with his newly created logo on them. "I love the new logo you've created for me. You're amazing! It's quite an honor to meet you, Lucille. You too, Lawrence," John said, shaking Lawrence's hand and then held Lucille's hand for a moment longer as he spoke, "I know a saloon is no place for a true lady, but maybe you two will allow me to buy your family dinner at a restaurant before too long." He released her hand. "And Lawrence, if you ever feel like it, hop on down to the Green Toad and I'll…" he paused, glancing down at Lawrence's missing leg. "I wasn't referencing your leg. I say that because it's what I say to people You're a lucky man to have such a beautiful and amazing wife."

Lawrence grinned. "I know I am. I'm getting more and more used to living without my leg every day."

"Listen, I'd love to get to know you, folks. You'll be seeing more of me around here." John finished his conversation and left the shop as Matt and Christine entered.

"Matt," Lucille said with a joyful smile, "I'm glad you and Christine came in. I made you a present. I hope you like it."

"Yeah, give it to him," Lawrence said with a touch of excitement. "We just wanted to say thank you for all you have done for us."

Lucille handed him a small cloth bag. "I hope you like it."

Matt noticed Jinhai and Ah See both stepping closer to watch him. He could hold the bag in his palm, but his thumbs and hands were wrapped tight in gauze and hurt to move them. He asked

Christine to open it. She gasped when she pulled out a black coffee mug with a gold U.S. Marshal's badge glazed on the side of it with his name and title encircling the badge.

"Wow! It's beautiful," Christine said with a very pleased expression to Lucille.

"I love it," Matt said, looking at the mug. "Now, there is no way anyone will confuse my cup with theirs around the office. Thank you. I love it!"

Ah See cleared his throat. "Jinhai says he is glad you are all here. He has a present for Lucille and Lawrence that he wanted to give them while you were here, Matt. He says it is because of you that he can give this to them."

"Me?" Matt asked with a narrowing of his brow.

Jinhai held a plate wrapped in plain brown paper out toward Lucille. He nodded once inviting her with his eyes to take it.

"What is it?" she asked while unwrapping the paper.

Ah See translated for Jinhai, "It is a gift from Jinhai to you and your family."

"Oh," she smiled and pulled the paper wrapping off the plate. Her smile faded and her jaw opened while her eyes widened as they stared in disbelief. She gasped, "It's the most beautiful thing I have ever seen. Thank you."

Ah See translated for Jinhai.

"Wow." Lawrence stood beside his wife, staring at whatever was on the front of the plate.

"Let us see," Christine said with a giggle.

Lucille turned the plate around. It was the same

plate with faint green vines and leaves with pink lotus flowers gently floating on a still black pond at night. Dewdrops on the leaves and flowers reflected the moon's light from the sky above that Matt had broken into five pieces when he threw Ah See against the counter. Jinhai had kept the pieces and melted the gold dust he had collected from mining the creeks down and used the gold to mold the pieces back together. The plate was a work of art before it was broken, but now it was stunning. Lines of pure gold weaved their way across the picture like a spider web blowing in the wind and truly enhanced the glazed painting far beyond anything Lucille had seen before. It was a work of art that was far more valuable than Lucille could accept.

Ah See translated for Jinhai, "Jinhai says we as human beings are like plates that are marred by time, scarred by tragedy and other people can often hurt our hearts. And sometimes, our lives can simply just be broken. Some people give up and throw their life away, but like that broken plate, life can be repaired and become more beautiful and more valuable than before. Your family had been broken, but you did not allow the seeds of bitterness to take root. The plate is Jinhai's gift as a representation of you and your family. He says, may you always remember there is still beauty in the darkness."

Lucille covered her mouth to control her tears flowing from her eyes. She set the plate down carefully and quickly moved around the counter to hug Jinhai. "Thank you," she wept. It was a plate that Lucille would never sell at any price.

"I know we talked about it yesterday, but something dawned on me last night," Christine said as she casually walked with her fingers interlaced with Matt's along the boardwalk.

"What's that?" Matt asked. He had slept much of Sunday and spent a few hours with Christine the evening before. They spent an hour reading the Bible together and left it laying open on his bedside table to invite him to pick it up when he awoke in the morning and when he went to bed. It never failed to amaze him how refreshed and alive he felt after spending time in the Lord's word and some honest prayer. Matt and Christine had a lot to talk about, but they agreed that they did not want to end their engagement or the love they had found together.

"I talked to Bella last night about what she said to you. She apologized and she really is sorry. But what I realized was she doesn't have any stories. My Grandpa had stories about his youth and all kinds of stuff. My Grandmother too. Bella's life has been taking care of young ladies and the dance hall. She has stories, but nothing too exciting. I don't know if we will ever be able to have children, but I will be Gabriel's stepmother and we will have grandchildren. We may even adopt some children if we don't have any of our own, or maybe not. The point is, I have interesting stories to tell now." She gazed at Matt with a whimsical expression. "Every bad thing that happened is like a crack in that plate Lucille had. It can break us, or we can choose to use it for good once we get through the darkness.

I really like what Jinhai called that plate, beauty in the darkness. I'll never be boring because of you."

Matt watched her hand swinging in his. "That's a part of the reason I love being a lawman. I don't know what will happen tomorrow or the next day. It keeps me from getting bored. If you want to talk about having stories to tell, I have a lifetime of them. But I'll tell you a secret, I hope to gain a lifetime of better ones with you right beside me. Thank you for having the courage to stick with me through it all. We've had some close calls and we're not even married yet."

"We'll have some more, I'm sure. All I know is Jesus is watching over us and I believe we'll grow old together just fine. I also know you'll always protect me."

"You better believe I will."

"Look," Christine said, pointing across the street. Joe Thorn moved along the boardwalk with his head down and appeared to be quite glum by his composure. "Billy Jo and I had quite a lot to talk about while sharing a room in the hotel. Joe pulled that ring you sold him out of the privy out there where they lived and gave it to her in a box with a letter saying how sorry he was and begging her to come home. They were supposed to talk today at lunchtime, and it looks like she told him to get lost. Good for her!"

"I hope she doesn't get tied up with Wes Wasson now."

Christine shook her head. "No. Your uncle Luther is taking her to the Oregon Coast as soon as his knee heals. He isn't bringing her back for a month or two. He wants her to stay away from here for a while. Which reminds me, where are we going for our honeymoon?"

He smiled, knowing she was as excited as he was to see the Pacific Ocean for the first time. "The coast."

"That's right. And I can't wait for that first glimpse of the ocean. I will be Missus Matt Bannister. And that's what I am excited about most of all."

Wu-Pen and his guards were dead. The gold stolen from the safe at the Engberg and Penn Assayers Office had been returned. Ah See and Jinhai agreed that the finances belonging to Wu-Pen should be shared among the victims of his crimes, including the families of the mine disaster and the family of Izu and Wang Chee. His thumbs would heal in a week or two. But more importantly, Christine was safe and right beside him. The one place he would always want her to be.

A Look At: Murder At Cluster Springs Raceway by John Theo, Jr.

Pulled straight from today's headlines!

A deadly auto accident at a southern Virginia racetrack draws private investigator Brandon Hall into a new case. When young race car driver Drew Schilling dies in a fiery crash, his politician father hires Brandon to investigate. Rumors about that it's a politically motivated murder, and NOT an accident as some would have the family believe.

When Brandon uncovers evidence which ties the raceway death to the rapidly changing political landscape in the United States, radicalized groups, promoting violence on college campuses and cities, just might paint a few more targets.

Enter the corrupt world of Washington DC politics, old Dixieland families, and the volatile culture wars unfolding within the United States.

What no one realizes yet, is that God is still in control.

About the Author

Ken Pratt and his wife, Cathy, have been married for 22 years and are blessed with five children and six grandchildren. They live on the Oregon Coast where they are raising the youngest of their children. Ken Pratt grew up in the small farming community of Dayton, Oregon.

Ken worked to make a living, but his passion has always been writing. Having a busy family, the only "free" time he had to write was late at night getting no more than five hours of sleep a night. He has penned several novels that are being published along with several children stories as well.

9 781639 772131